RENO

•••••

The crowd grew quiet. With one blow of the fist Jim Reno had destroyed the image Aaron Carr had spent a lifetime building. Reno had struck down the most formidable fighting man on Skull Ranch. And everyone who had seen it knew that Aaron Carr would never stop until he had destroyed the man who stood in front of him.

"You beat one man," old Carr said in a measured tone, and the blazing light in his eyes belied his forced manner. "I give you credit for being a fighter, Reno." Then he dipped his head once, his voice steady as a rock. "I give you warning now in front of this Valley, I'll smash you!"

GILBERT MORRIS
RENO

Tyndale House Publishers, Inc.
Wheaton, Illinois

Library of Congress Cataloging-in-Publication Data

Morris, Gilbert.
  [Drifter]
  Reno / Gilbert Morris.
    p.   cm. — (Reno western saga) (Jim Reno westerns series ;
#1)
  Originally published as: The drifter, c1986.
  ISBN 0-8423-1058-4
  I. Title.   II. Series: Morris, Gilbert. Reno western saga.
III. Series: Morris, Gilbert. Jim Reno westerns series ; no. 1.
PS3563.O8742D7   1992
813'.54—dc20   92-9438

Printed in the United States of America

98 97 96 95 94 93 92
 8   7   6   5   4   3   2

To Ronnie Earl Smith
"He which hath begun a good
work in you will perform it
until the day of Jesus Christ."

ONE

Stranger in the Valley

A powder blue haze of Indian summer swirled across the valley below the ridge where a rider drew rein. "Top of the trail, Duke," he murmured to the compact roan. He slipped to the ground in an easy motion, loosened the saddle's girth, and took a sip of water from a battered canteen. Pulling an old saucepan from the pack lashed behind his saddle, he filled it with the rest of the tepid water and grinned as the horse drank it noisily.

He put the pan back, then stretched his arms and leaned against an outcropping of yellow rock. The sudden lift of the arms threw the rounded muscles of his chest and upper arms into high relief. As he relaxed, it was with the total ease of a cat. Although he was of average height, the tightness of his muscles made him look smaller than the 175 pounds that sheathed his frame.

Lazily he took in the valley that lay below, noting the curving line of cottonwoods that banked a small river. His eyes were dark, almost as black as the raven hair that crept from beneath the brim of a worn gray Stetson. His face was wedge-shaped, tapering down from a broad forehead and high cheekbones to a chin that jutted and had a trace of a cleft. The eyes were sleepy, shrouded by jet black brows, and there was a youthful look which was countered by the weather lines slanting out from his eyes across his smooth olive skin.

For ten minutes he gazed at the valley, then tightened the cinch and mounted in one smooth, easy motion. He let the roan pick his way down the steep trail, but his eyes probed restlessly the burnt bronzes of the tree line which led downward. Wood smoke came to him and he turned instantly toward the south, the steely calm of his face broken by the hint of a wildness fitfully asleep. He had a way of absorbing the world with his eyes, a careful filing away of perceptions for future use.

For two hours he followed the dim trail, toward where the valley stretched for twenty miles with scarcely an undulation, only the cottonwoods and willows breaking the flow of the flat earth. Far to the west he saw a broad floor of grass banked by a continuous wall of low-lying hills. The ramparts of a higher range of snowcapped mountains barred the valley to the northeast, but far off he could see the thin spiral of smoke rising from a town.

"Must be Placid" he mused aloud, then a grin scored his bronzed face revealing white, even teeth. "Be nice if it lived up to its name, wouldn't it, Duke? I guess we could use a little peace, couldn't we?" Then he laughed out loud, slapping the roan on the shoulder suddenly. "That's what I like about talkin' to you, Duke—you always agree with everything I say."

Thirty minutes later the steep fall of the hills began to break, giving way to a gentle slope. The scrub oak and stunted pines of the heights gave way to the tall growth of heavier timber and for another hour he enjoyed the cool shade of the needle-carpeted trail. He stopped only once to pull a rifle from the saddle boot and knock two plump red squirrels out of a tall jack pine. He leaned over and picked them up without dismounting, stuffed them into his possible bag, then rode on until he came out of the timber into the floor of the valley.

Darkness fell like a curtain, but he had time to reach the river and set up a small camp by the time the stars pierced the sky. After hobbling his horse, he built a small fire out of dry wood and roasted one of the squirrels, instinct leading him to save the other. It was the gesture of a man who had known the bite of hunger, a small frugality which amused him for some reason, bringing a smile to his broad lips.

After he ate his small meal of squirrel and corn dodgers washed down with cool river water, he lay down on a thin blanket with his saddle for a pillow and listened to the sounds of the evening. The gurgling of the stream was broken once by a loud splash as a deer emerged and waded noisily into the willows. A full-throated bullfrog shattered the silence periodically, bellowing into the cool night air, and once there was a muffled squeal as an owl took a thumping rabbit not twenty yards from where he lay.

Gazing sleepily at the pinpoints of light overhead, he murmured out loud, "Wonder if there's some joker on one of those lying beside a river—looking at this old planet, wonderin' what's the next card to turn over?" He smiled, pulled his hat over his face, and dropped into a dreamless sleep. Once the sound of a shot floated from very far away to his ears. He awoke instantly, his muscles suddenly rigid. After a few seconds there was a sudden volley, the sound muffled by the distance, then nothing.

"Odd," he said softly. Slowly he relaxed, and didn't move until the sun struck his eyes with a dull red glow.

By the time the sun had cleared the eastern hills, he began to pass small herds of cattle. He'd seen a few on the slope of the hills, all wearing a strange brand in the shape of a skull. Most of them were in herds of less than twenty animals, but once he rode through a herd that must have held at least three hundred head, all of them fat with summer graze.

He saw no riders, but passed several old campsites marked by ashes and the tracks of a chuckwagon. All morning he rode steadily north, headed toward the town he had spotted from the rim of the mountain, and he passed through some of the finest grazing land he'd ever seen, thick with cattle bearing the skull brand. Later he saw a few cows with a Circle M brand, not many and not as fat as the Skull cattle, he noticed.

At noon he watered his horse in a small stream, and thirty minutes later spotted a small spiral of smoke rising to his left. He turned Duke's head and steadily advanced until he crested a rolling hill and saw a small house with a barn and a few small outbuildings nestled against a snakelike curve in a small stream. A one-man outfit, he guessed, and down-at-the-heels, at that. He took in the unpainted house, with the straggling fence that surrounded it, and noted that the barn needed a new roof.

As he hrode toward it, he saw two riders come out of the timberline which flanked the small ranch to the east. They were headed directly for the house and once they stopped and one of the pointed in his direction.

Pres Conboy drove his spurs viciously into his horse, grunting to the smaller man riding the paint, "Come on, Red. We ain't got all day."

He was a big man running to fat, but underlaid with thick layers of solid muscle. He held the reins in hands thick as slabs, and he wrenched his horse's head around so violently that the animal almost stumbled. Conboy jerked the animal's head up with a show of brute force, cursed, and spurred again.

He drove his horse at a run until he reached the yard of the dilapidated house, then jerked the bit back to bring the lathered horse to a sudden halt.

"That horse ain't gonna be worth much if you don't watch out," the smaller rider said. He was a thin-framed man, with crisp auburn hair and a pale face. He wore a fancy shirt stitched with elaborate care, creased trousers, a pair of snake-skin boots highly polished, and a gunbelt and holster to match. There was a fine crease in his fawn gray hat and a clean necker-chief around his neck.

"Let 'im die, then!" Conboy snapped. "He ain't no good anyway."

Red Williams shrugged. He knew that Pres Conboy would grind into a powder anything that would not serve his will—horse or man.

"No skin off my nose," he said. Then he glanced at the horizon. "You seen that gent comin' outta the hills? Looks like he's headed this way."

"Yeah. Keep an eye on him, Red."

"What we gonna say to Edwards?"

"Boone wants us to keep the pressure on these two-bit spreads. He says there's too many of 'em sproutin' in the Valley."

Williams grinned and touched the pearl-handled .44 at his side lightly. It was a caress, the way another man might touch a woman, and there was a sensuous pull at his lips as he breathed gently, "You want me to give it to him, Pres?"

Conboy grinned broadly, but shook his heavy head. "You'd like that, wouldn't you, Red? But not yet, Boone says. Just shake 'im up some—for now."

A man and a woman had stepped out of the house. They stood on the porch watching Conboy and Williams as they dismounted and came closer.

"Hello, Pres," the man said. He was thin, almost emaciated, and the bones of his face were starkly revealed by the gray skin. His hair was gray as well, dull and lank. The clothes he wore might have fit him once, but now they hung on him like loose sacks, and he seemed to tremble in the faint breeze that blew across the yard.

Conboy gave him a quick glance and slapped his hand against his meaty thigh. "Edwards, your cows are strayin' over on Skull grass. You been warned before, but I ain't gonna stand for it no more."

"Pres, I don't think . . ."

"I don't wanna hear what you think!" Conboy snapped. He stepped closer to the porch and grated out, "That bean-eater you got workin' for you gave some of my boys some lip when he come on Skull chasin' after some of them scrawny cows of yours. He won't be so smart next time, I guess."

"He's just a boy, Pres," Edwards said lamely.

"He's a dumb Mex!" Conboy exclaimed. "If he bumps into my boys again he may be a dead one."

Edwards answered, "You don't own the grass, Conboy. It's government graze." He stepped down off the porch and beside Conboy's bulk he looked like a boy. "You know we've kept what few cows we have inside the range we staked out. I haven't put up a fence, and Skull's got no claim on Circle M ground."

Edwards' face was flushed and he stared the larger man in the eye as he spoke. He wore no gun, and would not have been able to use if it he had.

"Watch out, Pres," Williams jeered. "He's gonna work you over if you don't act right."

Pres Conboy had one reaction when he was challenged, and his beefy face turned red at Edwards' words. His arm shot out and he grabbed Edwards by the shirt lifting him effortlessly up on his toes. "I'd like to wipe you out, old man," he said. "That's what I told Mr. Carr he ought to do to all you two-bit sodbusters! And if you let one more of your sorry cows drift onto Skull grass, I'll burn this shack to the ground, you hear me old man?"

He shoved Edwards back so violently that the older man fell sprawling, his head striking the single step of the porch with a distinct thud.

"Dad!" The young woman who had not said a word leaped off the porch and pulled his head up. She wore a homespun dress and her chestnut hair was in a coil of braids. She put her hand behind her father's head, and pulled it back out. She stared at the blood that stained her fingers, and turned a white face toward the two men. "Get out of here! Leave us alone!"

Red Williams laughed and said, "Aw, honey, don't be mad. Your daddy's all right. Here—lemme give you a hand."

He started to go to her, but she ordered, "Get away from here!" She turned to look at the ashen face of her father and saw that his eyelids were fluttering.

"Why, you just need a good man to help you, sweetie," Williams continued, nearing her.

"Company, Red," Conboy said, and both of them turned to face the rider on the well-knit roan who had ridden across the yard, stopping at the well.

Conboy and Williams turned fully around to face the rider, both of them alert as they sized up the man who was watching them. Both of them saw at once that he was not wearing a gun, but his hand was resting on the butt of a rifle. He was wearing good clothes, well-worn but still neat. The fawn-colored shirt with bone buttons fit like a glove, clearly revealing the strong shoulders and deep chest, and the butternut trousers had a faint stripe down the side of the leg. A thin black belt with a Confederate buckle, high-heel boots with fine stitching, and a gray hat held on by a thin leather lanyard made up his dress.

He just sat there, not saying anything, but there was something about the relaxed way he held himself that made Conboy nervous. Williams began to move to one side, but Press said, "Be still, Red!" There was nothing threatening in the man, but Conboy was feeling jumpy, which was unusual for the big foreman of Skull. He was not afraid of any man, but beneath his bullheaded skull was an animal craftiness that sometimes led him to exercise caution. He knew what he could do; he did not know what the man sitting on the roan could do.

Edwards had gotten to his feet, helped by the girl, and he said in a shaky voice, "Get down, young man."

"Maybe you better not," Red Williams said in a breathless tone. He was staring at the rider in a peculiar manner, and his right hand that hovered over the pearl handle of his .44 was trembling with eagerness.

"Red!" Conboy commanded loudly. "Cut that out!"

"Aw, Pres . . ."

"Mind me, you hear!" Conboy said strongly. He stared at the rider and said, "Just passin' through?"

"That's it," the man answered.

"I'm Pres Conboy, foreman at Skull. Guess you know you're on our range?"

"Sure."

The rider hadn't moved and suddenly Conboy was certain that this was no time to find out about the stranger's ability to unlimber a rifle. "What's your name?"

There was a noticeable pause, then the dark-faced rider said, "Reno." He added nothing to that single word.

Conboy studied that, then smiled briefly. "Guess that's as good as any. You lookin' for a job? I maybe can use a good hand."

"Thanks. Won't be here long."

Conboy waited for him to say more, but there was a bland indolence on Reno's face. Finally he nodded.

"That's a good idea—passin' on through. I'd stick with it was I you." Then he turned to Edwards. "You heard what I said. Next time you won't get off so easy. Come on, Red."

Williams argued, "Press, I think we better . . ."

"Shut up, Red!" He led the smaller man to the horses, and did not fail to notice that Reno's horse turned to face them. He didn't see that the man called Reno had given any pressure on the reins, but as they left the yard he muttered to Williams, "There's a lad as has smelled powder somewhere, Red."

"Pres, he didn't even have a gun, except that rifle. Why, I could have blown him right out of the saddle!"

"Mebbe, Red." Conboy shrugged. "You may get the chance."

As soon as the pair had gotten out of range, Reno turned the roan back to face the house.

"Get down," Edwards said. He touched the back of his head, stared at the blood on his thin hand. Then he smiled faintly. "Let me water your horse."

Reno slipped from the saddle. "Thanks. He is a little dry.

I'll do it." He led the roan to the trough beside the house, and after loosening the cinch he let Duke drink a little, then pulled him back.

"Here. You must be thirsty." He turned to find the young woman holding a gourd filled with water toward him.

"Thanks. I am sort of dry." He drank all of it, gazing at her over the rim of the gourd.

She was a small girl, but not frail. The simple dress revealed a full figure, and she had rounded arms with firm wrists and strong hands. There was a calm light in her hazel eyes which reflected a spirit not easily stirred. She had smooth, tanned skin, the color of pale honey on her face, but which lightened to cream on her neck above her bodice.

"I'm glad you came just now." He realized that she was thanking him for coming at a bad time, and that she would never mention it again, nor would she forget it.

Edwards called out, "Come on and set." He dragged a couple of cane-bottomed chairs out of the house, and plunked down in one. "Name's Silas Edwards; this is my daughter Catherine. You're called Reno?"

"Jim Reno."

"Be glad to have you sit down and eat with us. You must be hungry after a long ride."

Reno shook his head, not missing the fact that Edwards had made an attempt to find out where he was from, but said only, "I'm headed for Placid. How far is it?"

"Oh, you can make it in two or three hours. But we'd be pleased to fix you a bite to eat."

"Guess I'd better get on," Reno replied. He looked in the direction that Conboy and Williams had taken. "They might be back—you know that, I guess."

The older man seemed to sag. His face pulled down as he nodded and said slowly, "Yes, they'll be back."

Reno looked around the sorry spread, then toward the far grassland where Skull ran its herds. He looked at the girl and saw the despair in her eyes, and he knew all he needed to know about the Valley. He'd seen it before and he'd see it again.

"Might be best for you to move on, too," was his comment. It was a bitter word, and he knew it was a futile remark. The land was precious, like gold or silver, and men would die for it and kill for it. Silas Edwards, like a million others, wanted just enough earth to scratch a living from. But for every Edwards there was a Skull ranch which consumed thousands of acres in a huge operation.

"No. I'll not leave this place," the old man said. "I've left three places already, Reno. I'll stay on this one until I die."

The gray face was set, and the girl put her hand on the thin arm that rested on the back of the chair. "We'll be all right, Dad," she assured him quietly. Then she gave Reno a quick glance. "We could use some help."

It was, he knew, the equal of a scream for help from a lesser woman. This girl was reaching out to a stranger, and he knew that if it were not for her father she would have said nothing.

He shifted his weight, looked into her eyes, and murmured, "I'll be moving on, Miss Edwards."

"People always on the move!" she said suddenly, as if it were wrenched out of her very heart. "You're like so many others, never taking root!" Then she bit her lip. "I'm sorry. Good luck to you."

Reno nodded, then gave Duke another chance at the water. Cinching up, he stepped into the saddle and turned to face the pair on the porch. There was a fatal air about Edwards that shocked him, a desolation in the thin face. He shot a glance at the girl, and saw that nothing was hidden from her.

He found it hard to turn the horse around and ride out. "Good luck," he said finally. "I hope it turns out well for you."

"Good-bye," the girl called out. The man said nothing at all but sat staring at the crack in the porch.

A rusty windmill was creaking in the wind as Reno left the Circle M. The raw squawk of the bent piston grated his nerves, and he drove Duke away at a faster pace than was necessary. He dropped over a hill, but even long after the ranch was out of sight, he kept remembering the level gaze of the girl, and it stirred something so long forgotten that it took him a long time to remember the time when he would have felt obliged to stay. A long time ago, when he had been another man.

TWO

As the Sparks Fly Upward

October was Reno's favorite month, and he took his time getting to town, letting Duke amble leisurely down the slope. The trail from Circle M became a wandering road, then joined up with a well-traveled thoroughfare showing marks of heavy use.

He relaxed in the saddle, swaying in unconscious rhythm as the cool breezes off the mountains touched his face like soft fingers. He let his sleepy eyes rest on the orange and gold tips of aspens on a far-off range, marking it as a possible hunting ground. Even half-asleep he was constantly receiving messages—sights, smells, all the sounds that floated on the crisp fall air—he soaked them up, filing them away for future use.

As he drew closer to the town, he caught the sound of a freight train beating its way across the flat prairie, and paused to watch the smoke from the narrow-gauge engine coil up in a blue-white pyramid sharply etched against the powder blue sky. And as it always happened, he wanted to be on that train.

The road got more active as he cleared the final ridges of the rolling plain, and the tiny spreads he could see far off began feeding a small stream of farm wagons and riders toward the town. He was surprised at the traffic on the remote road until he realized it was Saturday. Market day for farmers—a break in the grim monotony of hard work for the whole family. A chance to talk, to look, to buy a little, to dip into the activity of the town.

A group of five riders raced by him, yelling and waving their hats. "Startin' their celebratin' a little bit early, Duke," he said, and a smile touched his long lips as he thought of his days as a puncher and how the Saturday nights were little islands of wild fun in the dull ocean of ranch work. "Wonder what it would be like to be able to go with that bunch, just yellin' and lettin' off steam?" he mused, and his face grew still and a little sober as he added: "Can't go back to being what you used to be—though I know some who tried. Seems like once you turn the page in the book, you can't ever turn it back again." He watched the riders enter the small town and fall off their horses to go into what must have been the saloon. "I wonder if those days were as good as I remember—or if it's just that I never have hit on something better?" Then he shrugged and spurred Duke into a gallop, putting the thoughts behind in the dust that rose from the road.

Entering the town from the south, he had a sudden feeling that he'd been there before—but he knew that was only because it looked like all other towns on the fringe of the frontier.

He passed through a thin scattering of houses, mostly unpainted frame shacks with sagging roofs and clothes strung out on rope lines. A street ran parallel to the main thoroughfare. He could see across the vacant lots where the more prosperous citizens had built—mostly white frame houses, and some having a second story.

He rode slowly down what seemed to be the main business district—in fact, the only one—passing a couple of rundown rooming houses, a few small shops, and a dressmaker. A large general store was already crowded with lookers—mostly women in drab calico, anchored by small children hanging to their skirts. Across the street a brick building boasted steel bars in the windows and a sign that said *State Bank* spread itself along the plank sidewalk.

The jail stood square at the intersection where a broad street cut across the main avenue, and there, Reno knew without looking, lay the other world of Placid. Turning left at the squat brick jail, he noted the row of saloons, mostly boarded up for the daylight hours, and the woman with a pale face and a low-cut dress leaning out of a window on the second floor of the Palace.

"Had to be here," Reno said. "Guess appetite never changes, no matter what else does."

He had a way of facing up to unpleasant things open-eyed, having learned some hard lessons about the futility of wishful thinking. Now as he looked at the saloons and the windows of the upstairs rooms, his mouth grew a little firmer, but he did not turn away. He had made some sort of peace with such things, a peace which was neither surrender nor acceptance.

The stable lay at the far limits of the main street, flanked by a gunsmith's small shop on one side and a hardware store on the other.

The hostler, an ancient, bright-eyed man with one arm, took his horse. "Fine-looking animal!" he said grinning. "I'll grain him real good."

"Thanks. I'll pick him up tomorrow."

"You ain't stayin'?"

Reno grinned at the quick question, but shook his head. "No. You know where I can find Thad Stevens?"

The hostler glanced at him with a startled eye. "The preacher? He'll be comin' to town tonight. Everybody does."

Reno knew his inquiry would be passed along, discussed, and that his presence would not be ignored. He wandered across the street, dodging the onrush of a florid-faced man in a bright waistcoat who drove a team of black horses down the street at full gallop. A barrel of apples caught his eye in front of a small store, and he bought two. Sticking one in his saddle-bags, he munched the other, savoring the crunchy meat and letting the sweet juices flow down his throat.

The hotel looked like all other hotels in towns all across the plains. Two stories, with a foyer flanked by a small saloon on one side and a cafe on the other. The battered desk was manned by a young man with the worst complexion Reno had ever seen. He tried not to look at it as the clerk asked, "Room for the night?"

"Yes. For tonight."

"Just one night? That'll be two dollars." He shoved the dog-eared register around, and pushed a pen across the desk.

The book seemed to fascinate Reno, and he read the names of some of the recent guests. Then he felt the attention of the pimpled clerk and signed the book with a sweeping signature: *James Reno*. He paused uncertainly, then added the words *Dalhart, Texas,* about the name.

"Take Number Eight—second to your right up the stairs."

"A key?"

"Been took off a long time ago. Put a chair under the door-knob. Anybody tries to come in, shoot 'im."

Reno smiled at the callous advice and made his way up

the rickety stairs to the room. It was no better and no worse than a hundred others he'd had. A sagging double bed, a wash-stand with a pitcher of water and a cracked basin, a battered table carved with the names of former inmates, and a chamber pot.

Throwing his saddlebags on the bed, Reno quickly pulled out his shaving gear and with practiced ease removed four days' stubble. He put the razor and soap back, took off his boots, and lay down on the creaking bed, falling asleep at once.

He slept for three hours without moving, relaxed as a cat. Then his eyes blinked open, and he sat up and stretched his muscles. He washed his face and put on his boots, then picked up his saddlebags and went downstairs. He tossed them over the desk at the clerk. "Keep that under the desk for me. I'll pick them up after I eat."

"Well, I guess that's all right. Best place to eat ain't here. We got an old roundup cook who thinks everybody's got iron stomachs. Go down to Mullins' place—he's got a Chinaman."

"Thanks."

"Say, tell Mary—she's the heavyset waitress there—to save me a piece of that cherry pie, will you? Say it's for Bar-ney."

"Sure." Reno wanted to tell the boy that with his complex-ion, pie was the last thing he needed, but he'd given up hand-ing out unasked advice.

It was only five, but already the sky was turning dark, so he made his way to the frame building with the simple sign *Mullins* beside the door. Two cane-bottomed chairs were tilted against the wall of the cafe, so he pulled one around, sat down, and watched the town come to life.

The streets were crowded now, and the narrow plank sidewalks spilled over into the dust with a mixture of farmers, women, riders, and a few Mexicans wearing their huge sombreros.

The pace of the town was speeding up, like a heartbeat, and Reno felt it as he sat there observing the crowd. He could feel the pulse of Grant Street down the way, the tinny pianos began grinding out the loud tunes, and he knew that as the night grew darker Grant Street would arouse like some sort of murderous animal. He had felt the blood-quickening power of such things before, and it suddenly occurred to him that the squat, ugly jail sat right at the crossroad separating Main Street with its lawful businesses from Grant Street, alive with a latent ferocity one blink away from violence.

He swung suddenly to his right, some instinct warning him that he was being watched. A stocky man of about forty-five was watching him carefully with a stare that was bold yet not quite steady. Maybe it was the cast in one eye, but he came to stand close to where Reno sat.

"I'm Bolin, the town marshal," he said, and paused as if he expected to be recognized. "You working for one of the trail outfits, are you?"

Reno stood up, taking in the black suit set off by a frilly white shirt. Bolin was dressed in the manner of Bat Masterson, and Reno suspected the imitation was conscious. "No. I'm just headed through to the coast."

"Yeah? Well, you got a long ride. But we got a few rules here. Check your gun at the jail if you come this side of town. . . ."

"What about if I go to the other side of town?" Reno asked with a smile, as if he knew the answer.

Bolin laughed, "Well, that's different. Man's gotta have a little fun, ain't he now? What's your name?"

"Jim Reno."

"Sure. Well, I run a tight little town here, but if you wanna let your wolf loose, do it on Grant Street. Understand?" He waited for Reno's nod, then moved down the street with a slight swagger.

Reno turned and went into the restaurant which had six square tables with red-and-white checkered tablecloths. A door at the rear led to the kitchen and a double window looked out on the yellow lamps that flickered out on Main Street.

Except for an elderly couple at the table by the window, there was no one inside. Reno took a seat and a short girl with red hair and a thick waist came over to wait on him. "Hello. What'll it be?"

"Your name Mary?" Reno asked.

"Well—" The girl was on guard instantly, stepping back as if he might grab her and take her to the mountains.

"Barney says to save him a piece of cherry pie."

She relaxed at once, a broad grin scoring her homely face. "Oh, Barney! He needs pie like I need a toothache!" Then she said, "The stew is real good tonight. And we got some fresh greens—probably the last we'll get."

"I'll have the stew and the greens, Mary—and a piece of cherry pie."

She giggled and disappeared into the kitchen, returning at once with a large cup of steaming coffee. Reno smiled. "You just saved my life." He picked up the coffee and tasted it. "I'll remember you in my will, Mary."

"A good tip will do." She grinned and went to wait on a young couple who entered and took a seat.

Reno sipped his coffee, then when Mary set the steaming bowl of stew and the plate of greens before him, he was suddenly hungry as a wolf. Instead of eating rapidly, however, he ate slowly, chewing every bite slowly, sipping buttermilk from a blue pitcher. Twice Mary filled his plate, then brought a piece of cherry pie and more coffee.

"This Barney's pie?" he asked the waitress and got the giggle he expected. He ate the pie and was drinking the last of his coffee when the door swung open and a party of five men came in.

A huge mountain of a man, at least four or five inches over six feet, led the way. He had to duck as he passed through the entrance, and Reno saw he would weigh around two-thirty or even more. He had cold blue eyes set in a square face, and he moved across the floor in a ponderous way, with a deliberation that brooked no opposition.

He seemed to fill the room, and when he spoke it was almost as if he shouted. "Pull a couple of these tables together."

There was no doubt at all that three of the four men with him were his sons, especially the oldest. He was a copy of what the father must have been at thirty. The same massive build, and even the same stolid, ponderous way of moving his body as if he intended to crash through a wall.

He reached out and picked up one of the tables by the edge, lifting it as if it were weightless, then put it next to another in the center of the room. "Lee, git a couple of them chairs."

The youngest man, a boy really, was tall, but had none of the bulk of the two older brothers. He was not over twenty, and there was an unfinished look about him. At thirty he might be larger, but he lacked the power of the older men.

The third son had the same square features and some of the bulk of the father. But there was a humor in his blue eyes that the others lacked.

The last man, Reno saw, was Pres Conboy. The big foreman met his gaze and stopped dead still, riveting Reno with his
muddy eyes. Then he sat down and ignored him.

After the men had pulled the tables around and arranged
the chairs, the older man said in a booming voice to the waitress, "Bring us something to eat, girl—best you got."

"Yes, Mr. Carr." The waitress answered nervously, then
scurried back through the kitchen door, obviously afraid of
Aaron Carr. There had been nothing cruel in his manner, only
a brusque indifference to someone who existed only to serve
him. He would treat his horse exactly the same way—firmly as
long as the animal performed his given service, but with no
affection. And Reno knew men well enough to realize that anything that drew breath and stood in Carr's way he would crush
with that same massive strength.

Reno had chosen a chair that put his back to the wall,
thus commanding a view of the restaurant. Resting his elbows
on the table, he sipped his coffee, but if his compact body was
idle, his mind was not. Without appearing to do so, he watched
the men across the room, his dark eyes taking in every detail,
and he automatically threw their strengths and their
weaknesses onto the scales, picking details and filing them
into his memory.

Conboy he knew, and from their conversation he picked
up the names of the other three.

Lee Carr, Reno noted, wore a fancy gun in a holster on his
left thigh despite the rule against guns on Main Street. There
was a self-conscious swagger in the way he threw himself back
in his chair, casting his eyes around the room, as if he wanted
an audience to be aware of how tough he was. His light blue
eyes touched on Reno, noted the lack of a gun, and with a

shrug ignored him. A wild young man anxious to prove himself, and who would, Reno understood, be very dangerous in his quest.

Frank Carr did not wear a gun, and there was an easy manner about his square face that the others lacked. Not that he looked soft—none of them did—but his broad lips had a tolerance which blended with the humorous light in his wide-set eyes. A man who could be a good friend, or a hard enemy.

The one they called Boone was the hard case. Not just the vast bulk which was overwhelming, but the grim set of his face which revealed no trace of compassion. It was not that he was tough; that was to be expected of most men in the country. It was the total lack of warmth, the deadly set of the jaw which, Reno knew at once, revealed the character of Boone Carr—a man who would expect no mercy and would give none.

Reno thought of the thin, sickly face of Si Edwards and the dark eyes of Catherine, and it saddened him to see the power and strength that lay poised to grind them to powder. For at the table across the room lay the might of the Valley, and he saw nothing in their faces that gave promise for the little people in their fragile world.

The men drank coffee, talking idly, and Reno paid little attention. He finished the last of his coffee, and was about to rise when the door opened and two women came in, one of them an elderly woman in a dark dress, the other young with the same blue eyes and broad brow that marked the Carr men.

"Where you two been?" Aaron asked as they piled the parcels they carried into empty chairs and took their places at the table. "You probably spent every dime I got." Although his words were cross, there was a light in the old man's face that came close to gentleness as he touched the shoulder of the girl and gave the older woman a smile.

"Stacy," Frank Carr said solemnly, "I swear if you get one more dress into that wardrobe of yours, the thing will plumb explode!"

Stacy Carr was a tall, fair girl, with the same ash blonde hair and blue eyes of the family, but there was none of her father's bulk in her figure. She had broad red lips and the pleasure she felt in the moment turned them soft, but Reno knew that the same quick response would show when she was angry. There was volatile quality in her mobile face, but Reno noted that she had little if any of her father's harshness. The sweep of her broad lips and the warm light in her eyes came, Reno saw, from her mother.

"Oh, we've got lots more shopping to do," she said. "You'll have to wait until we're through."

"Take your time, Stacy," Lee said with a grin. "We're going to church."

"Church?" she questioned with a twist of her head. "What in the world are you talking about? There's no church on Saturday night—and if there were, *you* wouldn't go there, Lee!"

"Now, Sis, you ought not to talk to your baby brother like that. How do you know I ain't up and hit the Glory Road?"

Stacy sniffed, then turned to Frank. "What devilment is he up to now?"

Frank shrugged, a sober light in his eyes. "Oh, the small ranchers and the farmers are having another one of their meetings." He leaned back in his chair and the humorous streak in him touched his lips. "Expect we all better sleep with our guns on, folks. Those big, bad dirt farmers are going to get us yet!"

"Don't be a fool, Frank!" Aaron said. He raised his massive head, and there was iron in his voice as he added, "I know they look foolish, but those hoemen and their two-bit spreads are more of a threat to Skull than the Indians or Texas fever."

"Dad, can you see Ole Swenson taking out after *us* with a six-gun?" Frank asked in exasperated good humor.

"No, not alone. But have you counted how many of those squatters have come into the Valley in the last year?"

"That's right!" Lee joined in. "And they're stretching barbed wire around the water now. I had to cut three just last week." He paused and said with elaborate unconcern, "Had to bust up one of the jokers."

"You shouldn't have done that, Lee," Mrs. Carr said. "You hurt that Donelly boy real bad."

"He won't fence off any more of Skull's water, Ma! Dad's right, Frank, about these people."

"Dad, you can't run them off with a gun," Frank protested. "They're not rustlers, and they're not fighting men."

"Wrong there, Frank." Pres Conboy shook his head. "Billy Sixkiller has done his share—and Ray Catlin over at Fishhook has killed two men that I know of."

"That was years ago, Pres, when he was a young man!" Frank protested.

Conboy lowered his voice, but it still carried to Reno. "The hoemen and the little ranchers been talking about bringing in some help. Some tough help, if you get me."

"Hired guns?" Frank asked skeptically. "They wouldn't do that. They don't have the money to pay men like that."

"They could offer them free grass and land—which would be Skull land."

"You believe that, Conboy?" Aaron asked suddenly.

Conboy shrugged and lowered his voice a fraction. "See that joker over there?" He nodded toward where Reno sat. "He was at the Edwards place yesterday."

"Don't mean anything," Frank protested.

"When he come to town a little while ago, he asked Charley Mott how to find Thad Stevens." Conboy demanded an explanation, and there was an angry look in his small eyes. "That preacher is the one who keeps the small fry stirred up. That's why we're gonna go to that meeting at the church tonight."

"You're not going to—" Mrs. Carr spoke nervously, a sudden fear in her eyes.

"No trouble, Mother," Aaron said, but there was a hard light in his eyes. "Things can't go on like they have been. If they're reasonable, we can find a solution."

Reno knew without a doubt what that "solution" would be—the settlers could sell out for practically nothing, or they could be harassed beyond endurance until they would have to flee.

He had seen it before, but it was not his problem. He stood up, put a dollar down on the table and walked to the door, feeling the stares of the Carr family pressing against his back. He was almost out the door when Lee Carr spoke to him.

"Hey, you! Hold it right there!"

Reno turned to face the tall young man who towered over him. Reno's face was still, and there was a looseness in his compact frame as he kept his dark eyes fixed on Carr, waiting for what would come next.

Lee Carr drew his shoulders back, and there was a brashness in his face as he demanded, "Who are you? What's your business in the Valley?"

A long silence ran through the room, broken only by the dim sounds from the street. Reno let it run on, not taking his gaze from Carr's face. Although he had made no threatening move—had not even spoken—there was a sudden intake, a breath plainly audible, and the men at the table stiffened as if some danger had suddenly presented itself.

Then Reno shrugged and a trace of a smile touched his lips. "Don't usually explain myself to self-constituted committees, but if you got that custom here, reckon I can put up with it. My name's Reno. I'm just a poor wayfaring stranger, you might say. On my way to the coast."

"You don't say!" Lee Carr grinned, looking at his family with a wink. "How come you're lookin' for Thad Stevens?"

Reno never moved, and when he spoke it was with a thin humor that cut at Carr's pride.

"Maybe I've just dropped in to sing in the choir."

It angered the tall man, and he reached out and tapped Reno's chest. "Think you can get away with that kind of talk? You're in trouble, fella."

Reno's eyes narrowed and he said in a summer-soft tone, "Well, as the Book says, man is born to trouble as the sparks fly upward." Then just as Lee Carr reached out to tap him on the chest again, the soft voice took on a steely edge and he warned with a direct stare, "Don't do that again, son."

A quick flush touched Carr's face and he opened his mouth and raised his fist, but Aaron's iron voice broke through: "That's enough, Lee."

"This joker is asking for it!"

"I said let it drop." Aaron Carr lifted his heavy gaze to meet Reno's eyes. "I take you at your word. If you're just passing through, we have nothing to say. But if you are more than just a visitor, I give you a warning now. Don't put yourself against Skull. You'll come out of a fight on the short end."

He had been dismissed, Reno saw, for the old man waved Lee to a chair and picked up a coffee mug, totally ignoring the man he had just warned. It was part of his character not to even consider that a man would need more than a simple warning, and he simply put the whole thing out of his mind.

A sudden wave of anger rose up in Reno, the rock-hard arrogance of Aaron Carr ruffling the smooth control of his face. He put his hat on and stepped through the door into the noisy current of people crowding the plank sidewalk. The incident soured him, and he decided to seek out Stevens at his ranch the following day rather than at the church. He expected nothing but trouble to come from the church meeting.

"Wrong move, Lee," Frank said as soon as Reno was gone. "You shouldn't have pushed at him."

"Don't be so soft, Frank," Lee snapped. "We got to put the run on these two-bit hard cases. You notice he didn't tell us why he wants to see Stevens, didn't you?"

Aaron nodded. "We'll wait and see. I'll have no trouble unless I'm pushed to it."

Boone Carr had said little, as was customary. He had watched the scene between Lee and Reno calmly, but there was a frown on his heavy face as he thought aloud, "Came to sing in the choir, did he?" Then he slapped his thick leg with a harsh laugh. "I guess maybe we can teach him a tune or two. And that preacher—I guess we better let him know it's time for him to be sticking to preaching." Getting up from the table he said with a heavy humor, "Come on, folks, we got to go to church!"

THREE
*A Man Can't
Keep Running*

Thad Stevens took inventory of the various faces of the small group gathered inside the church, and felt a stab of despair as several of them got up stiffly preparing to leave. He had been hammering at them for over an hour, arguing, bullying, sometimes almost begging them to stand fast against the common enemy. Now he left his place at the rough pulpit and walked down the aisle to catch a tall rawboned man by the arm.

"No, Ole, sit down. We haven't settled anything yet."

"No, and I don't think we're going to." Ole Swenson pulled away from Stevens' grasp and reached down to pull his wife to her feet, adding heavily, "I know you think we ought to keep on, Thad, but I got a family to think of."

Stevens was a large man, over six feet, and he moved awkwardly. There was a worried glint in his light blue eyes that did not escape his audience. He said hurriedly, "Sure you do, Ole, and that's exactly why you can't leave. You've poured six years of your life into that place of yours. It belongs to you and your family. Now if we'll just stick together . . ."

"Can't stick together all spread out like we are," a middle-aged man grunted sourly. He shook his head shortly, adding, "And if we did, what could we do against those tough hands Carr keeps on at Skull?"

Stevens threw his head back and declared loudly, trying to put confidence in his voice, as he did when he preached a sermon, "Fred, if we just hold on, there'll be some law in this valley soon. All we have to do is hang on."

Fred Flemming stared at Stevens, trying to find something solid, but apparently did not, for he grunted and got to his feet, saying, "I got to get home."

Desperately Stevens raised his voice and cried out, "You can't give up! Billy, what about you? You're not going to quit, are you?"

Billy Sixkiller had not said much, and even now he appeared not to have heard Stevens. His copper skin gleamed in the flickering lamplight, throwing the piercing eyes into relief, and the carved planes of his face did not reveal what was going on in his mind. He was one of the two men in the room who wore a side arm, and he had an air of total self-confidence as he slowly looked around the room. Finally he said, "I just don't think we can cut it, Reverend." A streak of savage anger broke the smooth lines of his face, and he said evenly, "I ain't goin' to let Skull run me off. They'll have to bury me first."

Andy MacIntosh stood up suddenly and said in a rich Scottish tongue, "That's vury weel fur you, Billy. You're a fighting mon. But the rest of us—except for Ray there—we're no hand to do anything like that." MacIntosh bit down hard on his pipe, and shook his shaggy head from side to side in thought, then suddenly beat his fist against his thigh, adding in an angry voice, "Still, if it come to that, and we have it to do, I'll do what must be done!"

"That's the way to talk, Andy!" Thad said instantly. He began walking back and forth, sawing the air with his heavy arms, urging the people to stick together. He was an earnest man, believing in his cause, but he did not have the gift of swaying men. And even as he began to see some spark of hope in the faces of the crowd, the door of the church swung open and Aaron Carr walked in followed by his three sons and his foreman.

Silence fell on the room at once, and most of the men sitting in the rude benches shifted uneasily as the big man paused and stared out at them.

Carr took his time, letting the pressure build up, then said loudly, "Preacher, I wasn't invited here, but I got something to say."

Thad stood straighter, and nodded to the big man. "You're welcome to, Mr. Carr."

Lee Carr snorted at that, but Aaron ignored him. "Now we might as well be honest. I never meet a man except head-on, so I'll say what I came to say."

"You don't have to say anything, Aaron," a slender man with silver hair suggested quietly. He took a step away from the wall, and his fingers brushed against the Colt on his leg. He was in his sixties, but there no was sign of the weakness of age on him. He was slim as a boy, and his steady dark eyes held the Carrs still.

"That's right, Catlin," Carr said harshly. "I've said it to you before. But I'm giving you one last chance to be smart."

"Save your breath, Carr," Ray Catlin said. "You're going to say that you're the big mogul in the Valley and the rest of us have got to eat humble pie."

"Dad, let me shut that old man's mouth!" Lee pleaded. He stepped forward, but ran into his father's iron arm.

"You be still, Lee." Aaron stared at the small group and said slowly, "I've talked to most of you before, and what I said is still true. This is cattle country. Always has been, always will be. You want to cut it up in small chunks, fence it off, tear up the land with plows. You won't do it."

There was naked power in Aaron Carr's voice and his words drove themselves like nails into the room. He did not raise his voice, but there was no modifying the stark power that lay in the man. He continued steadily, "I want to be fair, and I will be as generous as possible. I'll buy any of you out who want to leave."

"For ten cents on the dollar!" Silas Edwards shouted suddenly. He got up from his chair, shaking off his daughter's hand, and his thin voice rose in the narrow confines of the rude church as he lifted a bony finger toward the powerful rancher.

"You don't own the world, Mr. Carr! Sure, you've been here longer than the rest of us, but that's not everything. There's a whole lot of people moving into this country, and you can't kill all of them!"

Aaron Carr's face did not reveal a thing, but he replied at once, "I could kill a lot of them, Edwards. And I won't worry about it either. It's Skull land, and I won't let anyone take it away from me. That's what I came to say."

"You can't do it, Carr," Stevens said, and he made himself meet the iron eyes of the rancher steadily. He had to make a firm stand in front of his people, but despite himself he found the uncertainty that lay in him breaking out in his voice as he ended, "We'll talk about it, Mr. Carr. . . ."

"Talking is over, Stevens." Carr looked around the crowd with a thinly veiled contempt. "No more fence will be strung in this valley. Any new settlers will have to move on. And those of you here, I'm serving notice that if you get in the way of Skull, you'll pay for it."

Billy Sixkiller lifted his head saying in a knife-edged tone, "Carr, you know what I think of you. If you touch the Running Y, I'll rub you out."

There was a movement from Conboy, but Carr said, "Indian, I hope you don't mean that—or you're in deep trouble."

Conboy declared, "And you better think twice about bringing any hired guns into this valley. They won't live long."

"That goes for you, preacher," Lee Carr taunted.

"Me? What are you talking about?" Thad asked.

Aaron Carr cut off the debate. "The time for talk is past. I hope you're not foolish enough to hire some hard cases and fight Skull. We know you've talked about it, but let there be no mistake." The big man measured his words and there was a deadly calm in his eyes. "If you do bring in outside help, they'll be treated like outlaws. I look on you all as trespassers on my land. Up to now I've tried to live with you. Now that's over. If you're wise, you'll clear out."

He turned and the floor shook as the group stalked out into the night, leaving a tinny silence in the church.

"Well, that's plain enough," Josh Jordan said. He was the cook on Thad Stevens' spread, the Arrow. Small, bent, burned with a thousand suns, he got up and his voice was clear as he added, "God has just told us to get out."

"He means it," Ole Swenson said nervously.

"So do I," Billy Sixkiller said. He turned and walked toward the door. "You do what you want. I'm staying."

Everyone got up, and there was a sudden rush for the

door. Stevens tried to hold them, but it was impossible. Several of the wives pulled their husbands through the door bodily, and finally only Silas Edwards and Catherine were left with Stevens and Josh.

"I should have been able to hold them together, Silas," Thad murmured heavily. He slumped onto one of the benches and shook his head. "I just couldn't do it."

Catherine put her hand on his shoulder, drawing his gaze. She said warmly, "Don't be angry with yourself, Thad. Nobody could have kept the group together. They're afraid."

Silas looked tired. He shook his head. "Sure—and I guess they have a right to be. Aaron Carr will never back down."

"What do you think they meant about somebody hiring gunfighters?"

"I think Ray Catlin has said something about that. Nobody else that I know of."

"But Lee said something about *my* hiring a fighting crew." Thad shook his head and got to his feet. "Well, maybe we can meet again next week. See what we can come up with."

"Meet until doomsday, Skull will still wipe out anybody who gets in their way," Josh snapped. "Let's get on home."

First light was breaking when Reno picked up his saddlebags, made his way down the stairs, and walked to the stable. He had a sudden desire to be rid of Placid, and when the one-armed hostler brought Duke out, Reno saddled him quickly.

Swinging into the saddle he rode out the pitches the spirited roan always gave him in the morning, then asked, "Which way to Arrow?"

Charley Mott considered that, then pointed north. "Follow that road to the Snake River, turn east. Stevens' ranch is on the south bank, maybe ten miles."

"Thanks." He leaned over and handed the man a bill. "Keep the rest."

Mott watched the roan raise a cloud of dust, then turned and made his way rapidly to Frenchy's Saloon, disappearing inside and calling out, "Hey, Pete, you here?" When he came out five minutes later he was folding a bill, and there was a satisfied look on his face as he went down the street.

Reno let Duke run until the wild edge was gone, then settled down to the ride to Arrow.

Restlessly he searched the horizon to the west, having a sudden impulse to leave the country at once. But he did not, for the thing he had come to do was not accomplished. He had to see Thad Stevens.

As he had floated around town, making talk here and there, he had picked up enough to fill in the gaps on how things lay in the Valley. What he had heard made him wish that he was on his way to the coast, but there was a strong sense of a debt unpaid in him—something he didn't want to carry any longer.

He followed the dusty road, passing only a freight wagon and two prospectors on the way to town. When he got to the Snake, he watered Duke, took the apple from his saddlebag, and ate half of it. He fed the other half to the horse, then mounted and spurred Duke into a fast trot, a jolting pace that was uncomfortable but ate up the miles.

The country was good, he saw. Long rolling hills burnt sienna by the fall sun, and banked by the river flats with the emerald green of the willows. Far off the high rise of snow peaks caught the flash of the sun, and to the south, distant in the purple haze, he could barely see the summit of the hills he had ridden from to get to Placid.

A good land for cattle. Grass, water, not too hot except for a short season. He thought the winters would be biting, but not the killing kind he had known in Montana.

He had an eye for land, and all he saw pleased him. He was not a town man, and it took the open spaces and the dome of the sky to relax the tension that had built up in him even for one night's stay. He had known for a long time that he would have to live on the fringes of the world, and as he let the river and the plain delight his eye he wondered why he had wasted his life.

"What I need is to go to Canada, Duke, and keep going north until I get so far back in the woods the deer won't even run away." He smiled then, and the break in his humor made him look young. "Just one errand and we'll do 'er!"

Half an hour later, he topped the last rise, and there in a valley nearly a mile long lay what he knew had to be Arrow. "Not a bad looking place," he mused, and knew that he was seeing it without the one thing that destroyed its natural beauty—which was the long shadow that Skull threw over it. Aaron Carr would never sleep well with another man owning this fine section.

Two men were branding a small group of yearlings in the tiny corral over to the east of the main house, and they were so occupied with wrestling the feisty, bawling calves that he rode up and dismounted without their notice.

Standing at the fence, he fastened his eyes on the large man who was doing the heavy work, throwing the animals to the ground and holding them while the older man slapped the hot iron on them.

"Watch out, Josh!" Stevens snapped nervously. "You nearly stuck that iron on my backside. If you don't—"

He stopped so abruptly that Jordan got up suddenly, and both men stared at the visitor. Reno nodded and said, "Hello, Thad."

Jordan was angry. He was over eighty, but he had done his share of Indian fighting, and to be caught off guard went against the grain. He opened his mouth to cuss the dark-eyed man out, but then he glimpsed the shock on Thad Stevens' face and kept his mouth shut.

Stevens had an oddly helpless look on his face, and his color was bad. Ordinarily he had a sunburned tone, but now he was the color of old putty. His jaw was sagging, and when he tried to speak, nothing came out. Finally he pulled himself together and dropped the rope he had in his hand to go toward the fence.

When he got there, he opened the gate and stepped outside. Facing Reno, he did not speak for a long moment; then he said, "I never thought I'd see you again."

Reno shrugged his compact shoulders. "I guess not." The dislike on Stevens' face was so plain that he wanted to turn and leave, but he said, "Nice place you got here, Thad."

The words seemed to irritate Stevens, and he invited, "Come on up to the house. Josh, we can do the rest of these calves later."

"Might as well do 'em now," Reno suggested.

"No." Stevens turned on his heel and walked away, his back stiff and his jaw lifted higher than usual.

Reno caught the glance of the old man and said, "Looks like I wore my welcome out in record time."

Jordan was puzzled by his boss. He had worked on Arrow for five years, and although he had no patience with Stevens' preaching, he liked him as a man. He'd never seen Thad turn so cold toward anyone as he had to this stranger.

"Guess he et something that disagreed with him. My name's Josh Jordan."

"Jim Reno. Well, guess I better get my chore done and be heading along."

Josh turned and let the calf out into the corral, then said, "It's about time to eat. I got some stew on the stove."

"What kind?"

"Son-of-a-gun stew."

"That's the best kind, I reckon." Reno grinned. "If your boss doesn't throw me out, maybe I can wrestle a few bites down my throat."

He followed the old man into the house, and Jordan saw that Stevens was waiting in the living room, a cold look on his face. "I better dish up some grub," Jordan said, and dodged into the kitchen, not getting too far from the door as he began pulling the meal together. He knew every cow that walked on Arrow, and anything that touched Stevens or the spread he felt was his legitimate province.

Stevens asked bluntly, "What are you doing in these parts, Jim?" He spoke stiffly, and he did not offer the other a seat.

Reno let a little silence run on as he studied the face of the taller man. Then he said gently, "Well, I haven't come to stay, Thad, so you can relax."

There was a sudden reddening of Stevens' face, and he looked slightly ashamed of his behavior. "Well, I—I guess you caught me off guard, Jim. To be honest, I heard you were dead. About two years ago, I think it was, over in Sonora."

Reno's eyes clouded and he nodded slowly. "You just about heard right, Thad. Took a bullet here"—he touched his chest high on the right side—"but I pulled out of it." He then hesitated and said, "I've thought about you a lot, Thad, though you might doubt that."

Stevens nodded. "Sit down. Time to eat." He sat down in one of the battered kitchen chairs and slowly admitted, "I've thought of you pretty often, too. But seems like after you got out of the army, I didn't hear much about you."

A frown touched Jim's face, and there was a slight pause. "Just as well, Thad." He tapped the table softly with a forefinger and added, "I reckon I didn't do anything after the army you'd want to hear about."

Josh broke through the door with a large bowl of steaming stew. He plunked it down, saying, "You birds just sit there and I'll get the rest of the grub."

It was a good meal, but only Josh ate hungrily. Reno commended Jordan on the food, but actually ate little, and the owner of Arrow seemed preoccupied with some troublesome thought.

Finally, he said, "Josh, Jim is my half brother."

"What say?" Josh responded quickly. "I didn't know you had a brother."

"*Half* brother," Thad corrected, too quickly. "We had the same mother, different fathers."

"You sure don't favor none," Josh mused, considering their faces.

"No. I'm the black sheep." Reno gave Thad a strange look and said, "I didn't know you were a preacher."

For some reason the statement bothered the larger man. He shook his head quickly, and his face reddened. "Oh, Jim, I'm not a real preacher. Not ordained or anything."

"But I thought . . ."

"I just fill in. Pretty soon the church will be able to get a real preacher. I'm just a two-bit rancher trying to make it out here in these hills."

"I'm thinking of Lige," Reno said gently. "That was his dad," he explained to Josh. "He was a preacher, and I guess about as good a man as I ever knew." He leaned forward and his dark eyes probed at Thad. "Guess you remember how he never made any difference between the two of us, Thad?"

Thad nodded, "I remember."

"Not many men would have done that with another man's boy." Reno's face changed then, and it was strange how the thought he entertained softened the hard lines that had settled around his lips. A bitter smile crossed his broad lips and he said softly, "'Specially a maverick like me."

Stevens nodded slowly. "He always liked you, Jim. I guess it really went hard with him when you—" He broke off abruptly and was obviously feeling awkward.

"Don't mind, Thad," Reno said with a wry smile. "I went to the devil. That's the end of it."

Thad tried to get the conversation on another track. "Well, anyway, you did well in the war. Dad was real proud of you."

Reno shook his head. Reaching into his pocket, he pulled out something wrapped in a piece of soft brown leather.

Handing it to Stevens he said, "This is why I came looking for you, Thad."

Stevens fumbled with the string that held the small package together, finally removing a small miniature in a gold case from the leather. He stared at the face of it, and his face was still. Finally he looked up, and there was a tiny twitch in his left eyelid. His voice was not steady as he said, "I—I never had a picture of her, Jim." He turned the miniature toward Josh who

took in the sweet-faced woman in simple clothes, a woman
with Stevens' features in a refined way.

"Sure, I know," Reno said. He turned and stared out the
window, disturbed at the struggle Thad was having to cover
his emotion. "It was in my stuff when I left to go to the army,
but I never found it until I got to Virginia. After Lige died and
then Ma, I knew you ought to have it. But it was hard to get
things back home, you see, and then I just forgot it."

"It's good to have it, Jim," Stevens said. He smiled now,
and added, "You came a long way to give me this."

"No, not really, Thad." Reno stood up and gazed out the
window. "I'm going to the coast—Oregon, I guess, or maybe
Canada. Old Mrs. Cantrell told me where to find you."

There was a silence, and then Reno said, "Well, I'm on my
way, Thad."

"Why, you can't leave now, Jim!" Stevens was remembering his cold welcome and seemed determined to keep Jim
from leaving. He took him by the arm, arguing earnestly, "Jim,
you don't have to go to Canada. This is fine country. You can
stay here! Arrow isn't much right now, but we can work on it."

Reno smiled, and freed himself gently. "That's real fine of
you, Thad. Especially after all the grief I caused you and your
folks. But I've got to get away." There was a look of pain on his
dark, wedge-shaped face as he said almost to himself, "Too
many memories I need to get rid of, Thad."

Then he gave a little shake and took Thad's hand. "I'll
write you when I get there, Thad. Maybe you can come and
join me in the big woods."

"No, I'm here for good, Jim."

Reno thought suddenly of Skull, and knew that the same
thought was in his brother's mind, for there was a sadness, a

lostness in Thad's broad face. He didn't speak of it, but Reno saw that there was little hope for the future in the big man. He felt a stir inside that inclined him to throw in his lot with the small men of the Valley, but he ignored it, saying, "Well, good luck."

Both men followed him to his horse. He swung up and said, "Thad, don't be too proud to run."

Stevens stared at him, understanding at once that Reno knew about the trouble in the Valley. But he shook his head stubbornly. "A man can't always be running, Jim."

The statement caught Reno off guard. His face changed, and there was a sudden shame in him, as he realized that running was what he had been doing for a long time. But he shook it off quickly, saying, "I'd stay to help, Thad, but you're up against a stacked deck. I've played that hand before—and I can't do it again!" He leaned forward in his sudden earnestness. "Thad, I know all about turning the other cheek and all the other nice things you preach. But the trouble is, those things jut won't work. In another world, maybe, but not in this one. Give up, Thad."

Josh saw the strangeness of it all. Reno he had identified at once as the hard man, the one who could make things happen. Thad was the weak brother. But it wasn't working out like that. Thad, with all his insecurities and fears, was standing fast. It was Reno, with all his skill and strength, who was running.

"Better stay on, Reno," Josh said suddenly. He was not one to like another man quickly, but he found something in Reno very much like what he had been in his youth, and he didn't like to see the younger man throw it away. "Better to be dead than on the run from something."

Reno thought about that, then nodded. "I used to think that, Josh. Now—I guess I don't believe anything very much." He touched his spurs to Duke's sides, suddenly anxious to get away. "I'll write you from the coast," he called back, knowing full well he never would.

He traveled at a fast clip back along the bank of the Snake, and there was a confusion in his mind that blotted out the landscape.

Thad's words kept coming back like an echo: *A man can't always be running.*

He could not help thinking of the past few years, when time after time he had wound up running from something. Always thinking that sooner or later it would come to an end, but it never did.

He was a man who needed roots, who loved the land. Under favorable circumstances he would have led an even life as a rancher. But the trouble star he seemed to live under had led him down a turbulent stream, and now he realized he was tired to the bone with life.

He thought of going back, of beginning again with Stevens at the Arrow, knowing that the hard skills he had accumulated could be the difference between his brother living or dying.

But he did not turn Duke back to the east. He rode on, filled with dark thought, and because he was not himself, laying his customary caution aside, he did not see the horsemen who waited for him.

FOUR

Message from Skull

A raw shock of alarm shot through Reno as he came out of a shallow depression beside the river to find himself faced by four riders. Boone and Lee Carr, Red Williams, and a young rider he didn't know had spaced themselves along the trail, and he realized at once they were waiting for him.

As had happened so many times during the war, he was conscious of a strange silence, a foreboding of violence that threatened. His vision seemed to narrow, closing out the river on his right and the open plain on his left. Far off a hawk screamed faintly and the gurgling river purled softly on the gravel bar.

Lee Carr grinned broadly at Reno, and a streak of cruelty touched his thin lips. "Well, well," he drawled, "what have we got here?"

When Reno didn't respond, Red Williams said, "You should have kept on moving, Reno. You ain't very smart."

Reno stretched lazily in the saddle and said easily, "What's the welcomin' committee for, gents?"

His brain raced as he considered going for the rifle in the

saddle boot, but he knew he would never clear leather with the weapon. His only hope was to put them off guard and hope for a break, so he moved slowly and spoke mildly.

"Ain't no welcomin' committee," Boone Carr grunted, and there was a steady dislike in his heavy face. "I guess it's just the opposite."

"Yeah, we come to help you get started on your way out of the Valley," Lee laughed loudly.

Reno forced himself to grin, saying with a shrug, "Well, I appreciate your concern—but I guess I can limp along all by my lonesome. Matter of fact, I'm headed for the pass right now. This time tomorrow guess I'll have a good start on my way to Oregon."

"You're lyin', fella," Boone said. "Pres caught you at the Circle M already."

"Just happened by."

"You just 'happen' to go to Arrow?" Lee said. He shook his head and said, "We gotta make an example of this one, Boone."

Red nodded. "Lee's right. He ain't no pilgrim. Open up that saddlebag and you'll find he's packing iron."

Reno realized he was not going to get out of this by talk. Straightening up in the saddle he nudged Duke, and spoke to cover the movement the roan made toward the open plain. "I don't guess a man has got to explain himself to any self-appointed committees. I've told you—"

"Put a rope on him, Benny," Boone Carr commanded, and as the freckled-faced puncher built a loop, he added, "It won't wash, Reno. You're caught, and we're gonna rough you up."

Reno said quietly, "Now, let's talk about this thing. Why do you—"

Suddenly he drove the spurs into Duke's sides, pulling his head to the left, and the startled horse exploded in that burst of speed that only a quarter horse can show. Reno leaned forward over the pomme trying to avoid the loop he knew would come.

For a moment he thought he'd made it, and a thrill of fear shot through him as he expected one of the men to open fire on him. Then a rope dropped neatly over his shoulders, and before he could shake it off he was yanked violently out of the saddle.

He hit the ground on his shoulders, his head striking the earth. Instantly a roaring filled his ears while brilliant lights flashed across his vision. His lungs emptied with a whoosh and he heard someone shout, "Catch that hoss!"

Acrid dust filled Reno's nose and mouth as the rope bit into his arms, and a branch caught him across the eyes, blinding him with the searing pain. Although the ground was fairly level, he felt his hands being rubbed raw by the river gravel, and his body was snared once by a dead limb which snapped as the rider drove his mount steadily on.

The raging fury which rose up in his throat at the savage treatment of Skull gave way to a thick fear, and he struggled wildly to free his hands, but the rope bit into him like a steel band. *They'll drag me to death!* he thought, and not even the fierce baptism of fire at The Bloody Angle where the dead had been stacked like cordwood had made him so terrified.

An abrupt drop in the terrain flipped him over, and his head received a savage blow that seemed to blot out the world. He heard the sound of the horse's driving hooves only as a dim echo, and the pain in his battered body seemed to ebb. Out of the silence arose a strange roaring noise, and then he felt himself being jerked roughly to his feet.

"Hold him right there, Red. Grab that other arm, Lee."

Reno opened his streaming eyes, gasping for breath. His left shoulder seemed to be on fire, and he had no feeling in that arm. Boone Carr's square features filled his vision, a brutal determination etched implacably on his lips.

Without warning he pounded Reno's face with a ponderous blow that smashed Reno's lips against his teeth, driving his head back as if he had been struck by a pile driver.

The force of that blow was a mercy, for it stunned the helpless man completely. He did not feel the battering blows that Carr drove into his face, then into his body, held upright by Red Williams and Lee Carr.

On Boone Carr's face there was no anger. He smashed the helpless body of Reno as he might have split wood, with no emotion. Benny Lyons, the young puncher who had coiled his rope, stood with a white face as he watched the beating. Once he stepped forward and said, "Hey, Mr. Carr . . ." but Red Williams shoved him back, and he turned abruptly, mounting his horse and riding away at a dead run.

Lee Carr, who had been grinning at the beginning, finally said, "Hey, Boone, that's enough. We don't want to kill him."

"Hold him up," his brother answered stolidly. "You wanted this, and you ain't gonna chicken out."

He drove another half-dozen blows into Reno's face which was a mass of blood, then he drew back and sent a tremendous punch into the ribs.

"You broke something, Boone," Williams laughed.

Carr dropped his arms, stared at his fists, then looked around. "Where's Benny?"

"He took off," Red answered. "Let's get out of here."

"Where's his horse?" Boone asked.

"He lit out—too fast to catch."

Boone stared at the inert body of Reno. "Tie him on your horse, Red."

"What you aim to do?" Lee asked quickly. His easy smile was gone, and there was a strained look around his eyes. "We've done what we came to do. Let's light a shuck."

Boone stared at him, sucked on his lower lip. "You been walking around with that fancy gun for a long spell, Lee. Been acting tough, trying to turn your wolf loose. Now the first time you see a little blood you start shakin' in your boots."

"I—"

"We're gonna be sure those sodbusters learn what it means to stand against Skull!" He fished around in his pocket till he found a scrap of paper and a pencil. Going to his horse, he put the paper against the saddle. Only the sound of Reno's strained breathing broke the silence as he wrote.

"This ought to make it clear," he grunted, sticking the paper in Reno's shirt pocket. "Now, lash him down."

"Where we gonna take him, Boone?" Lee asked, as they put Reno's body across the back of Red's horse.

"We'll drop him off at the Circle M, I think," Boone said slowly. "Don't matter much which of them gets the word. Whoever it is will pass it on." He stared blankly at Reno, then as he swung into the saddle with grim satisfaction, "I don't think we'll have any more hired guns coming to the Valley. Let's get this done." There was a sudden pounding of hoofbeats, then silence flowed across the riverbank; soon a dusty timber wolf appeared out of the breaks, and paused to sniff warily at the blood marks on the river rocks.

When he tried to pull himself out of the dark currents, the pain flooded through him. It was easier to slip back into unconsciousness than to face the raw pain in his chest that sucked his breath.

Someone kept talking to him, a quiet voice that called his name, trying to draw him to the light. And there were hands that pulled at him, sometimes hurting him, but at times soothing the raw flesh with some sort of aromatic liquid that cooled his wounds.

Vaguely he knew that he was in a bed with cool sheets smelling of lavender, and through slits of his swollen eyes he recognized the passage of time by the alternating layers of light and dark that seemed to come from somewhere to his left.

He came to consciousness with a rush, as a hand touched his cheeks and a woman's voice asked, "Are you awake?"

"Yes," he answered in a scratchy voice. His eyes were hard to open, but he forced them wide enough to see Catherine Edwards leaning over him.

"Jim," she said, and a smile touched her broad lips. "How do you feel?"

He tried to sit up, but the movement sent a searing pain along his right side. "How—long have I been here?" he asked.

She took a glass of water and put it to his lips. As he drank thirstily she said, "Three days."

Reno drank all the water, and the effort of lifting his head tired him out. His eyes ran around the room, and he asked, "How'd I get here, Catherine?"

"You were delivered by Skull," she explained, and the gentleness of her lips hardened as she added, "They dumped you in our yard."

"Help me sit up," he said, and when she started to protest, he grew sharp. "Help me up!"

He drew his breath sharply as she helped him sit up, and the room reeled for a second, but he felt better having made even this small gesture of independence. "Wonder why they dumped me off on you?"

She reached over to a small table beside the bed and picked up a note. "This was in your shirt pocket, Jim. It says, 'Here's your hired gunman. The next one will be dead.'" She put the paper back on the table, and there was a light of pure anger in her hazel eyes as she said, "Skull, of course. They didn't need to sign it."

"Reckon not. You patch me up?"

"No, Doctor Moody came out the next day." She put out a hand and touched the bandage on his forehead softly. "You had to have stitches here—and a couple of your ribs are probably broken."

Reno shrugged, then said in a tired voice, "I guess it might have been worse."

She looked at him steadily, and there was a question on her lips, but she knew he would not welcome it. Instead she said, "You have to eat. I'll get some soup."

She left the room and Reno closed his eyes against the pain and dizziness that swept through him. He had been hurt before, so the pain was something that he could endure, but there was a deep anger that kept rising to the surface of his mind when he thought of the manner in which Skull had put him to the ground. To take a bullet in a battle or to get hurt in a fist fight—that was to be accepted as part of the risk of war and manhood. But to be held and smashed like he was nothing—that grated on him, and he had to drive the memory from his mind as he lay waiting for the food.

The soup she brought stirred his hunger, and he ate two bowls of it before he leaned back. "That was good."

She took the bowl back to the kitchen and returned with
a white enamel basin of water and clean cloths. "I need to
change the dressings," she said, and he lay still as she
removed the old dressings, washed the wounds and deftly
replaced the bandages. Without even asking, she bathed his
upper body, sponging him with the cool water in a competent
fashion. She pulled him forward once, holding him firmly
against her as she carefully avoided the bandages on his ribs,
and although she was calmly impersonal with him, he was
intensely aware of the firm curves and warm flesh so close to
his own.

"There!" she said with a smile. "Feel better?"

He nodded and was suddenly so sleepy he could not keep
his eyes open. "Yes . . . but . . . I . . ." He heard her laugh quietly, then he slid into a dreamless sleep, free from the restlessness of the past nights.

When he awoke again, his eyes were almost free from
swelling, and he found that he could sit up alone. Carefully, he
drew himself to a sitting position, and he was so pleased with
how much easier it was that he carefully pulled his legs from
under the cover and swung them over the side of the bed. The
movement hurt his side, but he cautiously put his feet on the
floor, and taking a deep breath, he stood up, holding on to the
bedpost with one hand and the wall with the other. Pain caught
at him, and the room swam for a second, but that passed.

He smiled, and stood there for a few minutes, savoring
the feeling. He was a man who hated to be dependent, and the
accomplishment pleased him. Already he was thinking of how
long it would take him to get out of the bed for good, but suddenly the door swung open and Catherine walked in with her
father. They both stopped and stared at him, then Catherine's

eyes snapped with anger. She ordered loudly, "Jim Reno, you get back in that bed!"

Reno felt like a five-year-old who had been caught with his hand in the cookie jar. "Catherine, I just—"

"You just hush up and get in bed!" she said, and with an angry gesture she pushed up a lock of her chestnut hair, adding as she stalked to stand beside him, "You aren't to be trusted, Jim Reno! I've worked too hard on you to see you get sick again, so you just mind me!"

Reno grinned weakly at Silas, who winked at him. "She's a hard woman, Silas," he said. "But I think I'm strong enough to stay up."

She pushed at him with a rigid forefinger and the pressure drove him off balance. He sat down heavily, and the room spun again, so that she caught him and with an easy strength she put his legs back in the bed. Then she laughed and said, "You're in great shape! Ready to break wild horses."

"Better mind her, son," Silas said with a straight face. "She's just like her mother—worse than I can say about making a man do what she wants."

"Well . . . ," Reno said quietly, and he looked up at the pair with thoughtful eyes. "I guess she can pretty well do as she pleases. I know I wouldn't have made it if you hadn't taken me in. I thank you."

Catherine's face suddenly was tinged with a delicate reddish hue, and she shook her head impatiently. "Jim, you don't need to thank us. Anyone would have taken you in."

He thought about that, then shook his head. "That would be nice to believe—but it's just not so."

Silas Edwards said quietly after staring at Jim for a second, "You don't believe in much, do you, son?"

"Not too much."

"That's too bad." Silas shook his thin face and commented sadly, "Hate to see a young man so hard."

Reno searched for a reply, but the dark streak in him was ingrained, and he could only say finally, "I guess if I'd met up with more folks like you, I'd have a more generous opinion of the world."

"There are lots of good people," Catherine stated firmly.

He refused to argue, saying, "Sure. Guess I been looking in the wrong places."

They sat down and talked for half an hour, then Silas said, "I've got some work to do. See you tonight."

When he had left, Reno said, "Catherine, your dad doesn't look well."

Her lips grew thin. "He has a bad heart—very bad. He had an attack two years ago that nearly killed him. But he won't slow down."

"He have much help?"

"Just Juan Renaldo. He's only seventeen, but a good hand. And there're a couple of part-time riders."

He looked at her directly, then said quietly, "You know Skull will never let you alone, don't you, Catherine?"

There was a sudden stiffening of her body, and she folded her arms across her breast in a strangely protective gesture. The light coming from the window caught her from the side, highlighting the planes of her cheekbones, and heightening the determination of her strong chin and firm lips. "I know. Oh, how well I know!" she breathed in a low voice, that was tense with a suppressed pain and underscored by anger.

"Can't you find another place?" he suggested.

"No! This place is our last hope, Jim! Can't you see that? If they would just let us alone, we could make it!" she cried suddenly, and there was a strange beauty for him in the way she lifted her face to the sun. "We could do fine . . . I could take some of the work off Dad . . . get some help. . . ."

He watched her as she spoke, and the thought was strong in him: *This is the strongest woman I've ever seen.*

Suddenly she stopped. "Sorry, Jim. I didn't mean to cry all over you. It's not your problem."

She turned and left the room, leaving him disturbed. He lay there all afternoon fitfully napping, but always coming back to her words, *It's not your problem.*

Caution had been built into him by a hard life, and he had erected a barrier around himself. Those few friends he once had had been taken by one means or another, and he had hardened himself to letting anyone get a foothold in his affections. A cold life, certainly, but it had been suitable—at least, up until now.

The old man's helplessness pulled at him, as did the beauty of Catherine. Not just physically, though that was very real. It was the courage and dignity that lay beneath her smooth face and firm body that made him wonder if he'd been wrong about his dark acceptance of life.

The next week went by slowly, even though he gained strength rapidly. He talked himself out of bed, ignoring Catherine's protests as well as the aches of his bruised muscles.

He was pleased beyond measure when Juan brought Duke back, having been more worried than he had cared to admit about the horse.

He limped around the house, his impatience driving Catherine to finally say sharply, "Well, go on then, Jim Reno, and kill yourself! I can't put up with your pacing anymore."

So he had driven himself, until within a few days he was helping with the chores around the ranch and getting acquainted with the neighbors who came in to visit. Most of them came to see Silas or Catherine, but he was an object of curiosity to them.

Thad had been there often, and he kept his silence for a few days, but Jim knew he would ask about the beating sooner or later.

It came when Reno was riding along the river looking for strays. Thad came from over a rise, having looked for Reno at the ranch. They chatted for awhile, then Thad asked directly, "It was Carr that beat you up, wasn't it, Jim?"

"Sure."

Thad was taken aback by the readiness of the answer. Then he said, "You know they thought you were a gunman I brought here to fight Skull."

"They said as much."

"Well, what are you going to do now, Jim?"

Reno flicked the stray he was driving with the end of his rope. "Leave here, Thad. Just like I intended."

It did not set well with the larger man, and he replied at once, "You don't figure you owe Si and Catherine anything?"

"Sure I do." Reno struggled to find the right words, then said with a shrug, "Thad, it's a lost cause. I could stay and go down with the rest of you. But I just don't see why I should do that."

Thad stiffened and his voice was thick with anger. "Jim, you've never been worth a nickel! Always did just what you wanted to do—never mind about anybody else!" Thad's eyes were bright as he went on. "Why, I spent my life wanting to be what you are. Everything came so easy for you—while I never could do anything right! Now you got a chance to use all that skill you picked up in the war—and other places—" He shook his head savagely. "If I could do what you can with a gun, I'd stop Skull!"

Reno said slowly, "No one man is going to stop Skull, Thad. Not me, not anybody."

There was a finality in his voice that shut off the plea Thad was about to make. He stared at Reno, and said in a low voice, filled with regret, "Jim, I've always been envious of you. Ever since we were kids. You had so much—and I had so little! But I wouldn't be you now for all the money in the world! You're a bitter, selfish man, Jim, and you'll die that way. I wish you'd get out of the country. Silas and Catherine haven't said anything, but I know they're hoping you'll stay and help them. But you never will!" He called back bitterly as he slapped his horse into a run. "Get out of the Valley, Jim! You're a sorry excuse for a man!"

"Looks like you're gonna live, Jim." Josh Jordan leaned against the faded barn watching Reno pitch bales of hay up to Juan in the loft. "How long's it been since Skull chawed you up and set you out on Circle M?"

Reno picked up a bale, holding it waist high. "Three weeks tomorrow," he answered. Effortlessly he sent the heavy bale up; Juan had only to move it into place.

"How's Silas feeling?" Josh asked. Thad had told him that Edwards had been having one of his bad spells, so he had come to lend a hand.

"I'd say not too well, Josh." Reno kept on working as he talked, and every time he pitched a bale, the breadth of his sleekly muscled shoulders writhed under his dark skin. His torso tapered down to a trim waist, ridges of hard muscles forming into squares across his stomach. Just as there was no spare flesh on him, there was an economy of motion as he worked steadily, lifting the awkward bales in one fluid movement, then exploding just enough of his energy to flip them upward with a smooth follow-through of his powerful arms and shoulders.

"He don't work like no cowboy I ever saw, Josh," Juan called down. His white teeth flashed in his brown face as he added, "Why, he even deegs post holes! What . . . !" He disappeared as Reno sent a bale flying over the lip of the loft, catching the little puncher in the chest.

Josh grinned as Juan emerged spitting straw. Then he got a serious look on his lined face, saying quietly, "I figured you'd be gone by this time, Jim—soon as you were able to ride out."

Reno paused, a quizzical look on his face. He drew a deep breath, gazing at the far-off line of hills that rose to the south. "Yeah, guess I thought so, too, Josh," he said finally.

"Couldn't nobody fault you, Jim. They shore left their tracks all over you." He glanced critically at the unhealed scars on Reno's face and the bruises still visible on his lean torso. "And I guess you know it'll be worse if they get to you again."

"They can be pretty rough, those Carrs," Reno said in a deceptively soft tone. "Especially when they got a man tied up so he can't fight back."

Josh paid no heed to the soft, toneless voice, picking up on the fire that gleamed in Reno's black eyes and the sudden hardening of the muscles in his face. He nodded slowly as if coming to some sort of conclusion, then he spat on the ground before saying, "You better git, Jim. Thad told me you wuz leavin', and he said you ort to stay and join up with the small ranchers."

Reno cocked his head, catching Josh with a quick answer. "He said more than that, didn't he, Josh?"

"Shore, but I'm makin' my own judgments. Reckon you sowed a plentiful crop of wild oats, and I seen enough men to know you ain't no tame cat." Josh's smile was knowing as he looked at Reno. "Way you make a show outta not packin' a gun might fool some folks, but I guess you've seen more'n a little action along that line."

Slowly Reno nodded, and his broad lips were scored by regret. "You read a man pretty well, Josh. Guess you've seen a few in your day."

"You got the marks, Jim. I been knockin' around for a long time, and allus noticed that some fellers just naturally take to the rough life. Why, I knowed Bill Bonny when he started out—just a green kid! But he had something in him even then, and I seen it." Jordan gave Reno a direct stare, adding flatly, "You got some of that in you, Jim. Question is—whut you gonna do with it?"

Reno laughed humorlessly. "Try to run away so far that I'll never have to fight any man, I guess."

"Won't do, Jim." Josh shook his lean face and added, "I reckon I know what's eatin' at you—old man Edwards." He paused, then dropped another word: "And that girl Catherine."

"I can't help them, Josh," Reno retorted, too quickly. He spoke again as if he were trying to convince himself rather than Jordan. "I'm in their debt. Nobody ever went out on a limb for me before like they've done. And if it were just work, why, I'd stay and help. But we both know Skull won't let it alone. This whole valley is a powder keg! Sooner or later there's going to be a war, and there's no doubt about who's going to win, Josh. Skull's just too strong."

Jordan nodded. "Sure, that's the way the hand reads, Jim, but you know it don't work like that, don't you? You seen enough action in the war to remember that lots of times a little bunch got their dander up and whupped the fire outta a big bunch."

"That's right," Reno admitted, "But—"

"And you know why, too, Jim. It was because one man with guts got up and said, *Let's go!*"

Reno didn't answer until he had pitched the last bale up to Juan. He put on his shirt, buttoned it, then turned to face the old rider. When he spoke there was a streak of regret in his chiseled face: "Not for me, Josh. I've done enough fighting to last me a lifetime."

"Wish you'd consider it—stayin' on, I mean," Josh said slowly. He looked straight into Reno's face and came as close as he ever would to asking a favor. "Way I see it, Jim, sooner or later it's goin' to come to a shootin' war. I think mebbe you could make the difference with these folks." He shrugged and ended, "But that's your say."

As Reno walked toward the house, he limped slightly, a reminder of Skull's treatment. Josh's words had disturbed him, stirring into life the thoughts he'd kept from his mind. Now he felt a restlessness to be gone from the Valley, on his way to the coast. He was, he realized, not going to be able to stay at Circle M for long. Skull would not permit it, for any resistance to its power had to be crushed at once. Word of the beating he'd taken had spread, so that if he didn't run, Carr would find a way to break him.

"Maybe I'm getting soft," he mused. But it was fear that actually convinced him to leave. Not fear of Skull's power; he had faced that sort of danger too often to be afraid. It was the fear that he would become what he had seen others turn into— merciless men, all the warmth of human emotion lost. A shiver went through him as he thought of some men who had learned to love killing, to lust for blood. Others had simply become animals, thinking no more of taking a human life than they would of shooting a rabbit. "I won't be like that!" he said under his breath, and going up the steps to knock on the door of the house, he made his decision.

Catherine opened the door, and he had that little shock that the sight of her sometimes brought to him—a gentleness which had so seldom touched his life that she drew his attention like a magnet.

"Come in, Jim."

"How's your dad?" he asked, stepping inside.

She hesitated and there was a quick fear in her eyes. "I don't like the way he looks."

"What did Doc Moody say?"

"The things I wanted to hear, I think," she said. "Keep him quiet—that's what it comes to. But you know he won't be still."

Reno shifted uncomfortably, searching for some hope to offer, then not finding any, said only, "I'm going to check on that bunch of yearlings over by the timber—you know, over close to the old Miller place."

Care left Catherine's face, replaced by a slow smile which made her look very young. Her warm eyes twinkled and there was a note of fond humor in her voice. "You know more about this ranch than I do, Jim. How'd you learn so much in such a short time?"

Reno felt trapped, for he had been playing a little game with himself, and he said quickly, "Oh, just kept my eyes open, I guess."

Actually he had been strongly taken by the ranch. Not for a long time had he been in the center of living an ordered life. As he had grown stronger, throwing himself into the round of chores that made a ranch alive, he had sometimes forgotten

Skull and its dark threat. He had let the violence of his past
slide away, and had entered into the life of the Valley. Branding, treating sick animals, putting up hay, riding early in the
cool dawn with Juan to locate some missing steers, eating at
the table with the crew with all the small talk and warm com-
panionship—all this flow of activity stirred a longing in him,
and he had thrown himself into the place as though it were his
own, a place to stay until he grew old and lay in a grave in the
small cemetery by the river.

Catherine caught the look on his face, and suddenly she
seemed to read this thought. "You like ranching, don't you,
Jim?"

"Yes. Better than anything."

"Why don't you . . . ," she said warmly, then stopped with
a sad look coming into her eyes. "But you'll be leaving soon."

"I'll stay until your dad gets on his feet, Catherine."

She shook her head. "No, I think you'd better go right
away."

"Why?"

"I guess you know. If you were going to stay permanently,
it would be one thing. But Aaron Carr can't let you go on living
here in the Valley. I've already heard that the word is out to get
you." She came close and he smelled the fresh odor of her
hair, and her presence triggered a little shock along his
nerves. "I don't want you killed, Jim."

It was in him to change—to forget his plans. For one long
moment as Catherine watched his dark face, she thought he
would. Then he nodded and said tonelessly, "I expect you're
right. I'll stay for a couple more days."

The light in her eyes went out, and she merely nodded as
he stepped back and left the house. As he mounted Duke and

started for the foothills, he no longer enjoyed the sun on his back, and already he was thinking of the trail that led out of the Valley, wishing he could be on it with no delay.

"You better wait until tomorrow to make your visit," Aaron Carr advised. He looked up at the sky, then down at Stacy. "Looks like it might blow up a storm, and it's pretty late already."

"Oh, Dad. Ruth is looking for me, and it's an easy ride."

"Never mind a thing I say," the owner of Skull grumbled, but he had a benevolent look on his craggy face. Giving her a hand up, he said roughly, "Ought to turn you over my knee."

Stacy gave him a smile and leaned over the saddle to kiss his cheek. "Too late. I'm spoiled so rotten you can't fix it."

"You need a man who'll whip the tar out of you regular," he shot back.

Those who knew Aaron Carr only as the ironfisted land baron who brooked no opposition would have been amazed at the easy tolerance he had toward his only daughter. He'd been hardhanded with his boys, but this laughing fair-haired girl was his weak spot, and he scowled to cover the affection he had for her. "I'm looking for a real man for a son-in-law. Going to give him a leather strop to use on you as a wedding present."

"Like the one you use on Mother?" she shot back gaily. Then waving her hand, she drove her buckskin mare out of the wide yard and down the road leading to Abe Frazier's Bent 6.

She passed several of the crew a few miles to the north, and her brother Frank pulled away from the hands driving two-year-olds toward some new grass.

"Where you headed, Stacy?"

"Oh, just over to see Ruth Frazier. Were going to the dance day after tomorrow in town."

"I heard Etta Reynolds beat your time with Ray Rogers," he said with a straight face but a gleam in his eye. "Ray said he was taking her to the dance and I meant to tell you, Stacy. I know it's tough getting dumped by a man, so if you like, I'll whip Ray and make him take you."

They had always been close, closer than any of the other family members. "You tend your own business, Frank," she sniffed. "I gave Ray his walking papers last week. Etta can have the leftovers."

He grinned at her, saying, "Better watch out you don't end up an old maid. But there's plenty of men around, I guess."

"Plenty of gophers and sidewinders, too," she said with a smile. Then she sobered and asked suddenly, "What about you, Frank? You still seeing May Swenson?"

Frank Carr at twenty-six was a highly eligible bachelor, but had never been serious about any woman. Not until the daughter of the nester Ole Swenson had blossomed into a serene, full-bodied young woman who had many of the young bucks fighting over her.

Frank straightened up in the saddle and stared at the distant hills. "Guess you know about how likely that is, Stacy."

"Sure, I know, Frank," Stacy said, and her wide lips were soft and maternal as she touched his shoulder. "I guess we're in the same boat, aren't we? Anybody we choose will have to pass Dad's inspection."

Frank laughed shortly, and his voice was bitter. "Can you imagine what Dad would say if I told him I was marrying a nester's girl? Besides, May wouldn't have me. She knows I could run her family out of the country any time."

"No, Frank, it won't come to that."

"Won't it?" he asked, then jerked his horse to a halt. "What makes you think it won't, Stacy?"

"Dad wouldn't do that," she argued, but there was no certainty in her voice.

"Better get moving, Stacy. Looks like a thunderstorm over there," Frank warned, then turned his horse away, and there was a slump to his broad shoulders as he left her.

Rolling clouds got darker as she drove her mare at a fast gait toward the Bent 6, and by the time she reached the rise of timber, dark shadows began to fall in bars from the tall pines. Her horse was still eager, so she took the trail at a fast gallop, hoping to clear the ridge and make the descent before dark. A rolling peal of thunder preceded by a bolt of lightning which licked downward and touched a tall tree made her anxious to get clear of the timber, and she drove her spurs into the mare.

Stacy knew the land thoroughly, but she didn't want to get soaked. Recklessly she swerved between pine and jack oak at full speed, enjoying the wildness of the ride, loving the weather, for she was not a calm woman, and the roar and crackle of a storm always delighted her.

Light broke at the end of the timberline, and she sped toward it, but suddenly her mare stepped into a pocket and she went flying through the air, able only to break her fall by hitting the needle-cushioned earth in a compact ball, which drove the wind out of her.

She sat up, shaking the dizziness away, and looking around for her horse. The mare was down, and Stacy got to her feet, hurting but with no broken bones. "Lady, are you all right?"

The horse was badly injured, and Stacy's heart sank as

she saw the right foreleg bent at an impossible angle, broken in all probability. "Oh, Lady!" she cried in the falling darkness. She bit her lip, for she loved this one best of all her horses.

She looked over to the west, thinking of what lay there. Only grassland, no settlers at all. To the east lay a small farm nestled in the foothills, but it was over ten miles away—too far. The Snake River lay ahead less than two miles, and there was usually someone following the banks.

She left quickly, walking awkwardly in the high-heeled boots, and was glad to leave the timber for the open plain. A city girl would have been terrified, but Stacy was born on the range, and as she made her way steadily along toward the river, there was no fear in her—only a great heaviness for the mare.

An hour later she came to the river, and the darkness had closed down, a moonless night and getting colder.

Turning west she followed the bank of the Snake, getting her feet wet and beginning to tire. Another half hour and the darkness was so thick she could not see her hand before her face. Only the infrequent bolts of lightning which lit up the sky gave her any view of the country.

Finally, just as she had decided to get under a tree and wait for morning, she saw a pinpoint of light in front of her. Eagerly she hurried toward it, and soon she was within hailing distance of a small fire.

"Hello the camp!" she called out, too wise in the ways of the country to walk in unannounced to a strange campfire.

"Hold it!" A voice challenged out of the ring of light, and a man rose, stepping to one side into the shadows. "Who are you?"

"Stacy Carr," she answered, and walked up to the fire.

She could not see the face of the man who stood in the shadows, but by the flicker of the small fire, she saw that he held a rifle in his hand. "I can't see you," she said.

The man stepped forward, letting the rifle drop beside the saddle close to the fire. "What are you doing out here alone, Miss Carr?"

"My horse is down," she said, straining her eyes to see his face. "I think her leg's broken." Then he stepped closer and she got a look at his face. "Oh—it's you."

"I guess so," Reno said. He did not smile at her as most men would have done. His face was lean, and the wedge shape of his jaw and the wide-set dark eyes gave him a wolfish appearance in the half-light of the small fire.

A flutter of fear went through her, for she knew of the beating he had taken at her brothers' hands. Alone with him, far from home and at his mercy, she made her voice steady as she explained, "I hate to trouble you, but I need some help."

He still did not move, and the silence ran on so long that a thrill of fear made its way through her, and she added, "I'll be glad to pay you."

Reno mumbled, "Skull can buy anything, I guess." Then he sighed. "Where's your mare?"

Stacy replied, relief in her voice, "About four or five miles back—in the timber."

"I'll go see about her. You sure about that leg?"

"I—I think so."

"Well, you know what's to be done."

Stacy nodded, unable to speak. Finally she said, "I'll have to go with you. You'll never find her alone."

He didn't answer but began saddling the horse staked out a few yards away. When he had finished he said, "Have to ride double."

"That's all right." She watched him mount, then put her foot in the stirrup, swung on behind him, and put her arms around his chest.

"Tell me where to head to the spot," he said, and let the horse follow the riverbank.

Stacy held on to him trying not to grasp him too tightly, but the gait of the mount, rolling and shifting as he picked his way through the broken ground, forced her to tighten her grip. The lithe muscles of his body were like steel coils as he rolled with the motion of the horse. Stacy pressed against his back, and the intimacy of the touch brought a flush to her face, making her glad of the covering darkness.

Finally she spoke up. "I think it's over there." She caught a glimpse of the rising timber and saw suddenly the huge dead pine she had passed as she came out. "There it is."

He drove the horse toward the spot, and soon they were beside the mare. He took one look by the light of a match, then was silent.

"It's—it's broken, isn't it?"

"I'm afraid so." He turned to her, and his voice ceased to be hard. "Take my horse," he said gently. "Head on back to the river. Go quick."

Blinded by a sudden rush of tears, Stacy grasped the reins and saw that he slipped his rifle out of the boot. She let the horse pick his way to the river and got off, hands tightly clenched. There was only the sound of wind and the rolling river, and then one shot came from the timber. She turned and buried her face in her arms, leaning on the horse.

By the time Reno came to stand beside her, her voice was steady. "Thank you. I couldn't have done it."

He mounted and pulled her up behind him without a

word, and neither of them spoke as they made their way back
to his camp. Once again she was forced to hold tightly to him,
and there was no way, she knew, that he could be unconscious
of her body pressed tightly to his, but he said nothing as she
slipped to the ground. He dismounted and tossed a few sticks
of wood on the fire.

"What can I do for you?" he asked.

She knew instinctively he would not take her to Skull, so
she said, "I was on my way to Bent 6, but it's a long way to go
as dark as it is. We'd have to cross the river."

"Not too anxious to do that," he said. "I was planning to
spend the night here."

"You're Jim Reno, aren't you?"

"That's right," he admitted.

She studied him in the darkness, then asked, "I suppose
you hate anything connected with our ranch?"

"Hating is pretty expensive, Miss Carr. I can't afford it. I'll
have to take you to the Circle M. You know the Edwards family?"

"Certainly. Catherine and I are friends." She saw a question rise to his eyes, but he said nothing. "Can we go now?"
she asked.

He pulled his gear together and tied it in the high limb of
a cottonwood. Dumping the remains of his coffee on the burning coals he reasoned, "Guess the rain will get this. We're
going to get wet." Then he did a peculiar thing. Instead of
swinging into the saddle, he said, "You get up. I'll ride behind."

She mounted, leaving the stirrup free, and then he
mounted easily, saying, "I guess you know the way."

Stacy nodded and moved the horse through the darkness.
He sat behind her, but he did not put his arms around her to

hold on. Swaying with the movement of the horse, he held the stiff leather of the saddle, and it seemed clear to her that he had known of her awkwardness, having to practically hug him, and he had found a way to ease the situation. Somehow it troubled her, for she had heard nothing good about Reno. If he had been rough or uncouth she could have met him head on, but that single act of courtesy—as well as the way he had handled the matter of her mare—made it difficult to look down on him as she might had he been different.

For a few miles they said nothing, and the rain began to fall, wetting them to the skin. "Turning cold. Be winter soon." He spoke idly, and she was curious.

"You're from where, Reno?"

The answer came after a noticeable delay. "From the South. Been gone from there since the war."

She asked him about the war, and he talked readily of it, telling her several incidents, making light of the hardship he must have known.

Finally as they got close to the Circle M she said, "We're almost there, Jim." A flash of humor touched her. "I guess if the homesteaders want to make an example of a Carr, the Edwards will have their chance tonight."

"I don't reckon they'll be too tough on you."

"No, I know they won't," Stacy said. "They're good people. I feel so sorry for Catherine. Her father is so dear to her. I don't think he's doing well, is he?"

"Not too good."

Then the horse stumbled and he caught at her instinctively, his arms clasping her in a steely grip. For one moment he held her tightly, his hard hands pressing against her firm flesh, and she sat very still, her breathing suddenly irregular, and she was shaken as she had never been by the touch of a man.

"Sorry, Miss Carr," he apologized, and removed his arms.

"That's—all right," she said lamely, then continued rapidly to cover the confusion that the moment had brought, "There's the house. They're still up. See the light?"

"Guess so," Reno said.

As they got to the yard, Stacy felt the need to express her thanks while they were still alone. She waited for him to dismount, then slipped to the ground, saying, "I am grateful, really I am."

"Don't mention it."

She shook her head, insisting on having her say. "No, you've been a gentleman."

He laughed at her then, pleasure in his black eyes. "That surprises you, doesn't it? That a common ordinary mortal not working for Skull could be a gentleman?"

She refused to argue. Taking his arm, she shook her head. She was a tall girl, and her eyes were almost level with his. "You're making fun of me—but you've got the right. I know you won't take money, but I'll always remember this time. And if you'll tell me a way, I'll make it up to you."

He leaned toward her, and she thought for a second he was going to kiss her, but he only said, "Maybe you could make things a little easier on Silas and Catherine. I'd consider that a fair trade."

"Done!" she said, and stuck her hand out like a man. He took it and she added, "I'll do that, and I'll find a way to make it up to you, too."

"Can you cook?" he asked suddenly.

"Certainly!"

"Well, you can bake me a cake."

"I will!" she laughed, and then she pulled at his arm playfully. "I'll tell you what, you come to the dance day after tomorrow and I'll not only give you a cake, I'll get you dances with the prettiest girls in the Valley."

He smiled at her, enjoying the light in her blue eyes which caught the light of the glowing windows. "What would your family say to that?"

She shrugged, and as the door to the house suddenly opened, she said firmly, "I'm not a child, Jim."

The door swung open and a figure filled the doorway.

"Who is it?" Catherine called out. She stared out into the darkness and there was anxiety in her voice. "Jim? Is it you?"

"Yes—and he's brought you a stray, Catherine," Stacy teased. She walked up to the porch followed by Reno, explaining, "My horse broke a leg, Catherine. Jim brought me in like a drowned kitten. Can you put me up for the night?"

Catherine's voice was steady, and she took Stacy's arm pulling her into the house. "Of course. Why you must be freezing in those wet clothes! Come along, and I'll get you some dry things."

Stacy resisted her long enough to say, "Jim, remember about that cake."

Reno waited until Catherine returned, then asked, "How's Silas?"

"A little better. He went to bed early." She gave him a strange look before asking, "How did you happen to find her?"

"She came walking into my camp. Good thing, too, I guess. Pretty bad night."

"Yes." She said nothing else, but there was a thought in her eyes that she kept back. "You better get dried out, Jim. Don't go back tonight."

"Tomorrow will do." He glanced toward the room where Catherine had taken Stacy, and mused as if to himself, "Funny. She's not like her brothers at all."

"She's a very beautiful girl, isn't she?"

"Didn't notice."

Catherine tapped him lightly on the chest and laughed softly. "Liar!" Then she sobered and said, "I like Stacy. Always have. But . . ."

Reno looked down at her, cutting her short. "Tough. I wish it were different." He left the house, going to the bunkhouse. A wry thought touched him as he was getting into the warm bed, and just before he dropped off, he wondered what sort of a face Aaron Carr would have when he found out that a two-bit rider had saved his daughter.

Maybe he'll make me a partner, he thought with a grin, then he dropped off, wondering why life had to be so complicated.

SIX
Skull Strikes Back

By Friday Silas was back at work, his face pale and drawn. He had hired Josh to help around the Circle M until he got better. He moved slowly, carefully, like a man who's had a hard fall and is afraid to test himself, but he smiled and was cheerful enough when he and Reno rode together looking for strays.

"Guess you'll be going to the dance tonight?" he asked as they walked their horses slowly along the trail.

Reno nodded and there was a faint smile on his face. "Guess so. I've done so many fool things, guess one more won't matter."

"Why, you need to be foolish, son," the old man said warmly. "You're a fool for work, and I want you to let go a little bit."

"All right." Reno almost told Edwards that he had decided to leave the next day, but the sickly face of the Circle M owner made him bite off the words. "Skull will be there, I expect. You figure they'll try to eat one of my drumsticks, Silas?"

"No, not at a dance." Then Edwards added, "But you better watch your back, son. And if you want a gun, I got a spare you can pack."

Reno let it go, knowing that Silas and others were puzzled by the fact that he never wore a gun. Finally he said, "I have a gun."

"Thought you might. Been wondering about it, too, if you want to know." Something was bothering Edwards. He sought for the right words then apparently shifted the subject. "This is good country, Jim. Man could do worse than put down his roots here."

It was, Reno knew at once, not a casual remark. Beneath the words lay an invitation to friendship, and there was a sudden desire to respond, to enter into the pattern of life on Circle M that had been so good for the past few weeks. Then he drew back, the dark side of his nature hardening the impulse for comradeship that struggled to find release, and he said in a tight and noncommittal tone, "Yeah, I guess so."

To Edwards it was like a door slamming shut, and regret flooded his faded eyes, but he said nothing more.

Got to get away was Reno's thought. *Longer I stay, the harder it'll be on him—and on me.* The last thought came to him strongly, and he decided to pull out early the next day. The decision, however, instead of bringing relief, only depressed him, and he was preoccupied and quiet the rest of the day.

The city fathers of Placid had big dreams, which were symbolized by the size of the city hall which would sit firmly in the center of town. Only the floor was built, the rest of the structure waiting for the boom that was sure to come.

The fresh smell of rosin and fresh-cut lumber was in the

air, and a line of lanterns hanging from a rope outlined the square where the dancing was to take place. The musicians—two fiddlers, a woman with a dulcimer, an ancient black man lovingly stroking a banjo, and two young men with guitars—were tuned up and ready to go.

Jim slipped off Duke and handed Catherine down from the buggy. She was wearing a simple dress made of gray silk with full skirts, but a top which hugged her rounded upper body and left her shoulders bare. Her face, which was usually calm, was stirred by the break in the hard work, and she glanced at Jim with a pleased smile which he returned.

"Save me a dance, Catherine."

"All right. Don't make too many trips to that bottle the Prince boys always bring to the dances."

"I'm a tame coon these days," he said, and then Silas appeared and led her off to a group of friends close to the refreshments.

He was caught off guard by how many men spoke to him as he went over to lean against the wall of the hardware store. He had not realized how many people had dropped by Circle M, and it stirred old memories of days when he had been surrounded by friends. As the fiddle broke into a fast tune and the dancers began to move across the platform, he felt the life beat of a people, which was always something he was drawn to. So much of his life had been spent in isolation. The habit of solitude laid fetters on him, but at times like this, when groups of people met to work or frolic, the vague sense of missing out on life became a sharp hunger that made him unhappy and restless.

"See the line's drawn pretty fine, Josh," he remarked once. The small ranchers and dirt farmers were gathered on the west side of Main Street, utilizing the plank sidewalk in front of the bank for visiting. Across the street, ranked in front of Neal Simmon's General Store, the owners of the large ranches took station. The division was natural, not one which had been organized, but it was an old story to Reno, and he knew that there was a division broad as the ocean separating the two groups.

"You got that right, Jim," Josh grunted. "All come for a party, but it's really two parties goin' on."

"Always like that." Jim suddenly straightened up, for Stacy Carr had left her partner and was walking directly toward him, a determined look on her face. She was wearing a pale blue dress and dark blue dancing slippers, and her hair was untied, cascading down over her bare shoulders.

She came to stand in front of him, and as he removed his hat, she smiled and said, "Our dance, isn't it, Jim?"

He hesitated, then said, "I believe so." Taking her hand he led her to the platform and as the band began playing a slower tune, he put his arm around her, and they began to move easily to the music.

The fragrance of her nearness revived old hungers, so that he had to bring his will into play. She brushed against him, and the sweet smell of her hair came to him.

"You're pretty tonight, Stacy . . ." His words brought a quick smile to her lips, but he added, ". . . but not very wise."

She glanced at the gathering of her people, knowing instantly that he was warning her that her act had been rash. "Do you demand that women always be wise?" she asked, smiling, and he saw that the impulsive streak that had brought her to him was part of her character. The tilt of her chin and the open-eyed freedom of her face revealed a spirit which would never be subdued.

He grinned and said with a look of humor in his dark eyes, "No, but this dance may be harder on me than it is on you. From the looks your dad is giving me, I don't much reckon he's going to offer me a partnership in his ranch."

He nodded at her father, and she saw that for once she had done something that had thrown him into a fury. His face was dark with anger, and the power to hurt that he had never shown her was naked in his eyes. Suddenly Stacy looked at the scar, still white against Reno's forehead, and said quickly, "I think I'd better go, Jim."

She intended, he knew, to protect him, to placate her father, but a sudden streak of wild rebellion cut across him like a whip, and he drew her closer.

"Our dance, I think you said." He was rewarded as she rose up to meet him, a quick smile on her face. In her eyes and lips he caught the undertow of her spirit, and he recognized a woman completely ready to meet him at all points.

When the music stopped she pulled away from him. "Thank you—for all you did for me that night."

"Is this your way of paying a debt, Stacy?" he asked.

"No!" she answered instantly. "Never think that, Jim." Then she whirled and left him to find his way to the refreshment table.

Thad was waiting for him, a strange look on his face. "Why'd you do that?" he asked, glancing across the street to where Stacy was listening to her father. "I thought you had more sense."

There was a harsh antagonism in Thad's voice, much the same as the day when Thad had called Reno a "sorry excuse for a man." Reno stared at the big man and said, "You like that girl?"

Thad flushed and bit his lip, then blurted out, "Guess you're the only one here who don't know how I feel about her. It's a big joke. A poor sucker like me falling for the daughter of the richest man in the country."

Reno was shocked at the raw pain on his brother's face. "Thad, I'm sorry." He asked quietly, "How does she feel about you?"

With a quick glance toward Stacy where she was dancing with a tall dapper rider, Thad said heavily, "We used to be pretty close, Jim. Went to all the dances together. Sometimes I'd just ride over and visit—things like that. She and her mother came to church a lot in those days."

He paused so long that Jim finally asked, "What changed all that, Thad?"

Thad's face altered, and he shook his head slowly. "Never have figured it out. Maybe she just didn't like me as much as I thought," he said, then tried to grin. "Guess I'll never find out now." The natural cheerfulness of Stevens seemed to fade.

"Take a try," Reno suggested.

"No. It wouldn't ever work. I'm a poor man, she's a rich girl. Even if that weren't so, she's Skull and I'm the man who's going to bump into her family sooner or later."

Reno shrugged, saying only, "Tough. Wish I could help."

As the night wore on, a steady trickle of men made their way behind the bank where the Prince brothers, Bob and Tom, dispersed a raw whiskey called "forty rod," which was said to be the distance a man could jump after partaking of it.

Several minor scuffles were halted in the early stages by wiser and cooler heads, but Reno, who had turned down Josh's invitation to partake of the liquor, saw that friction was beginning to build up.

Billy Sixkiller faced down a rider from the Flying R, but it had been a close thing.

Skull had moved in close as the argument flared, and riders from Abe Frazier's Bent 6 and T. R. Smith's Flying R had joined them. Sixkiller had a deadly look about him as he stood in front of a group of his friends, most of them small ranchers like himself. Tempers flared, and the Flying R hand was pressured into pushing the quarrel by the Skull riders, but he backed off, not ready to face up to the muscular half-breed who feared nothing that walked, and who was known to be a deadly hand with either fist or gun.

As the fight fizzled out, Josh murmured to Reno, "That ain't the end of it. I wish we could git outta here." He rubbed his arm and said, "I got me an arrowhead here that allus aches when trouble's comin'—and it's givin' me fits right now!"

Reno felt the same, but when the trouble came, he was off guard.

He was pressured into dancing with one of the homely daughters of John Malon, a tall girl who was not giving up on catching a husband even though she was over the hill, and Reno had given his full attention to finishing the dance and making his escape.

When he thanked her and stepped off the platform, he found himself on the fringe of a group of the small ranchers who were faced by Skull's men.

Reno made his way to the center of the open place and was surprised to see Thad facing Red Williams. Catherine was holding tightly to Thad's arm.

"Thad, don't fight with him," she was saying, but he was paying no attention.

"Williams, get out of here!" Thad ordered in a tight voice.

His face was pale as paper, and he was thinking of the gun in Williams' holster, but he was determined. "You're scum, and we won't put up with your insulting our women."

"Well, now, preacher," the gunfighter said, and he let his fingers brush the butt of the heavy weapon, "I guess you are callin' me out. Ain't that the way of it? You see what I got to do, don't you? Man can't let himself be insulted, can he now?"

It was an old story to Reno, and he ran his eyes quickly over the faces behind Williams. They were all grinning, and there was no doubt at all over the outcome. Only Billy Sixkiller would have been anything like a match for Williams, and everybody on the street knew it.

Aaron Carr or his son Boone had fostered the play, Reno knew instantly, and it was to intimidate the settlers, beating them into submission. Thad had become their leader, and with him crushed, the big ranchers could run the rest off with little trouble.

"I—don't have a gun, Williams," Thad said uncertainly. "But I'll get one."

"No, you won't, Thad," Josh said. He shoved his way into the open space and glared at Williams. "You're a tinhorn, two-bit, imitation badman, Williams," he spat out, "but you ain't gettin' Thad into no gunfight."

"Watch your mouth, old man!" Williams warned. "You ain't too old to die your own self."

Boone Carr took a step forward and said, "Stevens, you asked for this. Now you get that gun and you stand behind your words—or you can git outta the Valley!"

He said it to push Stevens over the edge, and it might have worked, for Thad's face burned, and he started to answer, but he didn't have the chance.

"Why don't you have a couple of your men hold his arms, Carr," Reno said harshly. He stepped out from the crowd, facing the Skull faction head-on. "That's about the only way you'd ever fight a man. You're a stinkin', rotten coward!"

There was a sudden catching of breath from the crowd, for Reno had left Boone Carr no choice. The huge man's face reddened and he snarled, stepping to face the smaller man, "Reno, you got off easy last time! I'm gonna finish you off this time. Go get a gun!"

Reno stood alone then, and he was a strange contrast to the vast bulk of Boone Carr. Reno was wearing a black suit, with a gray vest, and his raven hair curled over his broad forehead. He looked small next to the mountain of Carr's bulk, but there was something about the compact, muscular figure that brought a silence to the mob. He was smiling at Carr, as if this were something he had done often—and, even more strange, as if he were enjoying it. There was something darkly ominous about the way he stood there, commanding the attention of his enemy, his face relaxed as if he were thinking of a pleasant experience. His manner had its way with Carr, who shifted his feet and said, "Next time I see you, Reno, have a gun."

Reno glanced across at Billy Sixkiller who was watching him unblinkingly. "Billy, will you lend me your gun?"

A light flared in the dark face, and Sixkiller flipped his gun out and handed it to Reno.

"That's a nice piece, Billy," Reno said with a smile. He stuck the gun inside his belt and drew a snow white handkerchief out of his breast pocket, took one end of it, then offered the other end to Boone Carr. His voice was smooth and unruffled but direct as the muzzle of a rifle as he said, "I'll hold to this end of the handkerchief, Carr—you take the other." Then a light blazed in his dark face and he said in a voice that was soft as velvet, "Then we'll have a signal and we'll both pull our guns and blaze away."

Carr's face changed then, and every man in the crowd felt a chill at the idea of it. It was one thing to stand off and shoot at a man, but to link hands and take his fire from a foot away was a frightful thought. For one moment it looked as if the big man might take the offer, but the steady smile on Reno's face stopped his move.

"I ain't gonna do no such fool thing!" he said, and he stepped back adding, "There'll be other times."

Reno stepped forward and his arm moved so fast it was a blur. His palm caught Carr across the face leaving a white print there, and Reno said coldly, "You yellow dog! You're going to fight if I have to take a horsewhip to you!"

Carr turned pale, but once again he kept his hand away from his gun, for he had a strong conviction that if he pulled iron with this man he was dead.

"Fight him! Fight the man, or I will!" Aaron Carr stared at his son as if he were a stranger. "I thought I raised a man!" he grated out. "Wait until I get a gun, Reno—I'll see what sort of bluff you're running!"

"Dad," Stacy pleaded, but she was brushed back by her father's arm.

"I don't particularly care which Carr I take on," Reno taunted with a tight smile. "This dog of a son you got, why, he's pretty rough on men who are helpless. I'd sort of like to see what he could do with a man who's not tied up."

Carefully Boone Carr unbuckled his gunbelt, moving very slowly. It fell to the ground and he said, "I'll stomp you into the ground, Reno. Come on!"

The circle drew back and Reno tossed the gun to Sixkiller. Then he turned to face Carr.

"Bust 'im up, Boone!" Red shouted with a flash of hatred. Others from Skull began to call out for the huge man to break Reno up, and Carr knew that he had fallen in their sight when he had turned down Reno's challenge. But now he smiled, for he towered over the other man by six inches and weighed forty pounds more. He was, moreover, a rough-and-tumble fighter of reputation.

"I'm gonna break every bone in your body, Reno," he bragged with a wide smile, and he stepped forward driving his huge fist straight toward Reno's face.

A yell went up from Skull riders, and if the blow had caught Reno, it would have crushed his face, but it did not. With a small movement of his head he avoided the blow, and when Carr fell forward from the force of it, Reno struck the larger man.

Those who watched, many of them, did not even see the blow, for it was a short, not long, overhanded punch often seen in street fights. Reno triggered one punch that traveled no more than six inches, but every ounce of his weight was behind it, and it fell neither short of its target which would have meant a powerless tap, nor was it timed to fall too far past the chin of Carr—which would have been a sort of push.

The blow began in Reno's right heel which he planted firmly on the ground; it traveled up his leg and the V-shaped torso channeled the surge of power into the swelling deltoid muscles, which propelled the arm forward like a piston, exploding on Carr's mouth with a fearful power. It was even more destructive because it caught the full weight of the larger man as he fell forward into the blow.

A solid, meaty sound accompanied the blow, and Carr's head was driven backward at an impossible angle. He flopped backward, blood matting his heavy jaw, which dropped loosely, obviously broken. He lay on his back, and his legs twitched convulsively in the dust.

His heavy grunts of pain and his boots digging in the dirt were the only sounds to be heard. Reno stood over the helpless man, muscles clearly tensed and ready to destroy Carr if he got up, and a blazing battle light twisted his smooth face, so that not a man in the street had a thought of standing against him.

Josh Jordan caught Billy Sixkiller's eye, and they agreed silently about something. Then the crowd began to stir, finding a voice that ran like a tide over the street.

"Pick him up," Aaron Carr said in a dead voice. He did not watch as the men of Skull picked Boone up and carried him down the street, led by Doc Moody who took one look and said, "Well, he's lost some teeth—" then he stared out of his bleared eyes at Reno, and added, "but I'd have had to knock them out anyway, in order to feed him while we keep that broken jaw wired together."

Even after they left with Boone, who was beginning to struggle as he regained consciousness, Aaron Carr stood staring at Reno.

The crowd grew quiet again, a little breathless at this drama. Jim Reno had destroyed the image that Aaron Carr had spent a lifetime building. In a few seconds he had struck down the most formidable fighting man on Skull. And everyone who had seen it knew that Aaron Carr would never stop until he destroyed the man who stood in front of him.

Stacy Carr stood as if she were paralyzed. When the

trouble had begun, she had been filled with fear that Reno would be battered or even killed by the power of Skull. The destruction of her brother had been like nothing she had seen, and she stood there rooted, trying to understand how Reno's slim form packed the power to smash a man into a helpless heap with one blow.

"You beat one man," old Aaron Carr said in a measured tone, and the blazing light in his blue eyes belied the forced manner, "and I give you credit for being a fighter, Reno." Then he dipped his head once, his voice steady as a rock. "I give you warning now in front of this Valley, I'll smash you!"

Reno had slowly relaxed, and he waited until he was certain that the huge owner of Skull was finished. Then he nodded and said, "I expect you'll try," before he turned and walked away.

The crowd flowed away from the square quicker than seemed possible, and in a matter of minutes, Reno, Juan, Josh, and the Edwards were riding out of town.

After they had gotten clear of the lights of Placid, Juan exclaimed, "Mister Jeem, you should've keel that man! Skull never let you live! Not never!"

"Juan's right," Josh put in. "You been there when the fun started, I guess, so this ain't the end of it."

"No. Nothing like this ever ends," Reno said, and there was a bitterness in his voice. "No matter what else happens, if I stay, there'll be somebody dead."

"That'll happen whether you stay or go," Josh said thoughtfully. "But you'll be the target—the man they'll be sighting on."

If Reno heard, he gave no sign, and nothing else was said until he and Juan got back to the ranch.

Reno helped Catherine down from the buggy, and she said quietly, "I think Dad is feeling worse. I want to talk to you after he goes to bed."

She took her father's arm, and Silas, holding onto the rail surrounding the porch, pulled himself painfully up. Then moving very carefully, he went into the house followed by Catherine.

After Reno had unhitched the team and turned them into the corral, he stood leaning against the fence, empty by the explosion of violence. It was always like that, in the war and after other fights, but this time he was shocked by the utter emptiness that filled him. He stood there unable to move, and was taken off guard when Catherine said, "Let's walk a little, Jim."

She took his arm, leading him past the corral toward the stretch of stunted oaks that grew east of the house. She was not afraid of silence, and for a time they simply walked, listening to the wind coming up off the plains and rustling the dying leaves of the oaks. Finally she stopped and put her hands behind her back. The thin light of a quarter moon outlined the feminine strength of her body, and her voice was steady as she said, "Jim, I'm going to ask you something. I want you to stay."

From the moment he had first met this girl he had a sense of her depth. Now in her eyes and lips lay the powerful emotion which had attracted him. He felt the warmth of her spirit and he knew at once what she would say next, but he waited.

"I might ask you for my own sake, and for Dad, but it's more than that. It's all of the little people, Jim—the Swensons, Andy MacIntosh, old Mr. Matthews—all of them. They don't have a prayer if you go." Catherine suddenly looked full in his face searching for what lay behind his steady gaze. "I don't know if you're a religious man, and you probably think I'm wrong . . ." She smiled shyly, then continued, "I think God cares about people on this earth, Jim. I believe we're more than just puppets. I've been thinking that you . . ." She had trouble putting her thoughts into words, but finally she concluded, "You are the only man who can draw us together, who can help us survive."

Reno smiled gently, the edges of his eyes crinkling. "You think I'm some sort of messenger from God—an angel, maybe?"

"Don't laugh," Catherine protested.

"I'm not, but you're wrong." He stared at her and asked gently, "You really believe that everything comes out all right, don't you, Catherine? That the good will be rewarded and the bad will be punished?"

"Yes."

He searched her face for some sort of further answer, then asked, "Why do you believe that?"

"I guess—because I think it's true. And because any other way of thinking is so hopeless."

An owl sailed overhead, casting a shadow on her face, and the appeal in her large eyes flickered, then came back to him. "Will you stay?"

He looked her full in the face, then replied evenly, "No. I'm pulling out first thing in the morning."

The girl's firm back bent and her head dropped, but she said nothing, and Reno took her arm, trying to explain. He wanted her to understand, and knew that there was no way that she could, but he tried. "Catherine, if I leave, Skull will peck away at you. It'll be tough, but nobody will be killed. The worst that can happen is that you'll be forced to move. But if I stay, it'll be war." The steely bite of his fingers trapped her arm. "All-out war like you can't understand."

She raised her head, and silver tears glittered in her eyes. "I know that, Jim. We all know that. But do you think it's better to die a little bit at a time—or gamble your life with at least a hope that you can have something good in life?"

The question caught him painfully off his guard, for it summed up what his life had been for years. Now he knew there was nothing to do but run, for he could not bring himself to initiate a bloodbath on these people.

"I'm sorry, Catherine," he said stiffly. "I'll say good-bye now."

She tried to smile and failed, then whispered so softly that he almost missed it, "Good-bye." She turned and as she disappeared into the house, Jim Reno felt that he had lost a precious thing, but he knew no way to hold on to it.

Duke was not going to make the long ride unless he got new shoes, but Zane Keller, the blacksmith at Placid, had such a backlog he could not get to him.

"It's the contract with the stage line, Jim," he explained regretfully. "I got six teams and they got to be done today. Best I can do is get him shod by dark."

Reno nodded. "All right, Zane. I'll stay over and get an early start in the morning."

He had left the Circle M early, saying a short farewell to Juan, but he had avoided the house, not wanting to see Edwards' drawn face. Neither had he wanted to see Catherine, for he had nothing else to say, and he knew that the longer he lingered the more painful his departure would be.

He got a room at the hotel, ate breakfast at the café, then watched the blacksmith work on the horses. At noon, he went back to his room and sat on the bed, but his thoughts drove him out to walk the streets again. It was a strange thing for him, being unable to be alone with his thoughts, for it had been exactly the thing he had done with ease for a few years.

He sat down at a table in a saloon which was mostly empty, and played solitaire, conscious that he was the target of curious eyes after the fight with Carr. Nobody spoke to him, and he finally got up and walked to the edge of town, and on out past the loading yards at the track. Time dragged on, but finally he saw the sun beginning to dim, and he got his belongings from his room and paid his bill. When he got to the black-smith's, Duke was ready.

"Thanks, Zane," he said, putting the money for the job into his hand.

Keller dropped the cash into his pocket, taking in the gear Jim slapped onto the horse. "Pulling out, are you, Reno?"

"Headed for the coast."

"Sure. Well, I guess you know what you got to do." There was a note of discouragement in Keller's heavy face that attracted Reno's attention.

"You think I ought to stay?" Reno asked.

"Not for me to say." Keller shook his head. "But I was hoping . . ." He never finished his sentence, but turned to look toward the end of the street. He narrowed his eyes, saying, "That hoss is about used up. Ain't that Juan from Circle M?"

Reno wheeled, mounting in one fluid motion, and drove Duke toward where Juan had stopped, his horse flecked with sweat and about to fall.

"Juan! What's wrong?"

The Mexican's eyes were wide with fright, and he cried out, "Meester Jeem! You got to help us."

"Is it Silas?"

"Yes! I'm theenk he is dying! The riders came and they drive the cattle across the field—and Meester Edwards, he get out of bed and try to stop them!"

A cold feeling settled in Reno's stomach, and he asked tightly, "Was it Skull, Juan?"

"Yes, eet was the Skull men," Juan said in a high voice. "I got to get the doctor. . . ."

"Get him quick as you can, Juan," Reno said, and turned to ride Duke at a driving run out of town and towards the Circle M.

He drove the horse as hard as he dared, and when he pulled up into the front yard of the ranch, he met Josh who came off the porch. "Is he alive, Josh?"

"Just barely," Jordan said through tight lips. "Is the doc comin'?"

"Juan's bringing him. How'd it happen, Josh?"

"Skull drove a big herd across our hayfield, and you know how Silas was countin' on that hay to get the stock through the winter. Well, I was over to the west range, but Catherine says her pa got outta his bed and somehow staggered over to the field on foot. She heard him beggin' them to stop, but they just laughed, and when he pulled at one of them, they knocked him down. He never got up, Jim." A barren look crossed his weathered face. "Juan and me got him to bed, but he's not gonna make it this time."

The door opened and Catherine stepped out. "Jim? Is that you?"

"Yes." Reno went to her and she caught his hands.

"He's been asking for you, Jim."

"For me?" Reno was taken aback. "Why does he want me?"

"I don't know. He's so weak. Come quickly." She pulled him through the house to the bed where the sick may lay like a stone.

"Stay with him, Jim," Catherine said. "He may wake up. I want to send Josh over to get Thad."

"Sure." Reno sat down beside Silas and there was no movement in the still face for a long time. Then his eyes blinked open and he saw Reno.

"Jim?" he whispered, and his voice was so thin and reedy that Reno had to lean forward to hear.

"Yes. I'm here, Silas."

"Jim, I want . . . ," he broke off, and was about to drift off.

"Silas?" Reno asked, taking the frail hand. "You want me to do something."

The life was running out of the old man, and Reno started to pull his hand away, thinking to get Catherine there, but found he was gripped with surprising strength by the dying man.

"Jim . . . promise me . . . you won't . . . leave!"

Reno felt trapped. "Silas, you don't want me to stay. I'll bring trouble."

"Got to promise me . . . Jim! Please!" Edwards suddenly caught at Jim's shoulder, and pulling himself up in bed, he found a stronger voice and there was terrible desperation in his eyes as he cried out, "Please . . . Jim . . . you . . . only hope!"

His eyes begged and the light was dying out, and Reno suddenly exclaimed, "Silas! I'll stay! You understand! Catherine will be all right! I swear!"

Edwards' face, which was in a state of terror, relaxed, and a smile touched his gray lips. He let himself back on the bed, and he felt for Jim's hand, saying in a thin whisper, "Thanks, Jim! God will . . . help you!"

Catherine came in then, kneeling beside the bed, and her father reached over and stroked her face with his trembling hand.

"I'm . . . so tired . . . time for me to go home," and he smiled strangely, his face lighting up, the pain gone. "You'll be all right, Catherine. You won't be alone."

Then he whispered, "You've been . . . a good daughter." A sigh escaped his lips, his eyes closed, and his hand dropped to his chest.

"Dad!" Catherine screamed, and she took his hand in both of hers.

Reno waited for her to break, but she was very still, her head bowed, and there was a slight tremor in her hands; but after she had kept that position for a few moments, she reached out and placed a stray lock of her father's hair into place. Then touching his face with one quick gesture, she rose and turned to face Reno.

There were diamonds in her eyes, but her broad lips were smiling slightly. "He's all right now, Jim."

Reno wondered what kind of a faith could let a person take such a loss with so little grief.

Then she did weave slightly, and there was a weakness after all, for she said, "He's better off—but I'll miss him so!" and she looked suddenly so small and alone, that Reno stepped forward and took her in his arms.

"Maybe," he said gently, "I can help." And then there was a release, as her body shook with the grief that had to be expressed. Her face was buried against his chest, and she held on to him almost fiercely for a few minutes, then it passed.

Drawing back she looked up at him, saying softly, "Thank you, Jim."

He looked at Edwards and said, "I never saw a man die like that—so easy!"

"He was going home, Jim," Catherine explained. "He was always thinking about God and eternity. Now he's got what he always longed for."

Reno thought about that, and was greatly moved. Then he assured her, "I'll see to things, Catherine."

She shook her head. "You don't have to do that, Jim. I know you're heading out."

He said with a puzzled smile on his wedge-shaped face, "No, it's not like that. I made your dad a promise, so you'll have to put me on the payroll full-time."

Her smile, when it came, drove away the doubts that had risen in him, and he knew that, live or die, he was in the Valley to stay.

SEVEN
Law of the Gun

A raw wind sweeping over the flats drove fine dust into Stacy's eyes, and she turned abruptly away from the grave. A plain wooden coffin and a pile of red dirt was surrounded by a large crowd, but Stacy stood slightly to one side, for she was the sole representative from the large ranches. Resolutely she turned back, not missing a look of anger in the eyes of several mourners, but she held her chin high, forcing herself to listen to Thad Stevens who was standing at the head of the grave, his voice sounding thin as the wind whirled his words away.

"... So nothing any of us can say will change the destiny of this man," Thad was saying, "because what he is now is beyond man's reach. Sometimes it's hard to stand beside an open grave and think of the one we love, because his life has been spent in seeking the things of this world." Thad glanced at Catherine standing beside Mrs. Swenson, and he smiled. "But that's not the way it is with us today! Silas Edwards was a man who loved God, and was a follower of Jesus Christ. He made no secret of this. Everyone saw it, and that's why we can

stand here—knowing we'll miss him, but knowing that for
Silas, this isn't the end, but a beginning."

Stacy glanced at Reno who, like herself, was isolated from
the crowd. He was listening intently to Thad, and change
stirred his broad lips, a faint change cracking the habitual
serenity he imposed upon his cheeks. His jaws outlined the
long borders of his sharp-featured face, shelving squarely at
the chin. His eyes were black with a light in them that could
turn, as now, sharply penetrating. His high cheekbones were
smooth, and the intensity of his thought brought a line of tension to his brow. He looked, Stacy thought suddenly, like a
man who was hearing something very important for the first
time.

Reno looked up suddenly and caught her gaze; her face
reddened and she forced herself to hold his level stare for a
moment, then turned back to the speaker.

". . . None of us have any guarantees. As the Scripture
says, 'No man knoweth the day nor the hour of his death.' But
on the other hand, we do have one certain thing. . . ." He
opened the big black Bible, thumbed through it, and held the
wind-blown pages apart as he read in a solid tone. " 'In a
moment, in the twinkling of an eye, at the last trump: for the
trumpet shall sound, and the dead shall be raised incorrupt-
ible, and we shall be changed. . . . then shall be brought to
pass the saying that is written, Death is swallowed up in victory. O death, where is thy sting? O grave, where is thy victory?' "

A stiff gust of wind drove a tumbleweed across the cemetery, until it came to rest against the coffin, but the spell of the
old words held the group still. From where Reno stood he had
a clear view of Catherine, noting that her face, framed by a sim-

ple black shawl, was still. Not a movement stirred her features, yet there was a light in her fine eyes which revealed the serenity of spirit which had always seemed to Reno to be the rock bed of her character. Her lips, he saw, moved silently as she repeated Thad's words.

"'The sting of death is sin; and the strength of sin is the law. But thanks be to God who giveth us the victory through Jesus Christ.'"

Thad closed the book, nodded at the men who stood by the ropes, and they quickly lowered the coffin into the earth. Picking up a clod of earth, Thad said, "Dust to dust returns . . . ," threw it into the grave, and then turned to say firmly, ". . . but this man will live again!"

One by one the men and women around the grave filed by, each tossing a bit of earth into the grave, then left to stand beside the line of wagons drawn up a few yards away. Stacy hesitated, then followed suit, and as she passed by Catherine, she paused, then stopped and put her hand on Catherine's arm, saying, "I'm so sorry, Catherine."

"Thank you, Stacy," Catherine replied, and there was a firm smile on her lips. "It was good of you to come."

Reno had taken this in, and was waiting with the others as the daughter of Aaron Carr came back to where her horse was tethered to a scrub oak. He noted that there was a break in the crowd's talk as she came close, and he stepped forward and loosed the horse. Handing her the reins he said, "Good to see you, Stacy."

She nodded, and then smiled as she said, "I feel like a freak, Jim. Everybody blames my father for this."

"But you're not him," he murmured. "How's Boone?"

She bit her lip, then warned, "Be careful, Jim. He's a wild man! I—I think he'd kill you without a second thought."

"He'll try, I guess," he said, then as he looked at her a wry light touched his sunburned face. "Makes it hard for us to be friends, Stacy."

"Jim, get out of the Valley," Stacy said, then swung to the saddle and prepared to ride off. "This sounds hard, and I don't mean it to be callous." She looked around at the people close by, and shook her head. "Don't let these people drag you into something—" Then she halted abruptly, and with a look of bleak regret on her face, shook her head and drove her horse across the flat in a dead run.

They had been a target for curious eyes, but now as Catherine came back to the buckboard the attention fell upon her. She held to Thad's arm, but as she came up to the buckboard saying, "I'm ready, Jim," a stir of agitation swept the crowd.

Andy MacIntosh spoke for the others, his thin red hair furrowed by the breeze. "Catherine, what will ye do?"

Catherine paused and swept the faces around her steadily, knowing that they expected her to leave the Circle M. She let the silence run on, looking for the right word, the right tone, and then said firmly, "Why, I'm going home, Andy."

"But how will you manage?" Mrs. Flemming asked. She was a frail, sickly looking woman, the wife of Fred Flemming, as robust as she was frail. "You don't have any help, and you know—"

Catherine waited for her to go on, then when she didn't, asked, "Where would I go, Erma? It's my home. I'll be all right."

"You better think about it," John Malon urged. "I hate to bring it up at a time like this, Catherine, but you'll be alone at the place—and Skull won't have any respect for you."

Catherine said, "I'll stay, John." She said this so calmly, with such firmness, that there was nothing to add.

Billy Sixkiller was a man of few words, but he asked suddenly, "Jim, you gonna be leavin' like you figured?"

Reno stood there, relaxed and easy, but he sensed that everyone was waiting for his answer. He looked at Catherine, then nodded. "I'll be staying, Billy."

Ray Catlin asked at once, "You know you'll be the target, don't you, Reno?"

Reno reached out and handed Catherine into the buggy, then in one smooth movement mounted to sit beside her. He gave the crowd a serene look, nodded, and said, "I'll be at the Circle M. If anybody wants me, they can look there." Then he shook the reins, guiding the rig between the ragged tombstones to the road.

"He won't last!" Ole Swenson said as soon as they were out of hearing distance. "They must have twenty riders at Skull."

Josh Jordan said, "One man's all it takes—if he ain't afraid of dying!"

"What you figure, Thad?" Fred Flemming asked. "He's your brother, and he's a tough article. We all seen that when he cut Boone down. But he can't whip every man on Skull. They'll gun him down."

Thad gazed around the small group, reading hope in some faces that had been ready to pull out of the country. He nodded as if making up his mind, then said, "Jim and I haven't been too close the past few years. And he's been in some things I could never condone." His honest face was serious as he slowly added, "But I'll say this, if Skull sets out to get Jim, they better get ready to get hurt—because if just half what I've heard about him is true, he'll be there when the smoke clears!"

"Thad, you mean he's a gunman?" asked a small blonde woman, the wife of John Malon.

Thad thought about that for what seemed like a long time. "I don't want to call him that, Martha. He's a *fighting* man—and I think I see a difference."

"You're right there, Thad," Billy grunted with a trace of a smile on his lips. "Reno ain't no killer—but he's gonna be a regular wildcat when he makes his play!"

Reno kept the team at a fast clip all the way back to the ranch. Once he asked, "Sure you don't want to go stay with the Swensons a few days?"

"No. I want to go home," Catherine answered evenly.

"I want to get back quick as we can. Old man winter's almost here, and we don't have enough wood."

Catherine smiled, and when Reno looked at her in surprise, she shook her head. "It sounds strange to hear you say that: *We* need the wood." Then she turned serious and said, "I know you made Dad a promise, Jim, but I won't hold you to it. Skull won't kill a woman, but you're a man—and a marked man, at that."

There was a shortness in his reply. "I'm staying, so don't try to run me off, Catherine!"

"I—I wouldn't do that, Jim."

They got back to the house and he helped her down from the rig. "Go in and get me the biggest steak you can find, with lots of potatoes and a big pie if you can swing it." He grinned at her. He seemed very young at that moment, the edges of his hair showing raven black beneath his hat. The hat was raked back on his head, and he had none of the melancholy she had seen frequently. "I'll take Juan and we'll cut till dark."

"All right, Jim." Something was on her mind and she had difficulty coming out with it. "You can stay in the spare room if you like."

He shook his head. "No, I'll bunk with Juan."

"You have a sense of propriety, Jim."

He sobered. "I guess we got enough problems—without that one," he said, then he turned and led the team into the barn, leaving her standing there, and there was a warm light in her hazel eyes as she turned and went into the house.

Days flowed by so quickly that Reno realized with a shock one evening that Edwards had been dead for two weeks. He had worked hard all that time, up before dawn, eating a huge break-fast that Catherine cooked for him, and working at a driving pace all day, pulling the ranch together. The place had deterio-rated badly during Edwards' long illness, but little by little the fences were mended, the corral rebuilt, the cattle shifted to a new graze, and a mountain of red oak firewood grew outside the kitchen door.

"Jeem, you gonna keel us both!" Juan had protested, and Catherine had agreed, but to no avail.

"We can sit back and rest all winter burning firewood," Reno had said, and he did not tell the whole truth. He was caught up with it all—the work, the suppers, the quiet times on the porch watching the stars fire the sky, the visits to neigh-bors to help with haying or just to visit. The round of life made up of work and people caught at him, and he forced the thoughts of Skull from his mind, living and reveling in the sim-ple pleasures he had once known.

Barney Purtle, the young desk clerk from the hotel, came to work, having been fired from his job. "They said I was more interested in reading than in the work," he said defiantly to Reno after Catherine had hired him.

"You ever been a rider, Barney?" Reno asked.

"Well, not exactly," the youth admitted, "but I got all the stuff I need." He pulled out a huge box he'd brought to the bunkhouse and showed with great pride the huge batwing chaps, the violet-colored shirt, and the twin .44 Colts with the tie-down thongs.

Reno spoke without a smile, but his left eyelid dipped at Juan. "I can see you're all set, Barney. Bet you've read a lot about cowboys, haven't you?"

"Sure! And I'll do a good job!"

"Well, if you run into any wild elephants," Reno said picking up one of the huge pistols, "you ought to be ready."

Barney reddened, then said quickly, "Well, everybody knows there's gonna be trouble. I'm just gonna be ready, that's all."

"I hope not, Barney. I really hope there's no trouble," Reno said slowly, then he handed the .44 back to him. "Well, we better get to work."

Two days of bucking a saw in the green oak left Barney's hands blistered, but he never quit, and Reno said to Juan, "He'll make a good hand."

"If he leave them guns alone," Juan shot back. "Why you nevair wear no guns, Jeem?"

Reno didn't answer at once, but finally he murmured, "I don't like guns, Juan." And then he turned and walked quickly away.

He took one break from the ranch—Catherine insisted that they all go to the wedding of Ole Swenson's oldest daughter, Judith. Reno worked with Juan and Barney all morning, then they got dressed and rode over to the Swensons' place.

"Good night!" Reno exclaimed as they pulled into a yard packed with wagons, buckboards, and saddle horses, "I didn't know there were so many people. . . ."

"Oh, everybody likes Dave and Judith," Catherine said gaily. "All the women can cry and all the men can take a crack at that apple cider Ole makes. I hear it's got a bite like a bear trap, so watch out."

They walked into the center of the milling crowd in a large open space beside the large two-story house, and Reno found himself being greeted with slaps on the back and warm handshakes. He made several trips to a certain pin oak tree beneath whose gnarled roots a jug of Swenson's cider lay. The first time he took a sip it nearly took the top of his head off.

When he got his breath he said to Billy Sixkiller and Dave Melton, the groom, "That's—sufficient! I haven't had a jolt like that since a Yankee put a ball in my leg at Stone Mountain!"

"Purely for medicinal reasons," Billy assured him. "You might get snake bit."

Taking a very small swallow, Reno retorted. "The snake that could bite this hard ain't been hatched yet."

"Aw, Jim, this is my wedding day," Dave Melton protested. He was a sturdy, deep-chested man of twenty-five, with a pair of direct blue eyes and a shock of straw-colored hair that fell in his eyes.

"You keep on sippin' that jug, Dave," Sixkiller said, "and you won't be able to stand up for the preacher."

"Tend your own taters, Billy," Dave laughed, then took another pull.

"You got a good girl there," the half-breed said nodding. "You still gonna homestead the old Miller place?"

"Sure am."

"Could be trouble," Sixkiller warned.

"It's claimed land. I got the deed from Mr. Miller before he pulled out."

"You think Carr will read the fine print on that piece of paper, Dave?" Sixkiller snorted. "You know Miller pulled out because he was gettin' pressure from Conboy."

Melton's honest young face sobered, and he said, "Me and Judith done fixed up the place, Billy—got furniture and all the stuff we need. It's got a good spring and. . . ."

"Just why Skull and the Carrs will have a fit if you take it," Sixkiller argued.

"I'm gonna make my home there," Melton said stubbornly. He took another pull and Reno exchanged a quick look with Billy. They understood each other at once.

A traveling minister had been imported from Cedar Bluff, and he used the wedding as an opportunity to work in a sermon. With the bride and groom standing in front of him, he eyed the crowd who stood watching, then launched into a lengthy discourse—what was, in Reno's opinion, a leftover sermon. "Guess he's not gonna miss a chance at us sinners that won't be in church on Sunday," Josh whispered loudly to Reno.

He was a good preacher, though, and the import of his sermon was "Love thy neighbor." He knew these people, having been reared in the West, and he touched on the temptations and trials which he knew to be close to all of his hearers.

"He better hurry up or the groom's gonna fall down!" Josh whispered again, and Melton was indeed weaving from side to side in an alarming fashion. If he had not been propped up on one side by his bride and on the other by his best man, he would have fallen.

The preacher marked the swaying form of the bridegroom with a stern eye, then united the couple in a ceremony that was simple and eloquent. "You must love each other," he admonished in closing, "for you will be for each other in a way that is unique. You will live for Dave, Judith, and you will live for Judith, Dave," he said, and there was a gentleness in his voice that had been missing. "You will have to face the troubles that all men and women face. But God saw that it was not good for man to be alone, and that is why I pronounce you husband and wife. Love each other with all your hearts!"

There was a stillness on the yard, and Catherine was gazing at the pair, a broad, maternal smile on her lips.

Then one of the groomsmen let out a wild yelp, and the celebration began in earnest.

As the sagging tables filled with food were surrounded by the guests, Reno leaned against the well and watched, caught by the odd feeling the moment brought to him.

They were all there—Thad Stevens, Josh Jordan, Billy Sixkiller with his beautiful wife and two sturdy boys, Andy MacIntosh and his stern-faced wife trying vainly to keep up with all the young couples, John Malon of the Straight 8 and his large family, Fred Flemming of Box X, Ray Catlin, slim and distinguished, and many others.

Reno did not know them all, of course, but he felt the solidarity of the people. He had passed by such groups, but never sensed the solid bands which tied such people together. They would work together, marry their children in that society, bury one another. It was a life that he had once hated, longing for the adventure of war, then the search for excitement that drives a young man. Now he stood there, thoughtful, thinking of his past with a sudden bitterness that he did not let touch his easy smile.

Catherine came to him a little later, bearing two plates heaped high with food. "Let's eat, Jim."

He took the plate with a slow smile. "I'll wait on you when you get old, Catherine," he said humorously.

She tilted her head and asked, "Will you, Jim?" Her question brought the blood to his face, and she laughed. "Don't panic, Jim. I won't set my cap for you."

They sat down with a small group of friends, eating and talking at the same time. It was the easy talk of close friends, small, unimportant matters which were to be shared, and in the sharing there was such a warmth and ease of the moment. There arose in Reno a desire to have this kind of life, and the strength of his feeling shocked him into silence.

When he brought his mind back to the conversation, Thad was talking about the sermon the preacher had wedged into the wedding. "He did a good job. 'Love thy neighbor' is always a good word."

"Sure—providin' he loves you back," Josh said wickedly. He leaned back against a tree, a man who had seen sin in its many forms and knew the shape of it from memory. "If you turn the other cheek, why, that's plumb good as long as the other feller feels the same way. But if he don't . . . !" He didn't finish, but the look he gave Thad roughed up the younger man's feelings.

"Why, what good would it be to have a religion that only worked when things were going good, Josh?" he asked, shaking his head.

Billy Sixkiller was balancing one of his dark-eyed boys on his lap, feeding him awkwardly. He was a healthy man with a dark smooth face and a shrewd eye. A tough, quick-witted fighter with a gleam of affability and sound good humor in his brown eyes, he was serious now.

"It sounds good, Thad, and I know you mean it. But I'm wonderin' how it would hold up, this religion of yours, if Skull came to run you off your place."

This disturbed Thad, and he shook his heavy head stubbornly, saying with some heat, "It's not the same thing, Billy." He tried to find a way to state his feeling, but could only add, "A man can be a Christian and still hold up for what the Lord has given him."

Reno took no part in the talk, as they argued back and forth, and he felt somehow that this small circle of warmth and defense against the lonely arch of the world was somehow weakening, and soon, he felt, the momentary heat and light of the small society would fade.

"Jim, what you think?" Reno looked up startled to find that someone had singled him out, and they were all looking at him to hear his answer.

He felt trapped, and would have left the question unanswered, but there was an insistence he could not ignore.

There was a rocky determination on his face, and his voice was sad. "I thought a lot about killin' during the war. I guess maybe all of us did. Didn't take me long to get over my fool idea that we were all saints and the enemy was all sinners. I can still remember pullin' a trigger and seeing a man go down." He shook his head, adding, "I thought about it a lot, but I'd agreed to fight for what I thought was right."

He was quiet for so long, Catherine had to ask, "Well, what did you decide?"

He looked at her steadily and then swung his face toward the others. "All I've got to say is this: I set out a time back to be a man of peace. Now, well—I made a promise to Silas Edwards." He glanced at Catherine, then at Thad. "I'll take no gun as long as I'm let alone, but if there are those who won't let that be, I don't have any other way than to defend this ground the only way I know."

The sudden light of anger in his dark eyes silenced them all, and when he got up and walked away, Catherine said quietly, "I think we're wrong, Thad. All he wants is to be let alone."

"No, Catherine," Thad said slowly. "Jim has used all that's in him for wrong all his life. Now," he said almost in a whisper, "he'll have something to fight for that's good!"

"Amen!" old Josh Jordan murmured, and the fire in his old eyes burned brightly.

EIGHT
Valley Vengeance

Breakfast at the big house at Skull was a ritual. Aaron Carr sat down exactly at six o'clock at the head of the massive table set squarely in the center of the forty-foot room. Boone, Lee, and Pres Conboy sat to his left, while Mrs. Carr, Stacy, and Frank sat facing them.

The cook, a sallow-faced and ageless Chinese named Sim, kept the plates filled with eggs, biscuits, and ham, and refueled the massive coffee pot that sat next to Aaron. The talk ran freely around the table.

Lee Carr was telling how one of the young bucks he ran with had gotten into a scrap with a puncher from Bent 6 over a girl they were both courting, and the rest of the family listened with an air of amusement as they ate.

". . . So when Fred came out of Lily's yard, there was ol' Harry waiting for him!" Lee's handsome face was alive with a boundless energy, and he waved his fork around as he finished his story, ". . . and them two pounded each other until they got tired. Then when they decided to let Lily say which one of 'em she wanted, they went to get her—and that girl had left with Glenn Delancy to get hitched!"

Everyone laughed, except Boone. He sat there sipping milk through a straw, his face set in a stony stare as the laugh went around the room.

Mrs. Carr looked at him, and said, "Boone, I'm going to fix you some of my beef broth for supper tonight. Stacy thought up a way to grind up the meat real fine, and I know you get hungry for something more solid."

Nothing crossed Boone's face to show that he had heard, and Aaron said, "Been a hard time, boy, but in a few more days you can get that jaw unhooked." He waited for Boone to nod, but got no sign from his huge son.

Stacy glanced at Frank who shrugged, and everyone at the table felt awkward. Ever since the fight Boone had said nothing, but there was a raging anger in his eyes that revealed the inferno of wrath that simmered in the big man, growing more intense as the days went on.

"Boone's gone crazy, Stacy," Frank had said to Stacy a week after the fight. "He'll kill Reno the first chance he gets."

They were sitting on their horses on one of their frequent rides, and Stacy asked in a tight voice, "Do you think Dad will stop him?"

"Stop him?" Frank laughed harshly, "He'll probably help him!"

"But they can't do that," Stacy whispered. "They can't!" And she turned to this brother who of all the Carrs she loved best. "Dad's not like that, Frank. He's no murderer!"

Frank shrugged. "No, he isn't. But when anything touches Skull, he loses his reason."

Now, sitting at the table, Stacy felt fear as the steady light of hatred in Boone's face found a reflection in the light of the older man.

As they were about to get up from the table, there was a knock at the front door. Sim hobbled over, opened it, and Benny Lyons came in to stand awkwardly in the center of the room.

"Well, what you want, Benny?" Pres Conboy asked, irritated at the interruption. He valued the meals he took with the owner, and the sight of the small puncher standing there twisting his battered hat nervously got on his nerves. "What's so important it can't wait?"

"Well . . ." The freckled face of Lyons twitched nervously. He swallowed and blurted out, "You told us to let you know if any more homesteaders moved in on our grass."

"What are you telling me?" Conboy demanded.

"Well, you know the old Miller place at Whelan Springs?"

"What about it?"

"Somebody is livin' there now. They fenced off the springs, and Tobe said he had to take the bunch of yearlings all the way over to Bear Lake."

"Get those tramps out!" Aaron Carr's face burned with anger. He slapped his meaty hand flat on the table, rose to his full height, and shouted, "They're testing me out! Well, we'll settle this thing once and for all!"

"You want me to go take care of it, Mr. Carr?" Conboy asked eagerly.

"I want you to clear this Valley of those parasites," Carr replied in a grinding tone. "Skull is not going to be gutted by a bunch of ragtag hoemen. Do it today!"

Conboy licked his lips, then asked, "How far you want us to go?"

Aaron Carr's face was like a stranger's, Stacy realized with a sinking sensation. His cold blue eyes glittered in his craggy face, and there was a knife-edge of violence on his lips. He glared at Conboy, then said, "You heard what I said, Pres. If you can't handle a few farmers and two-bit spreads, I'll find another man."

Conboy straightened up, nodded, and said, "Just want it clear." He turned as he left the table and assured Carr, "By tomorrow there won't be a soul at Whelan Springs."

Boone got up at once and walked to the rack of rifles beside the door. He lifted a heavy Spencer that looked small in his mammoth hand, then began filling his pockets with shells from the drawer. There was a strange look of peace on his battered face that did not go with the action, and Stacy looked quickly at Frank.

"Wait a minute, Dad," Frank said quickly. "I can handle this. Let me go have a talk with these people."

"No. Too late for talk." There was an iron quality in his father's tone that silenced Frank, and he said, "Who are these people at Whelan Springs, Benny?"

"One of them Swenson girls—I forget which," Benny replied. "She married up with Dave Melton from over at Bluebonnet."

Stacy glanced at Frank, and was appalled at the pallor that tinged his ruddy face. Catching his eye, she pleaded with him to say something, to try to stop the thing before it went too far, but Frank was too much under the dominion of his father to take a stand.

She waited until the room had cleared, then ran to catch up with him as he stepped off the porch. Pulling him off to one side, she whispered urgently, "Frank! We've got to do something!"

"Do what?" he asked bitterly. There was a strength in him, Stacy realized, that had never been tested, and she tried to stir him to do what he had never done—stand against their father.

"You love May Swenson, don't you, Frank?"

He pulled away from her grasp, letting his anger spill out at her. "Stacy, mind your own business!"

"What kind of a man are you? If I loved someone, I wouldn't run away and let them get hurt!"

"Shut up!" Frank ground out, desperation haunting his face. "What do you know about loving anyone? And you think because Dad babies you, you could make him change his mind. Well, you couldn't—nobody can! Now leave me out of it, Stacy!"

She gazed at him as he walked jerkily across the yard, and a great pain filled her breast. Frank was the best of the Carrs, but he was too much bound by fetters of submission to their father to break loose.

She watched as they saddled up and rode out. Slowly she turned, and the confusion in her grew more intense as she tried to think of something to do. For over an hour she worked mechanically at her chores, coming up with no solutions.

Finally she threw down the ledger she was totaling and called to her mother who was in the kitchen, "Mother, I'm going out—be back for supper."

Without giving Mrs. Carr a chance to question her, she darted out of the house, saddled her horse, and rode out of the yard at a hard run.

"More eggs, Jim?" Catherine asked.

Reno shoved back from the table and grinned. "Better not. I've got a guilty conscious about sleeping so late as it is."

"You've been working too hard. The rest will do you good," she said while filling his coffee cup, then her own. She sat down and neither of them spoke for a time. He was a quiet man, and she was not a woman who had to have a constant flow of small talk, so the islands of silence which came as they were together were not awkward.

Finally she asked, "What do you get out of all this, Jim?" He raised one of his black eyebrows, caught off guard by her sudden question, and she went on slowly. "I know you're not staying for my money." She laughed and there was a sudden break in her serious eyes. "I haven't got any, you know that. And we both know you're going to run into trouble sooner or later. So what keeps you here?"

Reno shrugged his thick shoulders, and there was a hint of seriousness under his light words. "Why, I guess I got over-interested in you, Catherine."

"What?"

"I always get mixed up in things when I get interested," he said. Then he mentioned thoughtfully, "That was the way I got into the army. At first I didn't have any real burning desire to save the South. But I just got interested in the way things were going. So off I went."

She thought about that, then said: "I think you're a romantic, Jim Reno! You have a taste for lost causes—first the Confederacy and now me."

"Why, you're no lost cause, Catherine!" he protested. "And I'm no knight rushing in to save a damsel in distress."

They talked like that, their words placid and even like a smooth stream, and the thought came to Catherine with a shock, *Why, we're acting like a married couple!* And her face altered with the thought so strongly, he caught it.

"What's wrong?"

"Oh, nothing, I just . . ."

A horse ran across the hard-packed earth outside, and both of them got up and went outside.

"Why, Stacy," Catherine said at once, "get down and come in."

Stacy swung down, and there was a freshness in her face that contrasted strongly with the troubled look that marked her manner. "I can't stay," she said nervously. Tucking a tendril of her hair under her hat, she slapped the reins against the hitching rack, then hurried on, "I don't know any way to say this, but . . ."

When she hesitated still, Reno asked, "Trouble coming?"

"Yes!"

"Didn't think it would be too long," Reno commented slowly.

Stacy bit her lip, then with a tragic light in her fine eyes, she blurted out, "Skull is going to run the Meltons off the place at Whelan Springs."

"Oh, no!" Catherine gasped. She took Reno's arm, saying, "Jim, you've got to warn them!"

Stacy took in the two before her, noting the way that Catherine responded at once to the problem by reaching for Jim. She had not missed the manner in which they came out of the house, and she had the same thought that had touched Catherine, that they had the air of man and wife. Her thoughts were interrupted when Reno spoke up, the long lines of his face drawn sharper than before.

"When did they leave, Stacy?"

"Just after breakfast, about seven." Then she added with a sad air, "I guess it's too late. And I don't know why I came."

Catherine said warmly, "Why, you came because you care about people, Stacy."

"You wouldn't get that opinion from many people—not about a Carr!"

Reno said, "Catherine, I'll need Juan and Barney for a chore. You stay here until we get back."

"Yes, Jim."

The instant agreement caught at Stacy's mind, and she said abruptly, "Well, I'll—"

"Stacy," Reno interrupted, and his voice was warmer than she'd ever heard it, "listen to me. No matter what anyone says about the Carrs, and no matter what happens from this time on, I'll remember this best. You didn't have to come—but you did."

Catherine suddenly felt excluded as Reno stepped to Stacy's side, and she saw that his presence troubled the tall girl, for her fingers toyed nervously with the bridle and there was a look in her face that Catherine could not identify.

"There's going to be more trouble in this valley than any-one knows," Reno said, and he touched Stacy's arm gently, add-ing, "I'd give my right arm to spare you what's going to come—but all I can say is this: No matter what comes, I'm not your enemy."

"I know that, Jim," Stacy said huskily, and her reserve broke as she cried out, "I have to go! Be careful, Jim!"

She mounted and lifted her horse out of the yard. Reno turned. "That's a fine woman, Catherine."

"Yes. Mrs. Carr is the same. Frank and Lee would be all right if they had a chance." Her eyes clouded and she asked, "What are you going to do?"

He looked surprised. "Going to the Melton place." He

wheeled and ran lightly to the bunkhouse leaving Catherine to stare at him with a troubled face.

"What's up, Jim?" Barney asked. He looked up from where he was lying on his bunk reading a book. Seeing the intent look on Jim's face, he sat up and shot a look at Juan who was sitting lazily in a cane-bottomed chair.

Reno hauled his saddlebags down without a word. He pulled out a flannel-covered bundle and unfolded it. It was, the two men saw, a gun belt, and as he fastened it around his waist, there was a change in his manner that brought Juan and Barney to their feet.

"Skull is going to raid that spread by Whelan Springs."

"Dave Melton's place?" Juan asked.

"Yes. Now, Juan, I want you to go get as many of the settlers as you can south of the river. Barney, can you find your way north to some of the men there."

"Sure, Jim!"

"Find as many as you can, but don't wait around. Hit the spreads and leave word. I need Sixkiller and Ray Catlin bad—but get anyone who'll come. We'll meet at Swenson's place."

"What we do, Jeem?" Juan asked as he grabbed his hat.

Reno lifted a carbine from a peg on the wall, checked the action, then picked up a box of shells before saying, "We're going to war, Juan."

Barney's Adam's apple went up and down rapidly, then he whirled and pulled the heavy guns from a drawer and strapped them on with a look of nervous excitement on his young face.

"Barney, you just get the men," Reno said with a smile. "I don't want you to start this war."

He led them out and they rode off toward the west. Catherine watched with apprehension in her face. As Reno swung aboard his mount, she whispered, "Come back. I'll be praying."

Reno paused and considered that. There was a hard line in his jaw, and he rested his hands on the pommel, looking at Catherine. There was a cloudy look in his dark eyes, and he was slow to speak. Finally he said, "I rode a thousand miles to look for what I thought I wanted—which was a quiet life. Now I'm right in the middle of another war. And you're praying for us, and I'd guess Mrs. Carr and Stacy are praying for their men." He shook his head, and there was a grim look in his face. "I guess you'd better pray hard, Catherine, because what I'll have to do from now on won't look too good in my books."

"Jim, if you have doubts," Catherine said quickly, "don't go."

He stared at her, shook his head, and stated flatly, "I haven't been much of a man for praying and religion, Catherine, but I never set out to do something that I didn't give it all I had. Sometimes," he said regretfully, "some of the things I did weren't worth much. But I think this is. Man like me, why, he doesn't have anything else, so he has to have pride. So you pray—and I'll do what has to be done."

Duke tried to break into a run, but Reno held him back to a ground-eating gallop. Whelan Springs was, he knew, about ten miles east of Placid, about five miles north of Billy Sixkiller's ranch. Silas had drawn a map of the Valley showing all the spreads, fastening it on a wall of the bunkhouse. Reno had always had a knack for getting the feel of a country from maps—a skill which had served him well during the war—and now he considered the lay of the land, thinking how he could best get positioned to come up on Meltons' place. He decided to ride directly west as far as the dip of the plains, then take the north route marked on the map. It led to the northeast section of the Valley, and he thought that by the time Juan and

Barney got a bunch together, he could find the ranch. If a break came, he could get to Melton before Skull arrived. He had no idea of a fight—just getting the young couple away was his idea.

For three hours he followed the map he'd put in his mind, turning sharply as the country rose to the mountains in the southwest. The rocks began to shove themselves upward through the thin soil as the country rose, and he forded a creek that he figured must join the Snake, remembering from Edwards' map that there was such a creek named Barebones Creek. He rested his horse for half an hour, allowing him to drink the icy water, then forged ahead steadily.

He thought suddenly that he had done this often during the war—marching or riding for hours or even days, and it always ended in the mindless and obscene explosion of battle. This, he decided, would be no different, and the thought of throwing himself into bloody action brought a grim cast to his dark cheeks, but he did not turn his head or slow his horse.

Crossing a thick growth of pine that carpeted the foothills of the mountains, he emerged at the crest of a range of low-lying hills, rolling carpets of brown fall grass, and there beyond the last lifting of a sharp crest he saw a body of men suddenly top the summit and gallop steadily along the ridge, disappearing into the valley that lay to the south.

"Skull," he said softly, then spurred Duke for the first time, and the fiery quarter horse drove along the rise and fall of the country in a dead run.

Ten minutes later, Reno pulled up at the top of a rise in the middle of a thicket of trees. Below him in a sweeping valley he saw what he knew was Melton's place. And he saw, too, the woman who was trying to hitch a pair of half-wild horses to a buggy, and he saw the still figure of a man lying close to the house.

He galloped Duke down the slope and came into the yard at a run. Piling off the horse he ran to the woman who turned to him with a face pale as paper. She started to run, but he caught her by the arms, saying, "Judith! It's all right! I'm Jim Reno!"

She stopped, then a trembling shook her frame and she fell against him weeping helplessly. "He's dead! They killed Dave!"

Reno freed himself and ran to where Melton lay face down on the ground. He pulled him over carefully, and saw at once the bullet wound high on the chest. He saw, too, that Dave wasn't dead, but the breathing was slow and labored.

"He's not dead, Judith, but he's hurt bad. We have to get him inside and get this bleeding stopped."

She came at once, relief in her face, and together they got Melton into bed and the flow of blood staunched. As they worked, she told Reno how it had happened. She was still in a state of shock, not believing the crude violence which had shaken her world.

"You keep him still," Reno said. "I'll go for the doctor. That slug has got to come out."

He mounted the tired horse, and the shadows were getting long as he pulled into Swenson's yard.

The yard was crowded, and Reno noted at once that Juan was there with Billy Sixkiller and two men he had met at the wedding.

"You been at my girl's place, Reno?" Ole Swenson asked at once. "She all right?"

"Dave's been shot, Ole," Reno said wearily. "Judith is fine. Dave needs a doctor bad."

"Charlie, go get Doc Moody," Swenson commanded a tall young man instantly. "Kill the team if you have to." Then he turned to Reno, saying, "Coffee over here."

Reno followed him to the same large table that had held the food for the wedding. He wolfed down a huge sandwich and swallowed several cups of scalding coffee, telling what he'd seen.

"Now who did it?" one of the men asked.

"Do you need to ask, Hank?" Sixkiller grunted.

"Skull." Reno nodded. "Judith said they rode in and told them to get off. When Dave started to argue, one of them pulled a gun and shot him down."

"Know which one did it, Jim?" Sixkiller asked.

Reno took a swallow of coffee, and then his voice was soft as a summer breeze as he nodded. "I know."

He said nothing more, but something in his tone made Sixkiller nod as if he found something satisfying in the words.

"What we gonna do?" Swenson asked hopelessly. "No law is ever gonna touch Aaron Carr."

"We'll wait until the rest of the bunch gets here, I guess," Reno said. He settled down, his back against the wall of the house, listening to the talk, but taking no part. It was an old story to him, and he thought a lot about Stacy Carr and how she'd looked as she'd made herself tell what her father was planning.

Thad and Josh pulled in, then an hour later Barney came galloping in with Ray Catlin and another man in tow.

It was almost dark as they stood around the fire that someone had built up in the yard, and the women ducked back into the shadows, the boys edging in so as to miss nothing. "We have to go over to Mason City for a U.S. Marshal," John Malon said.

"Lot of good it'll do!" Sixkiller snapped. He flung a stick he'd been digging in the dirt with into the fire and added, "No law is gonna help us; you know that, John."

"Weel, John's got a point," Andy MacIntosh said slowly, pulling his hand through his whiskers, "but I think maybe Billy's right."

"Can't live like this!" Fred Flemming insisted, shaking his head. "If they'll do this, they'll do anything."

Thad had said little, but now he stepped into the light of the fire, and he was more certain than anyone had ever seen him. He spoke so defiantly that two or three of the men looked at each other in surprise. "We're not going to Mason City to get a marshal. We're going to take care of this ourselves."

"You been eatin' raw meat, Thad?" Ray Catlin grinned. He was one of those dapper men who managed to look as if they'd just dressed for a funeral or a wedding. "How you think we're going to go up against Skull?"

Thad flung his head back and said, "Nobody here hates violence worse than I do. But it's what we've come to. Every one of us has known, I think, that sooner or later we'd have to fight or run."

"And you say fight?" Ray asked curiously.

"Yes! We have no other choice!"

"Sounds like a good way to get us all killed," a short heavy man named Kilmer suggested. "I'm no gunfighter, and neither are you, Thad."

"No, that's right, Mack, but I'm ready to learn."

"Think on it, now," Swenson urged cautiously.

"Why, I haven't done anything but think!" Thad said angrily. Then he turned to Reno. "Jim, you know about this sort of thing. Can we win?"

Every eye moved to Reno who was standing to one side, listening to the talk. He turned now and his dark eyes reflected the shadows of the falling evening. He seemed to be studying the group, weighing them in some sort of scale. Finally he shrugged and said, "I don't know, Thad."

"But will you help, Reno?" Ray Catlin asked instantly. "I been in a scrap or two, but this time I won't follow anybody I can't trust. And I say now that you're the only man here that I'll follow."

"I guess I'll say amen to that," Billy said. "What about it, Jim?"

Reno stood there, a bitter smile on his wide lips, but he said, "I'm out to break or be busted. With you or without you, I'm going to have trouble with Carr."

"That's all I want to know," Billy said with a grin. "What do we do first?"

Reno looked around and saw that he held the small group. They would follow him, and it would be his responsibility when they died. It would be his head the blame fell on when they shed the blood of Skull men. He could turn and walk away from it now, but he knew he never would.

"The one thing I know is this, you won't win by playing games with Skull. They've got too many men and too much power. You can't expect any mercy, and if you expect to come out on top, you can't give any."

"Who wants to?" Catlin asked.

"All right," Reno said. "Who knows where the Skull crew is about this time?"

"I do," Flemming answered. "They're over toward Black Oak pass. You know that big house they got over there?"

"Don't know it," Reno answered.

"Well, it used to belong to a man named Hooper, but when they froze him out they took the house and use it from time to time for sort of a line cabin. Big nice house, too."

"You sure about that? That they're there?"

"Been working the herds there for two or three days. Guess they ain't left."

"Well, let's get at it," Reno said, and then he smiled. There was a looseness about him, and the gentleness of his smile was a wonder to all of them. He had a wildness that could be felt, and they had seen him explode when he struck Boone down. But now he was almost boyish-looking in the half-light, and it came as a shock to hear him add, "Some of us might not come back, so if you got good-byes, get them said."

The words came like a chill on some of the men, but he saw at once that there was a tough fiber in others. He realized that some of them would quit when the going got rough, but men like Billy and Ray Catlin were the same kind he'd seen during the war. Such men would charge an emplaced gun as if they were facing toy pistols. They died hard.

Some of them would have to.

NINE
Over the Edge

"What we waiting for, Jim?" a voice rasped impatiently out of the darkness.

"Jest hold your taters, Barney," Josh answered from his position to the left. "They's two or three things about this leetle game you ain't learned yet."

Reno smiled at the exchange, remembering an elderly sergeant in his troop who had sat down on raw trigger-happy recruits, and he knew that Barney was in good hands.

A ray of pink broke over the crest of the hills to his left, and five minutes later the house below was clearly visible. Still he waited, ignoring the restlessness of some of the men behind him. They were nervous, most of them afraid, not having been tested under fire, and he said quietly as a thin stream of smoke spiraled out of the clay chimney, "All right. Watch your feet."

Slowly the small group picked its way down the slope, and only once did a man slip, sending a rock tumbling down toward the house. He cursed, and Sixkiller said instantly, "Shut your mouth, Bones!"

According to Flemming, who had been inside the house many times, there were two bedrooms upstairs and one downstairs. The front door opened into the large room that served as a living room and dining room, and a door led off to the left to a bedroom, one at the rear to the large kitchen.

"Billy, you take a couple of men and go in the back. Try to get up to the back door without spooking anybody, and if the door's locked, you knock it down when you hear us come in the front. I'll let out a yell so you'll know when to make your play."

"Yeah," Sixkiller grunted. He gestured to MacIntosh and John Malon, then silently led them off to the side, their movements shielded by a narrow line of cottonwoods close to the house.

The other men herded close to Reno, their eyes wide open in the morning light. Ray Catlin was calm, but there was a glitter in his eye as he smiled at Reno. "What's the plan?" he asked quietly.

"I want to catch them off guard," Reno said. "No shooting if we can help it."

"What if they start shooting at us?" Barney whispered with a nervous look at the house. He was skittish and Reno knew he could be just the one to open fire at the wrong time.

"They won't be armed yet, Barney," Reno explained patiently. "That's why I wanted to catch them off guard at breakfast. If we're lucky, they'll either be in the kitchen or at the table."

"What if some of them are upstairs and get to their guns?" Fred asked.

"Then we'll have to take care of them," Reno said. "But we go in quick and get the drop on those downstairs. Ray, you take Josh and see if anybody's still in those bedrooms."

"Sure."

"No talking now. When I bust in, stay close as you can with your guns out."

He led them to the house, and slowly stepped up on the porch, trying not to give any warning; then the others stepped up. As he stood with his hand on the door, he saw that the windows were shuttered and closed, so no one could have seen their approach. Inside he heard the rumble of several men talking. He nodded at those behind him, then drew his gun, checking to be sure they did the same.

He hit the door with his shoulder, sending it flying open, then took three quick steps inside, followed by Ray who moved at once toward the stairs to the left of the room.

"Hold it!" Reno shouted at the top of his voice and the men around the table froze. There were seven of them at the table, and the cook was caught with a huge pot of coffee in one hand and a pan of biscuits in the other. Pres Conboy had a fork loaded with eggs half-lifted to his mouth, and his eyes were wide with shock as the armed men swarmed into the room, guns out and steady.

Ray took the stairs three at a time and disappeared, but his voice floated downstairs, "You jokers just drop everything! Move downstairs." Two punchers came down with Ray urging them on. "Get over there with the others."

Sixkiller stepped through the back door pushing a fat puncher without a shirt in front of him. "This is the catch, Jim," he said, looking at the Skull riders.

"What do you think you're doing?" Conboy blustered. He lunged to his feet shoving his chair backward with a crash and stepped forward to face Reno. "You can't make this stick!"

"You just keep on talking that way, Pres," Reno said calmly. "I like to see a man who thinks positive."

"What's the ticket, Jim?" Ray asked. "You want to hang them here or somewhere else?"

"That's a bluff, Catlin!" Conboy shot back. "Now, you birds get outta here!"

"Likes giving orders, don't he now?" Josh taunted, and there was a fierce light in his eyes. "Which one of 'em shot Dave, Jim?"

"Don't make any difference which one it was," Sixkiller said, his dark face ominous. "Why don't you keep on talkin', Conboy? Nothin' I'd like better than to put a slug right between your eyes!"

"Everybody outside!" Reno ordered at once. He knew that the situation was tense, and he wanted to get the prisoners into the open. "Move out."

Sullenly Conboy led the way, having no choice, and the rest followed. They stopped in the yard uncertainly, shivering in the cold morning gusts. They were ringed by the ready guns of the men, and there was a silence as everybody seemed to wait for something.

One of the Skull riders was a tall, thin individual with a wispy beard showing amber traces of tobacco juice. He had a pair of hard eyes the color of lead, and he said, "Have your fun, but ain't a one of you gonna have anything to laugh at for long."

"You gonna rub us out, Spade?" Ray asked solemnly.

The lean lips of Spade moved only slightly as he spat out, "Your ticket's punched, Catlin." He gave a venomous glance at Reno, adding, "You won't always have the drop. You're a dead man, Reno!"

"Give him your gun belt, Barney," Reno said at once.

"Jim!"

"Don't worry, Barney, he won't get to use it," Jim said,

and the smoky light in his dark eyes was a thin veneer barely masking the rage he had nursed ever since he had found Dave Melton in the dust. "Take the gun, Spade. I'm curious to see if any of you Skull trash can face up to a man with a gun on him."

"Gimme that iron!" Spade grated, and as he buckled it on there was a sudden agitation in the group.

"Jim, don't do it," Ray said, and his apprehension broke the customary calmness of his smooth face. "He's scum—why give him a break?"

Catlin was telling him, Reno knew at once, that Spade was a dangerous man—a fact which he had not missed. The lean face of Spade was filled with total confidence, no fear breaking through, and Jim needed no more evidence to know that Spade had been in this situation many times, and probably had never lost.

"What about them after I get you?" Spade asked with a gesture at the guns of the guards. "They gonna let us go after I finish you off?"

Reno said with a smile, "You fellows stand back, and if he puts me down, let the whole bunch go, you hear?"

"Jim . . . ," Billy started to argue, but Reno cut him off.

"That's it, Billy." Reno moved back and Spade turned and walked ten paces in the other direction. The crowd moved off to the left getting out of the line of fire, the Skull men still under careful watch.

"Kill 'im, Spade!" one of the captured men yelled. Then there was a silence as the two men faced each other.

Twenty feet separated Reno and Spade, and the light now broke clear over the mountains, the sky rosy and golden to the east. Only a slight breeze sent the dust drifting across the yard, and except for the stamping of the horses in the corral and the far-off cry of a lost calf bawling for its mother, there was no sound.

Spade was drawn over, hunching forward with his thin body tightly outlined against the sky. His arms were out from his side, and his hands were spread out like huge claws over the twin butts of the low-slung Colts. He trembled with the tension of the moment, but there was a confident smile on his thin lips as he stared at the man facing him.

Reno stood erect, relaxed, and his arms were down at his side. A curtain of what appeared to indifference kept whatever he was feeling concealed, and his eyes were open, steady, and calm, as he looked across at the Skull rider.

"Anytime you feel like it, Spade."

The words were not out of Reno's mouth before both of Spade's claw-like hands slapped at the handles of the Colts!

Ray Catlin saw the move, and a flash of despair shot through him, for Spade was as fast as his reputation. But as Catlin's eyes shifted to Reno, he saw something he had trouble believing.

Reno waited until the slap of Spade's hands on the guns came, then he did two things, but so smoothly that it looked to Catlin's startled eye like one motion. Reno's draw was so smooth it was deceptive, but in one twitch of a motion he gripped the gun, and all Catlin saw was a blur as the gun came up. But at the same time, with the same motion, Reno was twisting his body to the right and raising his arm. Most gunfighters shot from the hip, but at the end of Reno's lightning draw he was standing in the classic dueling position—body turned to the side to present the least possible surface to the bullet of an opponent, arm straight out with the gun aimed unwaveringly at the target.

Two shots close together rang out, and Spade, whose guns were only half clear of the holsters, was knocked over backward as if smitten by a giant hand.

Reno slipped the gun into his holster effortlessly, and watched as Spade thrashed in the dirt. His legs were kicking and he was grunting loudly, an ugly sound in the stillness of the air. Reno remembered a man who had taken a bullet in the stomach in the wilderness battle in Virginia. He had made that same mindless sound until the fire swept through the underbrush, silencing him forever.

Two of the Skull crew ran over and pulled him to a sitting position. He had two stains of red beginning to blossom, a violent scarlet against his gray shirt. One was in the very point of his skinny right shoulder, the other on his left, closer to the neck, but lower down.

Neither of the wounds were critical, but the almost insolent ease with which Reno had drilled him cast a shock on every man in the yard, even the settlers.

Sixkiller's Indian eyes glittered and there was a fullness to his lower lip as he stared, first at Reno, then at the wounded man. He said, "Well, well," and added in a steady voice, "I wonder who he'll get to wipe his nose for the next two months?"

"Want to have a try, Conboy?" Reno asked.

The hulking foreman of Skull said nothing, and there was a pasty look around his lips. He stared at Reno blankly, all the arrogance driven out of him by the sudden challenge.

"Guess he'll tuck his tail," Catlin said. "What's next, Jim?"

"Get a team hitched, some of you. We're going to deliver this bunch to the law."

While some of the Skull riders were hitching a pair of saddle horses to an old wagon, Billy said, "Jim, you know it won't do no good to go to the law. Carr owns it all in Placid."

"Sure—but I want this country to see Skull eating dirt."

"Yeah!" Billy smiled, pleasure running across his broad face. "I can see that. But what then?"

"See how she goes, Billy."

In less than fifteen minutes, the buggy was loaded with the wounded man. His wounds had been roughly dressed, but he kept moaning loudly at intervals, a raw sound of fear that raked the nerves of Skull's crew.

"Want to let 'em saddle their horses, Jim?" Josh asked, waving at the mounts in the corral.

"No," he reflected, and then he looked directly at Conboy, saying, "Take off your boots, Pres. You're going to be a barefoot boy again. The rest of you do the same."

The words shook Conboy and he shot back, "You can't make us do that, Reno!"

"I'll bet I can, Pres," Reno said. "If I get softhearted, all I have to do is think about you birds shooting down Dave unarmed."

"It wasn't me!" one of the Skull men said at once, a scared look on his face.

"Shut up and take off those boots!" Reno cried out, and he took one step toward the Skull crew. There was a streak of raw anger that flowed out of him, and he cut at them recklessly in a way that none of the settlers had seen.

"You're pretty proud, and you've been doing a lot of pushing. Skull has been having its own way, nobody to stand against it. Hear this—when I see any of you again, it won't be a walk to town you'll be facing—I'll kill you."

Reno snatched the buggy whip from the socket of the wagon and it whistled through the air not six inches from Conboy's nose. "Next time, Pres, I'll open you up. Now get those boots off!"

Ashen-faced, Conboy pulled at his boots and the rest of his crew followed suit. One look at Reno's face was enough to convince them that he would do exactly what he said.

"Move out!" Reno shouted, and the prisoners stumbled awkwardly out of the yard followed by the mounted guard. They were all horsemen and walking was not what they did well. By the time they had covered two miles their feet were blistered, their legs aching, but there was no mercy in Reno's face.

"Pretty tough, Jim," John Malon said, catching sight of a bloody track in the dust from the blistered feet.

"Tough?" Reno murmured. He turned to stare at Malon, a grim smile on his lips. "No, this isn't tough, John. But it'll get that way pretty quick."

"You're right about that!" Josh nodded. "When we drive this bunch up the street in town, why, old Carr will have to make his play."

"Guess we know what to look for." Reno shrugged. "Anybody know a nice way to start a war or to fight one, I'd be glad to hear it."

"Jim's right!" Ray said. "But it's a little scary, I don't mind telling you. It's like going over the edge of a cliff!"

"Yeah," Billy mused, and there was a cynical droop to his lids as he murmured so quietly that only Reno heard it: "Hard time is, after you go over the edge, waiting 'til you hit the bottom!"

"How's Dave doing, May?"

It had taken Frank Carr the best part of an hour to steel himself to the point that he could walk across the street to where the tall daughter of Ole Swenson sat outside the big white house occupied by Doc Moody and a crusty house-keeper.

Frank had agonized over the shooting of Dave Melton, riding for hours trying to think of what he might have done to prevent it. In fact he had been taken completely off guard when Red Williams had pulled a gun and shot the helpless man down, thinking that at the worst Melton might be rouged up.

May Swenson had first caught his eye at a picnic, and he had pursued her as he had other girls. It was a game, the woman to run and the man to pursue. And May was a beautiful girl to pursue. Yet her beauty had not been the only attraction, for to his surprise, beneath the beauty of the girl was a woman with wit and a love for life that fascinated him. He had not, of course, openly courted her, but at every meeting the magne-tism of her spirit drew him, so that he grew gloomy with the hopelessness of it all.

Now he stood before her, hat in his hand, his face twisted with embarrassment and shame.

"He won't die, Frank," she said, and there was no anger in her soft blue eyes, only pain and a regret that rived him like a sword.

"May!" he cried, "I didn't know! You know I wouldn't have been a party to a thing like that!"

She touched his arm, and said, "I know, Frank, but . . ." She bit her lip and continued, "I don't think it would be wise for us to talk together anymore."

"May, don't say that!" Frank said. "You must know how I feel about you."

"I know," she agreed, and then a wave of sorrow swept across her face and she shook her head. "But we both know nothing can come of it."

"We can leave the Valley."

"No, this is your home—and mine. We can't run. You know that, Frank."

He would have said more, but she looked over his shoulder and her lips met firmly. She said, "There's your father. You'd better go."

He turned and across the street Aaron was standing beside Stacy, glaring at him. With a glance at the departing form of May, he whirled and walked across the street.

"Finished?" Aaron asked sarcastically.

"No!" Frank said and his face reddened as he stood eye to eye with his father. "I'm not finished, Dad, and you might as well hear it now. I'm going to marry that girl if she'll have me!"

"No, that won't be," Carr said at once, his temper ruffled. "I won't have my son taking up with that trash!"

"Dad! She's not trash!" Stacy broke in, but her brother had been pushed too far.

"Let's get it straight right now!" Frank said, and there was a jerk in his voice as he went on. "I went with that bunch to run a man off his place. I didn't go to shoot a helpless man down. And if that killer Williams wants to try it with an armed man, why, I'm ready."

"You're a fool, Frank," Carr half shouted. "Do you think—"

"I've always been proud of my family and of Skull. But no more! A bunch of hired killers, that's what we are."

"You can leave the ranch!" Carr shouted. His face flamed and his words carried across the street to where a group of men turned and stared at the Carrs.

"Mean that, Dad?" Frank asked, and he was still as he waited for his answer.

"Get your things and clear out!"

"I'll do that!" There was a strange pallor on his face, but Stacy saw that nothing now would make him back down. "I'll be moving into the old place on Wolf Creek. It's free graze—but if you think Skull can take it away from me, why you just send your hired killer to have a try."

He turned and walked away without another word, and Stacy felt sick. On the one hand she was proud of him for standing for the right, but she knew that her father was unbending in his pride. Even now he stood there, his face frozen in rage.

"Dad, don't you think . . ."

He swept her words away. "He's a weakling, always has been!"

"No, Dad!" Stacy flashed out at him, and he turned to stare at her, this unexpected attack taking him off guard for once. "He's not a weakling. He's got some gentleness in him, and you've never understood that a man can be tough and still have a gentle side."

"Are you talking about me, Stacy?" he asked. There was a ring of incredulity in his voice, and he looked confused. "Have I ever hurt you?"

She moved in close and put her arm around him. "No, you never have. Can't you see you've been gentle with me all my life? And that's what's in Frank, Dad."

Aaron Carr stood there, his face a study in confusion. He was not a complex man, for he believed in himself and his rules with an iron will. Nor did he see himself as a cruel or unjust man. His fights had been simple in one respect, and that was that he had faced up to what he thought to be an evil or a threat to his home and family.

Now he was shaken to find that this battle was not to be the simple test of force he had thought. Deep down he saw in Frank the man he had been in his youth, and although Boone was the most like him physically, he knew that Frank was the one he wanted most to carry on his blood.

Stacy's face turned up to him, swaying him, and he started to say something; but just at that moment somebody down the street called out, "Look at that!"

Both Aaron and Stacy glanced across the street to see everybody running toward the end of Main, and one of Skull's riders paused long enough to say, "Mr. Carr, you better come quick!"

Stacy followed as her father plunged onto the street, headed for the small crowd that had already collected outside the jail. He could see a wagon and several mounted men, but it was only when he got closer that he saw with a shock that Pres Conboy and part of the Skull crew were standing in a small group, apparently exhausted.

Shouldering his way through the crowd he emerged in the center, and saw that Jim Reno and a group of settlers and small ranchers were keeping a close watch on Conboy and the crew.

The crew, he saw, was played out. One of them simply slumped into the dust, too tired to stand up, and all of them had feet cut to ribbons by the rough terrain. Peering into the wagon he saw Slade moving from side to side and moaning hoarsely, his shirt a red splash of color that contrasted violently with his ivory face.

"What's this?"

Mack Bolin stepped out of his office taking in the scene with one glance. He darted a look at Aaron Carr, then at Reno. "Who shot this man?"

"I did." Reno's glance was laid on the marshal like the bore of a rifle, and a mutter went around the crowd.

"There's a law against that," Bolin said grimly. "Gimme your gun, Reno."

"It was a fair fight, Bolin," Ray said at once. "We got a dozen witnesses that Spade went for his iron first."

"Jim never even started until Spade's guns were half out of leather." Josh grinned. "It was a real sight to behold!"

"Well—" Bolin was stymied, and he looked again at Carr who was standing stock-still, his face an image of shock.

"Any law against shooting down an unarmed man, Mack?" Sixkiller asked.

Bolin ducked involuntarily. He could not admit any knowledge of Melton's shooting, but everyone in the crowd was aware that he knew the truth. "I got no authority outside the town," he muttered weakly.

"Then shut up about takin' a man's gun!" Ray snapped.

Reno sat there silently, his eyes locked with those of Aaron Carr. He knew as well as anyone that Marshal Bolin would take no stand. That was why Reno had paraded the Skull crew into Placid, and that was why he had been cruel in his method. He understood that the Carrs of Skull would never listen to any argument but force.

The owner of Skull stood there, every eye fixed on him. He had been in such positions often, and now the old habits reasserted themselves. He put the thoughts of Frank and the words of Stacy away, and bent his will against Reno as he had done so many times before.

"You have declared yourself, Reno," he said in a steady voice, but his face was like flint. "I take your attack on my crew as I always have, and from now on, look to yourself." He swept the men on horseback with his burning eyes, as if memorizing their faces. The authority in Carr's voice was unmistakable. "Consider yourselves warned—all of you!" Then he looked back at the wagon and said, "Get him to a doctor."

"Just a minute, Carr!" Reno slid off his mount and there was a dangerous look about him, even though he made no moves toward the weapon on his hip. He paused before the huge form of Skull's owner, and even though he had to tilt his head back to look him squarely in the face, there was nothing submissive in the act.

"I want everybody in the Valley to know what's happening," Reno said forcefully. "You've given me a warning, and now I give you one, Carr."

"I don't need your warning!"

"No? You better understand this: There's nothing you can do to us that we can't do to you. There's nothing you can take from us that we can't take back from you."

"Bluff!" Carr reddened. "You can't make it stick, Reno!"

"No? Listen, Carr, I went through two range wars, and it was rough! But I'm telling you now, that no matter how many men you hire to get the job done, when the smoke clears, we'll be there!"

Then Reno looked at Stacy, whose face was pale, and said, "I regret to have to talk like this before you, Stacy."

Carr wheeled and walked away with giant strides and after one strange look at Reno, Stacy turned slowly and followed him.

"Come on," Reno said. "Let's get out of here."

"What about this man?" Bolin asked, staring at Spade.

Josh spat into the dust and said dryly, "He ain't the last one that'll be brought in like that. Some of 'em won't make it this fer. They only have to go as fer as that graveyard."

"Let's go," Reno repeated, and the men followed him down to the square. He got off his horse, and the rest followed his example.

"Well, we're out of the frying pan, at least!" Ray said with a grim smile.

"Into the fire," Malon agreed. He wiped his forehead, and there was a tremble in his hands and a nervous tic in his eye. "Boys, I don't mind tellin' you, this has left me feelin' plumb shaky!"

"Always does," Reno replied. "Long as you get shaky *after* the trouble, you'll be all right, John."

"But how we gonna fight that big bunch, Jim?"

"Bite 'em on the tail and run like the devil, John," Reno said with a smile. Then he added, "I want all of you to stay ready. The only thing we don't know is the time and the place Skull's going to hit."

"That's right, we got to stay organized," Billy said. "When one of us gets hit, he runs away. No trying to be a hero, right, Jim?"

"That's it."

"You got any guesses about what Carr will do?" Ray asked.

Reno nodded. "I think he'll come to Circle M."

Josh said at once, "My thinkin' exact, Jim. Now I say we all go along with you."

Reno shook his head. "It may not be right away, though I don't think it'll be long."

"I'm goin', and you ain't takin' me out of it," Billy insisted rebelliously.

"Me, too," Ray spoke up, and Reno smiled knowing that the two loved a fight.

"All right, but no more. The rest of you get home, and if we need you, I'll send for you."

They broke up and Reno said, "I'm going to get some extra shells from the store."

"Meet you at Frenchy's Saloon," Billy said grinning. "I'm packin' a big thirst."

With a wave of his hand, Reno left them and walked directly to Simmons' General Store. Neal Simmons was standing behind the counter, his eyes veiled. Skull was his big customer and he asked curtly, "Do for you?"

Reno got the shells, then said, "Simmons, there'll come a time when you speak a little more softly to people who don't ride for Skull."

Simmons reddened, but Reno walked out before he could answer.

"Jim!" He heard his name, and looking toward the alley he saw Stacy standing there.

"Stacy, what . . . ?"

"We don't have time to talk, Jim, but I want to tell you one thing." Her lip trembled and she forced herself to speak more slowly. "I—I know what's coming, and I don't want you to hold back. But will you look out for Frank?"

"Frank?" Reno was puzzled. "What about him?"

"He's leaving home. Taking up a place over by Wolf Creek. I know some of the settlers won't understand. His name is Carr—that's all they'll see, and I want you to help him."

Reno stood there, and finally said, "I'm sorry about all this. Sure, I'll go see Frank. It couldn't have been easy for him."

"It's not easy for any of us, Jim."

They were alone in the alley, and the presence of the girl disturbed him. The violence of the past hours had drained him, and he found himself looking at her in a strange way. She was vulnerable, desirable, and suddenly the sense of her femininity came so strongly to him that without willing to do so, he took her arms and pulled her gently forward.

Her eyes opened wide and her lips parted. She did not resist as he slowly put his arms around her, drawing her close. His lips fell on hers, gently at first, then both of them were caught up in an instant when the sounds of the town seemed far away. She pressed against him with a sweetness that matched the yielding of her lips and the fragrance of her hair, and he felt her hands close behind his head as she pulled him closer.

Then, as it began, it ended, and both of them stepped back. Her hand was on his chest, and she whispered, "Jim, what is it?"

He struggled to frame his mood in words, then muttered, "I guess we're both crazy, Stacy."

"No!" she breathed in agitation. "Don't say that, Jim. Everything I love is falling apart!" She touched his face. "You're the one thing in the whole mess that makes any sense!"

"Stacy . . . ," he began, but tears filled her eyes, and she shook her head.

"I have to go," she said thickly. "Be careful, Jim!" Then she left him, and he walked slowly toward Frenchy's Saloon with a heaviness in his step.

"It's a long war," he mused slowly. "And there's not going to be any winner. There never is."

TEN
Cabin-Raising

Fitful gusts of wind with a threat of cold drove the new-fallen crop of dead leaves around the feet of Stacy's horse as she rode toward Wolf Creek. She had waited for nearly three weeks for Frank to come back to Skull, but when he had come, it was when she was gone to town. According to Lee, he had piled all his belongings into a rickety spring wagon and left without more than a short word.

"Didn't he say anything at all?" Stacy had asked Lee.

"Just said to tell Mother he'd be back when he had time—for a visit." Lee had shifted and glanced at his sister with a puzzled look. "He ain't really gonna try to make a go at that two-bit spread, is he, Sis?"

"You know Frank when he gets stubborn."

"Oh, sure, but this is crazy! He'll starve to death and break his back. I don't get it."

Stacy had answered, "It caught Dad off guard. Frank's always been such a good son. But I could have told Dad one thing—when Franklin Robert Carr does get an idea, he sets his foot down hard enough to make the welkin ring!"

Cresting a knoll that lay banked around a bend in Wolf Creek, Stacy saw her brother digging a posthole. She rode down the slope thinking wryly that she'd been more accurate than she'd known in her statement.

He looked up suddenly, and the scowl on his face broke. As she slid off her horse he threw the posthole diggers down and said, "Well, I guess you know the worst, Sis." He stepped forward holding out his broad hands which were covered, she saw, with blisters both old and new.

"Frank!" she said, taking them in her own hands, and shaking her head. "These look *awful!*"

He put his arm around her and drew her over to the weathered shack, saying ruefully, "A cowboy has to be a teetotal idiot to do this kind of thing!"

"Haven't you got any gloves? You ought to put some salve on these blisters."

"Wore out two pair of gloves already." He waved at the line of postholes that outlined the place, and there was laughter in his fine eyes as he said, "See those blamed holes? I quit on every one of them, Sis! Then I got mad thinking how all the small ranchers and settlers I've laughed at all my life could have put this fence up in no time."

Stacy looked around, noting the small house weathered to silver and listing to one side. A barn off to her left was propped up by a series of pine poles, and the doors were sagging beyond control. A garden plot someone had hopes for once was taken over by ragweed and sage, and the yard around the house was littered with cans and trash: one of a thousand failures that once had been a high hope, but now was slowly falling back into the earth. Another ten years or so and nothing would mark the spot except a few rusty nails and a well filled in with dust.

"Not much, is it?" he said, catching her gaze. His smile faded, throwing his features into relief, and Stacy realized from the set of his jaw that Frank was totally committed to this task.

"You have to do this, Frank?" she asked, knowing better than to urge him to give up. She knew him as well as he knew her, and the stubborn streak that he had masked with an easy smile had not been hidden from her.

"Yes."

"But—why? Oh, I know Dad is stubborn—and wrong, too, in this case."

He shook his head. "It's more than a mistake, Sis. I could put up with that. But his whole way of thinking is going to destroy him! I've tried not to think about it for a long time." He tried to smile as he added, "Now I cut my picket. It all got too raw, Stacy, and when Williams cut down on that unarmed man, it was just too much."

If Stacy had been less perceptive, or if she had been convinced that Frank was wrong, she might have tried to argue, but she was too wise for that.

"Well, I've come to ask for a job. You need any help, Mr. Sodbuster?"

He gave her a quick smile, realizing that she knew him too well for him to protest. "Sis, I've worked on this place like a slave for three weeks and you can't even see it."

Stacy turned to her horse and pulled a heavy canvas sack from behind the saddle, saying, "I'm the new cook. Bet you haven't had a good meal since you got here."

"Sis, if you got anything to eat in that sack that won't stick in my craw, I'll make you half-owner of my vast estate!"

She laughed and went inside, not surprised to find it cluttered and filthy. All morning she worked cleaning and scrubbing, and by the time Frank came in at noon to eat the meal she had prepared, she had made enough difference in the place to cause him to open his eyes wide.

"I don't believe it!" he exclaimed. "Why, it's actually clean!"

"I guess if you can dig postholes, I can scrub and clean!" she laughed. "Now, sit down and pitch into some of this chili."

They sat down together, and he said, "My stomach thinks my throat's been cut, Sis. I've never been so hungry. . . ."

He got up suddenly, and went to the door. "Somebody coming," he said, looking out. "It's Stevens." There was a sound of a horse crossing the yard, and he greeted the rider, "Hello, Thad. Get down and come in. You're just in time for some grub."

Thad replied, "Hello, Frank. I've been meaning to come over ever since you moved in, but . . ." He paused as he entered the room, and when he saw Stacy, his face altered. "Hello, Stacy."

"Hello, Thad. Pull up that other chair."

"Well . . ." Thad's manner was uncertain, but as they both urged him, he sat down and let Stacy fill his bowl with the spicy chili. They all began to eat hungrily, and Frank noticed that Thad said little to his sister, but he stole a glance at her from time to time.

Finally Thad said, "I guess you know just about everybody in the Valley is talking about you."

Frank nodded. "I can guess."

"Most folks think you'll patch it up with your father."

"Sure." Frank nodded again. He scraped the bottom of his bowl and filled it again from the large pot on the stove. Then he grinned and asked curiously, "How you figure it, Thad?"

Thad shrugged. "It would make more sense than busting your back on a small spread. I can tell you a little about that!" Thad did not look toward Stacy, but somehow she felt that the statement was aimed at her.

"You know what a hard worker Frank's always been, Thad," she said. "Are you saying he can't make it on his own?"

Thad looked at the palms of his hands, callused and tough as boot soles. There was a small smile on his full lips as he looked at the pair. "It's not a matter of working hard. It's the rest of it that wears you down."

"Tell it, Thad," Frank urged at once. He put his spoon down and gave his full attention to the tall man across from him.

"You've always worked hard, Frank, but you never had to live with what a small rancher or a farmer faces. You always knew that you had a place at Skull, always knew that no matter how bad things got, you'd have a home and plenty to eat. But it's not like that for most people." Thad clenched his fist, and there was a sadness in his eyes as he went on softly.

"What if the crops get eaten by the bugs? What if a drought fries the grass and you have to watch your little herd shrivel to skeletons? How are you going to get the money to pay that note at the bank? And if you can't pay it, where are you going to go for help?"

He rubbed his thick forefinger across the top of the table and Frank admitted, "Yeah, I see what you mean, Thad."

Stevens shook his head sadly, and then he looked at them adding, "I hope you never have to find out what it's like, Frank, to watch a wife try to feed children on not enough to go around. And then, as if that's not enough grief, there's . . ."

Stacy knew what he almost said, and she murmured,

"And it's worse when ranches like Skull threaten to destroy anything you build—is that it, Thad?"

He hesitated, then nodded. "Yes, that's the worst. We were all expecting an army to come after we roughed up Skull's crew. What happened, Stacy?"

She stirred restlessly, and Frank did not miss the hungry glance that the visitor gave his sister when she stared past him out the window. "Boone wanted to do just that, but Dad stopped him."

"That's good," Frank said in surprise. "Maybe Dad's changing."

"No, he told Boone that Skull had to wait until the trouble died down," Stacy corrected. "I think he's afraid that a U.S. Marshal will come over. But I think he told Boone to be ready to hit the next man who puts up a fence—hit him with all Skull has."

"That'll be me," Frank said.

"No, Dad will never touch you." Stacy got up and began putting the dishes into a pan of water, and there was a fear in her eyes as she said, "But there's another thing. Right after the trouble, Boone went away for two days. When he came back, he had this rider with him. But he's not a rider, because he never works."

The two men looked at each other, and Frank asked, "Who is he, Sis?"

"His name is Kincaid. He spends all his time either in town or practicing with a gun."

Thad stared at her, then said, "There's a man by that name with quite a reputation. Comes from Val Verde. I hope it's not him."

"Dad would never hire killers!" Stacy protested.

"What about Red Williams?" Frank shrugged. "Dad lets Boone and Conboy hire the men. You know that."

There was a silence, and Thad got up saying, "Well, I came to invite you to a cabin-raising, Frank. A bunch of us are getting together to put up a house for Nate Smiley. He's got four kids and they don't need to go through another winter in the shack they're living in."

If Stevens had offered Frank help, it might have been different, but this appeal drew him. "Sure, I'll come."

Thad's face got a little tense, and he asked uncertainly, "Stacy, if you'd like to come . . ."

"Thanks, Thad. I'll tag along with Frank."

A smile brightened Thad's face. "Good! I'll see you there!"

After they heard his horse leave the yard, Frank caught a strange expression on Stacy's face as she looked toward the door. "You know, Sis," he said slowly, "I used to think that you and Thad were getting pretty thick."

"You did?"

"I wasn't wrong, was I, Sis?"

"No." Stacy got up and walked to the window, staring out, and there was an odd note to her voice as she added, "No, you weren't wrong, Frank."

"What happened?"

She gave him a tired smile, then shook her head. "Thad's a proud man, Frank. He felt like he didn't have enough to offer me. But that wasn't really it. He just couldn't . . ."

When he saw how hard it was for her, he murmured, "He couldn't stand up to Dad, was that it?"

She nodded, then said, "A woman wants a man who's not afraid. And I guess there's not a man in the Valley who has the nerve to face up to Aaron Carr."

Frank shook his head slowly. "Asking a small rancher to take on Skull—that's a pretty stiff test! I'm just beginning to get an idea of how helpless a feeling it is. But for what it's worth, Sis, I guess Thad loves you. You feel that way about him?"

"I—I thought I did." Misery was in her face as she suddenly looked across at Frank. "But it won't come to anything."

"Maybe not, but you can't blame Thad for being a little jumpy about taking Dad on. Everybody is."

Stacy shook her head and asked, "What about Jim Reno?"

Frank nodded slowly and mused, "Yeah—what about Reno? Now there's a different breed of cat!" He turned to leave, then wheeled to give her one last thought:

"Reno and Skull are going to collide somewhere along the way—and it's going to be downright fatal for one or the other!"

"That Barney! He gonna wear those guns out, Jim!" Josh grinned and waved toward the bunkhouse where Barney was practicing his draw. "That do take me back some. Guess I musta spent half my time doin' that when I was a kid. You too, I bet!"

"Sure," Reno said with a smile. "I started my misspent life early."

They were waiting for Catherine to finish the pies she had been working on for the cabin-raising. Thad stuck his head out the door and said, "All ready. Let's get loaded up. If we don't get there pretty soon, the cabin will be up and done without us!"

Reno and Josh helped wedge the smoking pies firmly into the wagon, Josh saying, "Mebbe we ort to 'test' this one, Catherine, jest to be sure it's OK."

Catherine slapped his hand sharply as he lifted the cloth off a pie. "Keep your grubby hands off that pie, Josh Jordan! Nobody eats until the roof is on the house!"

"Aw, that's the trouble with you womenfolk," Josh complained. "Too dad-blamed serious!" Raising his voice he bellowed, "Barney, put that hogleg up 'fore you blow your foot off and let's git!"

All the men rode their horses, and Catherine drove the spring wagon, which was loaded with food and tools. The small procession swung east to pick up Mrs. Dodson, a widow, and her oldest son, Clarence. By keeping the horses at a brisk trot they were halfway to the site before eight.

"There's the Carrs," Thad said, as a pair of riders emerged from a belt of cottonwoods and turned to join them.

Frank looked a little tense as he rode up, not knowing what reception he might receive, but Reno put him at ease with a wry remark, "Hello, Frank. How's the posthole business?"

They all laughed and Frank's face relaxed. He joined in the idle talk and Stacy got in the wagon with Catherine and Mrs. Dodson.

As they were getting close to the Smiley place, Barney said, "Jim, I've been practicing my draw."

"Noticed that, Barney."

"Well, what I want to ask is, which is best, you think, two guns or one?"

"Better use two, boy," Josh teased. "One won't shoot fer enough!"

But Reno was serious. "I've seen some pretty handy folks using two guns, but if you know what you're doing, I'd say one's plenty."

"Yeah, I notice you only carry one. Can I see your gun?"

There was a slight hesitation that they all noticed, then Reno slipped his gun from the holster and handed it to the boy.

Taking it eagerly, Barney felt its weight, sighted it, then exclaimed, "Why, this is a .38! Almost everybody I know packs a .44—or bigger!"

"Fine if you're huntin' buffalo," Reno said with a soft smile. "But a .38 slug in the head is a mighty sure persuader."

"Say," Barney said, looking at the gun, "there's something funny about your gun."

"Barrel is two inches longer than on most guns," Reno said. "More accurate at a distance."

"Most gunfighters don't give two whoops 'bout that!" Josh snorted. "Pull iron and blaze away 'til somebody's down— that's the ticket. Why, I seen five men get in a real shoot-out in a saloon in Dodge City. All of them pulled their smokepoles and lemme tell you, the air was shore thick with smoke!"

"How many got killed, Josh?" Barney asked, his eyes wide.

"One of the gamblers clattered over at the other end of the room and got a little finger blowed off," Josh laughed, "and some winder lights got busted. None of them jokers got a scratch!"

"Aw, you're lying again, Josh," Barney said.

"Maybe not," Reno commented. "It's one thing to shoot at a tin can, and something else to send a man off to hell with a bullet."

"Jim," Frank interrupted suddenly, "you ever hear of a gunfighter named Kincaid?"

"There's a Kincaid I knew once," Reno answered. "Why you asking?"

"Stacy says that he's working at Skull."

"Think it could be the man you know?" Thad asked.

"Maybe. If it is, he won't be overjoyed to see me. We never did get along."

"Could you beat him?" Barney asked quickly.

Reno turned to face the young man, and something he saw saddened him. He shook his head and when he spoke it was with regret. "Nobody knows that, kid. It's a sorry test of a man—seeing who can get a gun out of a holster first. Most of the men who've gotten good at it have been ruined. Either they got killed, or they turned into mad dogs. If I had my way, I'd never pick up a gun."

"I didn't know you felt that way, Jim," Thad murmured.

"Hey," Juan said breaking the silence that spread itself over the group. "Looks like we're late."

The clearing they rode into was a beehive of activity. Crews had already cut the logs and several men were busy cutting them to length and hewing the mortises at the ends. Some had wanted to hew them square with a broad ax, but winter had caught them and there was no time. "Have to haul plenty clay and wattles to fill the chinks, Nate," John Malon was telling the rail-thin Smiley as Reno and the others dismounted and plunged into the work.

"What you do best, Jim, on this cabin building bit?" Ray Catlin demanded.

"Making shakes."

"Well, I've never had a man who could make 'em as fast as I can nail 'em up," Ray challenged. "A new hat says I'll have to twiddle my thumbs waitin' on you to get me some shakes."

"I need a new lid," Jim shot back. "You pick a crew and I'll stay with Barney, Juan and Frank."

"Losin' team has to eat second table?" Catlin grinned.

"Sure."

It put a spice in the work, and they joined the rest in getting the walls up.

The corners of the house were already squared, and four corners men carried the corners up ladders while the rest were left on the ground to lift from there. The first timbers were rested on the foundation stones, notched at both ends by the corner ax men. The next two were notched on the underside, then placed to fit the saddles of the lower ones. The wall of logs rose higher and higher, carried by the men on the ground, until it got too high; then two small logs called "skid poles" were rested against the side of the wall and the timbers were scooted into place by means of push poles and ropes.

By noon the walls were up, and after a quick break for lunch the rafters were set in place. The chinking was a later labor when other chores less pressing were done. There was a doorway, stopped by a temporary blanket, and a window opening in each end closed by canvas until glass could be bought. The fireplace took a large part of one wall.

"Now I'm gonna show you how real men can put a roof on a house, Reno!" Ray said. "I figure you and that sorry crew of yours will be eatin' with the women and kids!"

The cedar logs which had been brought in to use for the shakes had to be cut into lengths, and four men were set to work at this task. Reno had picked up a froe which was used for riving the shakes. It was simply a straight steel blade with one sharp edge and a hole on one end holding a wooden handle.

Reno looked around and saw that practically everybody had slowed down work to take in the contest. He felt the edge of the froe, grinned at Frank, and said, "I sure am looking forward to that grub. Got no intention of letting Ray and that sorry-looking outfit he calls a crew go first."

"They haven't got a prayer, Jim," Frank said with a broad grin. There had been several hard looks as he had ridden in, but as he had joined into the work of raising the cabin walls, the looks had been more surprised than otherwise. Now, looking at Reno, he saw that both of them felt good about the thing. Relief washed over him freely, for he had known the world of Skull, and nothing else. There had been a ray of doubt as to whether or not he could win a place with these people. Now he knew that he could.

One butt lay on the ground and Frank, taking an ax, split it in two with smooth easy motions, then into quarters, and finally into eights. "There you go, Jim," he said and fell to the crosscut saw with Juan hanging on to the other end for dear life.

Reno picked up one of the V-shaped pieces, balanced it against a stump, and placed the froe on top with the blade running toward the smaller end. He gave a sharp rap to the dull side of the blade with a wooden mallet, at the same time twisting the froe as it went into the wood. As the blade slid down through the block he kept hitting the end that stuck out and directing the direction of the edge so that very quickly a thin shake fell to the ground.

"Boy, that feller can rive a shake!" someone exclaimed. "You better call a prayer meeting of your fellers, Ray!"

Catlin saw that Reno was an expert, for the shakes were almost falling off the slab, and no sooner had he finished one length of the cedar than another was feeling the bite of the froe.

"There's a bundle for you to start on, Ray," Reno said,

grinning as he picked up an armload and handed them to Catlin. "Better get to it."

"Come on, you fellows! He can't last at that!" Catlin practically ran up the ladder. Getting into position, he began nailing the shakes into position with the rough handmade nails. "Keep 'em comin'!" he shouted as he finished a layer and moved to the second course.

All afternoon the race went on accompanied by a series of lively insults, jeers, and cheers from the crowd as they took sides in the contest.

Reno worked like a machine, looking up from time to time at the steadily growing pile of shakes, and at the roof yet to be done. Straightening up slowly, he walked over to stand looking up at Ray, sweating despite the cool November wind that was raking off the clouds in the north. He remarked loud enough for all to hear:

"I wear size 8, Ray. And I'll see that some of the leftovers get saved for your boys!"

Ray looked up with a startled expression on his thin face, then looking sheepish and angry at once, threw his hammer as far as he could with a whispered oath.

A laugh went up from the crowd, and Reno and his crew, including Frank Carr, were beaten around the shoulders with hard hands until they all begged for mercy.

Nate Smiley had dug a pit close to the cabin, in which a deep bed of coals, three days burning, had accumulated. Over the pit he had erected a scaffolding of poles from which hung the butchered chunks of half a dozen deer and calves. Over the same fire, also, was a series of huge iron pots containing potatoes with their jackets on and half a wagonload of squash.

"Let's eat!" someone howled, and after Thad had pronounced a brief blessing, they attacked the food on the trestles.

Reno was joined by Catherine as they piled their plates high with food. Backbones, hog jowl, sausage, fried ham, chicken, cornbread, preserves, biscuits, pumpkin pie, butter-milk, and a huge vat of coffee began to flow from the table into the hungry workers.

"You sure are missing some good grub, Ray," Jim called over to the losing crew that was standing awkwardly to one side waiting for the others to be served, and a laugh went up at their expense, but it was a good-natured kind of fooling.

"Where did you learn to make shakes like that, Jim?" Catherine asked.

"Did a lot of it when I was growing up, but I put in a sum-mer at a mill in Oregon."

"What's it like out there, Jim?"

As they finished, he told her about the coast, and they took their plates to the big tub, dumping them in. "Let's walk," she suggested. "If I sit down I'll go to sleep."

"Sure."

They made their way through the clearing, passing by a huge stump that Stacy, Thad, Frank, and May Swenson were using for a table. "Beats digging postholes, doesn't it, Frank?" Jim smiled as they passed.

The big man grinned. "You got that right! Sit down and help me with this pie."

"No, I'm full as a dog tick," Reno said with a shake of his head. "Me and the boss lady are going to walk it down."

As they walked away, Catherine noticed that Stacy's eyes were following Reno. She saw also the look that Thad had given the tall girl by his side, but said nothing.

Reno, however, said, "They make a nice looking couple, don't they—Stacy and Thad?"

"I always thought so."

"Old Thad, he's got a real case on that girl." Then he glanced at her quizzically, asking, "You figure he's got a chance with her?"

Catherine took his arm as she stepped into a shallow hole, and she did not remove it as they went on. She was a quiet girl, and he had learned that she seldom gave her opinion without serious thought, so he waited until they had gotten to the edge of cornstalks dancing briskly in the last rays of the day.

"Everyone thought they were in love once," she said slowly. "Of course, Thad's slow. Not like you."

"You think I'm a fast worker, Catherine?" Jim grinned. His white teeth made a track across his dark features in the failing light, and he shook his head in mock sadness. "Like the Book says, 'Dead flies cause the ointment of the apothecary to send forth a stinking savor: so doth a little folly him that is in reputation for wisdom and honor.'"

Catherine stared at him in surprise. "You know your Bible, Jim."

"Used to," he corrected. A single plaintive cry floated across the darkness of the prairie, the desolate cry of a timber wolf. He listened to it as if it meant something, then added as he turned to face her, "My dad was killed when I was just a kid, and my mother married Lige Stevens two years later."

"How did your father die?"

Bitterness threaded Reno's voice as he said, "Shot down while he was holding up a bank."

"Oh—Jim, I'm sorry!" Catherine said, and she held more tightly to his arm.

"Well, I never knew him. But Lige Stevens was a better

father to me than he'd have been. I know that now, but I didn't back when I was a young man studying for the gallows," he said grimly. "Lige was a preacher, and a good man. Wasn't his fault I went bad. He used to try to tell me what would happen if I kept going the way I was headed, but he never turned me away, not even when just 'bout everybody else did."

Catherine leaned slightly against him, and he caught the fragrance of her hair as she said, "I'm glad he didn't, Jim."

They walked on, coming to a split rail fence containing a mare and her foal. The moon was just beginning to glow, and Catherine's face was silvered by its light as she stretched over to rub the nose of the colt.

"Reverend Stevens taught you the Bible?" she asked.

"Yes. Believe it or not, he even made me like it. He never was an important preacher, but he had a way about him. Religion wasn't something to do on Sunday. He was a walking Sermon on the Mount." Jim shook his head, adding, "I guess he never gave up on me, Catherine. I was in the army when he died, but Thad said just about the last thing he said was, 'Tell Jim I love him. Tell him I'll be waiting for him.'"

A fiddle started tuning up back at the clearing, a thin sound that brought back some memory that held Reno still. But when he finally turned to Catherine, she was holding her fist against her lips to keep from crying, and two silvery tracks made their way down her cheeks.

"Why, don't cry, Catherine," he said. "Shouldn't have mentioned it."

"No, it's all right, Jim. I—I guess I was thinking about Dad. He was the same way."

The sound of a banjo joined in with the fiddle, then a guitar began to find the melody. Darkness was complete, but there was an orange moon turned upside down in the west, and overhead the stars made icy points in the sky.

Suddenly her closeness came to him as a shock, and he saw in her the perfection, the grace, and the warmth that had been growing into his awareness during the long months he had known her. She was the strength and the completeness and the glory that a man dreamed of, but never expected to find. He drew her close and kissed her, suddenly taken off guard by the wild, fiery flavor which she released without restraint. Taken by surprise, or suddenly willing—this he never knew—she gave him all he asked for, then pulled herself away.

He stepped back, shaken by the rush of powerful emotion she had stirred in him, and said, "I'm not sorry, Catherine."

She did not answer at once, as was her habit. She sighed and put her hand on his arm, saying, "I'm not sorry either, Jim."

"You're still grieving over Silas."

"No, that's not it—and you know it."

He had no answer for that, then as the music broke into full strength he smiled and said gently, "It's time to be foolish, Catherine."

He led her back to the circle of light thrown by several large bonfires close to the newly finished cabin, unaware that few in the party did not take notice of their arrival. He had made a place in their imaginations, and everything he did was of note to these people.

Thad said nothing, but he felt Stacy move restlessly as Reno led Catherine to the group of dancers who had begun to move to the sound of the music. About ten or twelve couples in an irregular formation, standing around the clearing in some semblance of a circle, began swaying as the music started. A thin-faced farmer in bib overalls stepped up beside the musicians and began calling the tune:

"Coffee grows on the white oak tree:
  The river flows sweet brandy-o;
  Now choose the one to come with you,
  As sweet as sugar in the candy-o.

"Two in the center and you'd better get about,
  Two in the center and you'd better get about,
  Two in the center and you'd better get about,
  And swing that lady 'round!"

And as the singers reached the line "As sweet as sugar in the candy-o," a young man grabbed a pretty girl in a red-and-white checkered dress by both arms and gave her a violent spin around the circle. He did just what the song told him to: "And swing that lady 'round!"

Then the first stanza of the song was repeated and the girl in the ring chose a short young man wearing a violet colored shirt, who in turn selected a girl for his partner as he stepped to the inner circle. Without losing a step, the two couples traced a figure eight on the ground and were in their proper places at the center when "candy-o" was reached by the caller. Then came the order from a dozen throats:

"Four in the center and you'd better get about,
  Four in the center and you'd better get about,
  Four in the center and you'd better get about,
  And swing them ladies 'round!"

Reno and Catherine lost themselves in the dance. They

met in the center of the circle following the traditional scheme of the old game to the letter. Another couple stood facing each other some four or five feet apart. The second boy took a position a few feet behind the first young man, and the second girl took a position behind the first girl. Then boy number one took his girl's hand and passed her on the right, and they circled so as to meet and to pass at the same spot, followed by the second couple tracing a figure eight on the floor. Then the coffee verse came and the last couple coming in selected another couple to join them. Now three couples were in the center and the whole crowd sang:

"Six in the center and you'd better get about,
Six in the center and you'd better get about,
Six in the center and you'd better get about,
And swing them ladies 'round!"

Thad suddenly turned to Stacy and asked, "Want to dance, Stacy?"

She was taken off guard, and her eyes were wide as she looked up at him and said, "It's been a long time, Thad."

"Come on," he urged, and soon they were making the intricate patterns of the dance in the circle. As Reno caught a glimpse of his brother he saw a light in his face that had been absent for a long time.

"Look at that," he murmured to Catherine.

"Yes. It's good to see."

They saw Frank pull May Swenson into the center and her face was alight with pleasure as the tall man swung her like a feather through the dance.

For two hours the music went on, and there was a relief

from the terrible pressures that life brought to bear on the earthbreakers and the small ranchers.

As they finally left the clearing, Reno said as he helped Catherine into the wagon, "Wish this could go on forever—but tomorrow's coming."

She caught at him, holding his arm fast, and forced him to face her. "Tomorrow will come, and trouble with it. But we're not alone, Jim."

He never knew if she meant him or her faith in God, for she mounted the seat and spoke to the horses, causing them to move out across the prairie toward the Circle M.

As they followed, Thad said quietly, "It was like old times, wasn't it, Jim? Like when we were growing up?"

"Sure." There was a long silence and then he added, "Those times came to a bad end for me, Thad. Wouldn't like to think that would happen again."

Thad said only, "I guess every man makes his own heaven."

After a long silence Reno thought with a sharp stab of regret, *His own heaven—or his own hell!*

ELEVEN
Barney's Place

Winter was a threat that reached out of the hills, touching them with a bitter cold breath, driving the ranchers to days that stretched from the dark of morning until long past sundown. November, which had begun sleepily with brisk mornings that turned into warm afternoons, suddenly was transformed into wolf-sharp winter weather that struck the land with blue-black cold.

Reno led Barney and Juan at a driving pace, trying to get set for what he felt would be a killing winter.

Josh, with the wisdom of a mountain man, had felt the same. Sniffing the cold breath that swept down out of the hills, he had growled at Reno, "This ain't gonna be no picnic! I figure this winter is gonna be a genuine killer if I ever seen one!"

"How you know that, Josh?" Barney had asked.

"Why, ain't you seen how thick the acorn shells is, boy? And I ain't never in all my days seen such thick fuzz on the caterpillars!"

Barney stared at the old man with a doubtful look on his youthful face, then asked Jim, "He's lying again, ain't he, Jim?"

"You jest wait, boy!" Josh shook his grizzled head, adding, "I mebbe could mistake a few signs, but this here Apache arrowhead I tote around in my arm ain't never been wrong. And it says they's a stem-winder of a he-winter over in them hills ready to pounce on this valley any time!"

Reno had not missed the troubled expression that had crossed Barney's face, but it was two days later before the young rider opened his mind. They were replacing the wire on a fence, Reno pulling the strand tight with the team while Barney drove the staples in. Finally they finished the job and on the way back to the ranch Barney, who had said little all day, asked, "Jim, you know Mary Bolling?"

"Redhead that waits tables at the café? Sure."

"Well . . ." Barney shifted uncomfortably on the hard seat of the wagon, pulled the collar of his red plaid coat up around his ears, and finally said, "Well, what I want to tell you is that I'm real serious about her."

"That right, Barney?"

"Sure! I mean she's a real nice girl, Jim, and I been thinking about her a long time."

"How does she feel about you?"

"She likes me a lot, Jim." A warm light glowed in Barney's eyes, making him look even younger than his years.

"Sounds like a good thing to me."

"Yeah, but the thing is, Jim, I want us to get married and have our own place."

"You do it, Barney," Reno said, slapping the thin shoulder of the boy. "We'll keep our eyes open and sooner or later there'll be a piece of ground, and then . . ."

"Jim, the thing is, I already got a place!" Barney's voice got excited and he waved his arms as he went on. "Maybe you don't know the place, being new around here, but there's a little place just east of Billy Sixkiller's ranch. Not a big place, you know, but nice. Last week I heard that the folks that used to own it wanted to sell out. They left about two years ago to go back to Texas, but they came back to see if they could find a buyer. Mr. Duke—he's the old fellow who owned the place—he couldn't find anybody with the cash, so when I talked to him, we worked out a deal." Barney faltered slightly, and he struggled to tell Reno what the listener could easily guess. "Well, what I mean is, Jim, I bought the place."

Reno tried to think about the country lying in that direction, and he asked finally, "Where'd you get the money, Barney?"

"Oh, I had a few hundred dollars saved up, and Mr. Duke is going to let me pay the rest out. We got a paper drawn up and everything."

"Well, Barney, you've had a taste of what ranching is like. Guess you know you don't always eat too high on the hog." Something was troubling Reno, and finally it came to his mind. "Isn't that section east of Billy used mostly by the big ranches for late graze?"

"Oh, sure. Mr. Frazier of Bent 6 has been using some of it." Then he hesitated and added, "And Skull has some stock there, too."

Reno shook his head. "You know how they'll take it if you move in on their grass."

"But it's my place!" Barney protested.

"Sure, but you know what happened to Dave Melton."

"They won't move me off!" Barney said, and there was a hard set to his young face. "What I'm saying, Jim, is that I'm moving over there tomorrow—if it's OK with you. I know there's not a lot of work left around the Circle M, so do you think Miss Catherine will mind if I go?"

"No, that part is all right," Reno said slowly, as they pulled into the yard. "But I don't think you ought to go right now. Wait until spring."

"Can't do it, Jim." Barney jumped down and opened the gate, then came back with a smile on his face. "I already got me some stock," he said, then added, "Just twenty cows and a bull I got from Jess Masterson. He said he couldn't carry them through the winter."

Barney stood there looking up at Reno, and there was a light in his eyes that Reno recognized, for he himself had once been young and full of hope. He thought of himself and it was painful for him to remember how he had been battered by life until that hope had faded. It left him with a dark strain of fatalism that had eaten away at him for the past few years, and with little of the boundless optimism he had known when he was just beginning. He almost told Barney to forget it, that the game wasn't worth the effort, but the slight form of the young man, and the plea for understanding in the gentle eyes, changed his mind.

"You do it, then, Barney!" he said and jumped to the ground lightly, slapping the boy with a hard hand. "Maybe you'll be the next cattle baron in these parts. When's the wedding?"

"Oh, Jim, I ain't even asked her yet!" Barney laughed self-consciously. "I got to get the place fixed up and get me a little money. Can't ask a girl to start with nothing."

"Why not?"

"Why, you wouldn't do that, would you, Jim?"

The question caught at Reno, and he sobered, then shook

his head. "No, I reckon not. But I'm for you, Barney." He smiled at the beaming light that shone on the boy's face when he spoke, but as he put the team up he was wondering how long it would take Skull to make a move against Barney.

After supper Barney told Catherine his plan and Reno could see that beneath the smile she had for him, she was worried.

After Juan and Barney left, she sat in the kitchen drinking coffee, and she asked, "Will they let him alone, Jim?"

He shrugged. The fatigue of the steady work had planed his features down, hollowing his eyes, leaving lines around his mouth. He leaned back in the chair, and she wondered again how he could be so utterly relaxed at times like this, and so tightly drawn at others.

"No, I guess not." He grasped the cup in both hands and moved it on the checkered tablecloth as if he were totally engrossed in it. Then he shoved it to one side and looked straight into her eyes. "Catherine, I think I'd better pull out."

The words sent a sudden shock through her for which she was totally unprepared. After losing her father she had felt completely alone, but somehow she felt that she had been strong enough to pull herself through it and go on living. But now, as he spoke the easy words, she knew suddenly that Reno had been her anchor. Her dependence on him had been a subtle thing, and only now that the thought of going on without his help, without times like this of talk, and even without that strong physical attraction that had stormed her when he had kissed her—without him, in fact, life seemed drab and empty.

All of this she concealed, not taking her steady gaze from him as she asked, "Why, Jim?"

"I'm going to draw the bees, Catherine," he said, then laughed shortly. "Not that I'm all that sweet, but Boone Carr will never stop as long as I'm in one piece."

"Maybe he'll change. Stacy hopes so."

"No, he won't. A bullet through the head—that's what will change Boone's mind. Sooner or later there's going to be trouble, and no matter who else is involved in it, Boone will try to wipe me out."

"But you can't keep on running all your life, Jim!"

"Catherine, if I'm here, Skull will wipe out the Circle M." Gently he added, "It's your home. How would you feel if you lost it?"

She replied evenly, "Not as bad as I'd feel if I lost you, Jim."

He smiled and shook his head, then got up from the table. The lamp threw his shadow high on the wall as he came to stand over her, and with an unusually gentle motion he let his hand fall on her shoulder.

She sat very still, hardly breathing, and finally he said, "You think about it. I got nothing to lose, but you have."

He left quickly and Catherine unconsciously reached up and touched the place where his hand had fallen on her shoulder. For a long time she sat there, then she slowly pulled the worn black Bible off the shelf close to the table. Her hands trembled as she slowly turned the pages, and her lips moved faintly as she read until the wick began to smoke. Then she turned the wick down and sat in darkness, and her thoughts were long and like nothing she had known.

For Stacy, home had always been Skull. The boundaries of the huge ranch had been her world. Her family and the crew made up the fabric of her life, and except for a few close friends in town and on the larger ranches, nothing had ever stirred the even tenor of her days.

Now, all was changed, and she realized that her whole existence was on the razor edge of disaster. Her father had been a rock, never failing to furnish with his rocklike stability a sense of total security. Now he seemed to be blind to the chaos that hovered over his life.

Her mother was worried about Frank, but was so dominated by her husband that it never occurred to her to doubt his judgment.

More than anything else Boone was a grief to Stacy. She had never felt the affection for him she had for her other brothers; he would have rejected it if she had shown such a feeling. Always she had been half afraid of him, for there was a cruel streak in him that ran close to the surface.

But since he had been humiliated by Jim Reno, there was something in the man that frightened her badly. He said little, but even after his broken jaw healed enough to permit Doc Moody to remove the wires, there was a strange fanatical look in his eyes.

Then when he brought Kincaid to the ranch, Stacy knew that nothing would change him.

Stacy had tried to speak to Aaron about it. "Dad, he's a hired killer. He never works—just practices with that gun of his."

Aaron patted her shoulder absently, saying "Takes hard men to keep this place going, daughter."

Toward Kincaid she behaved as she never had toward any of the hands. He was always around the ranch, and one day he had boldly accosted her with, "I'm Bob Kincaid." He waited for her to speak, and when she merely stared at him, he smiled and said easily, "You're Stacy, aren't you? Boone told me about you." When she still kept silence, he gave a broader smile, the expression of a man who was accustomed to easy conquests among women, and murmured, "We might go to one of the dances in town some day, you think?"

He was a large man, just under six feet, sleek as a seal with muscle that swelled the tight silk shirt he wore open at the throat. There was something of the dandy in his dress, and in the ornate silver handle of the Colt at his side, but he was one of the most masculine creatures Stacy had ever encountered: a smooth brown face, piercing brown eyes, and a pair of full red lips almost concealed by a drooping moustache. Small ears set close to his head and an aquiline nose gave him a hawklike expression, and as he watched her she saw that he was totally aware of his power over women.

Slowly she said with a steady look into his eyes, "I don't go to dances with the hired hands."

It broke his composure, as she had known it would. The full lips tightened and there was a higher color in his cheeks as he said, "Too good for me, are you?"

"I'm glad you understand that, Kincaid. Now we won't have to talk to each other anymore."

She gave him an indifferent look that was not a reflection of her feeling. The man's whole body had tensed like a cat about to spring, and she realized if she had been a man he would have left her dead in the dust.

From that moment she had realized that his pride would compel him to have his try at her, and she hoped he would make it in front of her father. It was the one thing that would arouse the owner of Skull enough to fire the man.

Kincaid was a womanizer, but he confined his chasing to the women of the town, nursing the certain knowledge that one day Stacy Carr would pay for the way she had treated him. But he said nothing, not even to Williams or Boone.

One day the three of them had stopped at Frenchy's Saloon for a drink after putting a small bunch of steers in the loading pens. It was one of the few times Kincaid had volunteered to do any work. He worked now only because he was bored and knew that after the cattle were shipped the crew would spend the rest of the night in town.

"You better rest up, Bob," Red Williams said. "All that work is liable to put you in bed."

Kincaid had a feline smile, and he turned it on Williams, saying, "I try to stay good at what I do best, Red."

Boone and Williams gave each other a quick look, knowing that he meant handling a gun. Boone nodded. "You do that, Bob. We got plenty of nurses for these critters."

"You got something special for me, don't you, Boone?" Kincaid asked languidly, his eye fixed on a woman across the room wearing a scarlet dress. "I don't suppose you're going to pay me forever to loaf around Skull."

He had been at loose ends, having left his job in New Mexico where he had spent a profitable time enforcing the will of a railroad on some stubborn landowners. They had all sold—except for the three he had killed—and when Boone had sent for him to come to Placid, he had had nothing better to do.

He did not know Boone, did not know the situation in the Valley, but when Carr had met him at the hotel there had been an instant understanding that someone was becoming a nuisance to Boone Carr. "You don't have to lift your hand to any of the work, Kincaid," Boone had said, and then his voice had gone dead as he added, "But there's one little chore I need you for."

Kincaid had shrugged, not concerned in the least. "Who is it, Carr?"

When Boone had answered, "I'll let you know when the time comes," the gunman had taken the money and thought nothing about the man he would kill.

The woman in the red dress was a new girl in town, and he pursued her in a careless fashion, edging the cowboy who had been with her out into the cold with a single look out of his hard eyes.

She called herself Francie, and he was enjoying the game as she sat down at the table with him, so much so that it annoyed him when Red's voice said, "Boone wants you, Kincaid."

"Not now," he answered shortly.

"Better come. I think it's business." Red's face, when Kincaid swung to face him, was alive with a rare excitement, and his hand caressed his Colt handle in anticipation.

Kincaid glanced at Boone who was standing near the swinging doors looking out, and there was a strained attitude in his body. Kincaid shoved the girl away and walked quickly to join him. Looking over Boone's shoulder he saw a man walking down the street. It was dark, but by the lanterns on the sidewalk he saw that there was a woman with him.

"That's your meat, Kincaid," Boone whispered.

"Now?"

"No. But I want you to know him."

"All right." Kincaid slipped through the doors and positioned himself against the building, seeing that the pair would pass within a few feet of where he stood. Pulling his hat down over his face, he rolled a cigarette and lit it.

The woman was on the inside, and she would be closer to him, but the lantern over his head cast a strong yellow beam directly on the spot where they would pass, so Kincaid waited and presently they stepped into the light.

Perhaps he moved, for the man pulled the woman back with his right hand and stepped suddenly in front of her, face to face with him.

There was one instant when Kincaid almost went for his gun, but he saw in one glance that the man was unarmed. He relaxed and there was a smile on his smooth face.

"Hello, Jim."

Reno took his time, finally nodding slightly and saying, "Hello, Bob."

Although both men seemed idle and relaxed, there was a wire-thin tension in Kincaid's voice as he said, "Didn't expect to see you again—not after Abilene."

"I guess you haven't wasted much time looking for me, have you, Bob?"

"That's right." An old memory probed at Kincaid and he straightened up, coming off the wall in one smooth motion.

Reno smiled and said softly, "Bob, you shouldn't let things bother you so much. But I can see you have a few scars."

This ruffled Kincaid, as Reno had known it would. He licked his lips, and there was a flicker in his eyes that changed his whole appearance, making him predatory, and there was a stiffening in his gun arm, a tenseness that he at once revealed as he stared into Reno's face.

Finally he nodded and forced himself to say, "See you around, Jim."

He wheeled and stepped back into the saloon. There was

a line of anger in his jaw as he walked over to Boone who had retreated to the bar.

"Carr, why didn't you tell me it was Jim Reno you wanted rubbed out?"

Carr was so surprised at the anger in Kincaid's voice he took a long moment to consider his answer. "I didn't think it mattered to you." Then he shot a hard look at the set face of the man before him. "Does it make a difference?"

Kincaid nodded. "Yes. Oh, I'll get him, you can bet on that," he said quickly as Boone started to speak. "But it'll be different than what I figured."

Red Williams had edged up, taking in the last part of the conversation. He slapped the bar and said in a rash voice, "Why, he can be had, Bob. I been trying to tell Boone I could handle him."

A strange smile touched the full lips of Kincaid, and then he laughed. "Williams, you'd make a sorry-looking corpse— which is what you'd be if you stood up to Jim Reno."

Williams turned pale. "I don't see so much in that joker!"

Kincaid signaled for a drink, swallowed it, then said softly, "I guess you heard of Bill Tombs?"

"Tombs? Sure I have," Williams said. "Who hasn't? He made Wild Bill take water once over at Dodge—and he punched Sam Williamson's ticket—which wasn't so easy!"

"You think so, Red?" Kincaid asked with a tight smile. "Him and two other pretty fair hands met up with Reno down in Tucson—when the smoke cleared all three of them was buzzard food and Reno didn't have a scratch."

"He's good, Red," Boone said. "From what I hear from those who seen him put Spade down, he's quick as a blink."

"Just about." Kincaid nodded.

"So what'll you do?" Boone shot the question at Kincaid.

"So I'll get him. That's what you're paying me for." There was an air of certainty in Kincaid, and he had a straight-grained nerve that nothing could shake.

"All right." Boone thought about it, then shook his head. "It's got to look good, Bob. The old man is right about one thing: Sooner or later we're going to have some law in this thing, so I want it to look like self-defense."

"I know how you can set that up, Boone," Williams broke in.

"How?"

"I guess you ain't heard about that kid that worked for Circle M—what's his name? Barney something."

"What about him?"

"Earl told me the kid bought the old Duke place, said he's moved into it."

Boone thought about it, and a light stirred in his dark eyes. He nodded and said softly, "Yeah—I think you may have something, Red."

"Reno is real close to the kid, so I hear." Red grinned wickedly. "I think he might be real upset if someone put him down."

"That's a thought." A cruel smile creased Boone's face. "That sure is a thought." He glanced at the two and asked, "You two feel like a little ride tonight?"

Kincaid shrugged. "Your show, Carr."

"Yeah, I think we might have a little fun out of Barney Boy," Williams said, and the three left the saloon and rode out into the darkness.

The sound of a horse moving at a fast clip across the yard

awakened Reno, and he rolled out of bed, the gun on the table beside him falling into his hand.

"What's up?" Juan asked sleepily.

"Hold it down, Juan!"

The horse pulled up outside the bunkhouse, the sound of its labored breathing cutting the silence.

"Jim?" a voice called loudly, "Jim, you there?"

Reno stepped to the door, opened it, and lowered the gun. "Billy, is that you?"

Sixkiller was a faint shape in the darkness. Dawn was beginning to fire the eastern hills, and as he stepped down from his horse, Reno saw that his face was set with anger.

"What's up, Billy?"

"Light a lamp, Jim."

Juan scratched a match and the golden glow lit up the room. Sixkiller said hurriedly, "'Bout three this morning a bunch came out of the bottoms. I heard 'em coming, and by the time they pulled up in the yard I was about ready to open up. Then one of them shouted, 'Here's a present for Reno.' Then they rode off."

A sudden cold feeling touched Reno, and he asked, "Was it Barney?"

Sixkiller nodded. "They'd dropped him in the yard like a sack of grain, Jim. If I could have seen in the dark, I'd have cut loose on them. But they rode off."

"How about Barney?" Reno asked quickly.

The dark face of Billy Sixkiller twitched with anger, and a light blazed in his stolid face. "No good."

"Is he alive?"

"Just barely—at least he was when I left," Billy said. "My woman is good with hurts, but he's all busted up, Jim!" He took a piece of paper out of his shirt pocket and handed it to Reno. "This was stuck inside his pocket."

This is what anyone who gets on Skull grass will get! the crudely written note said.

Reno stared at it, noting the bloodstains on the edges, then he looked up at Sixkiller and there was a fierce light in his black eyes that the Indian had never seen.

"First, we take care of Barney."

"I sent Leo to fetch Doc Moody."

"All right." Reno looked down at the gun that was still in his hand, and there was a bitterness in his face that turned his mouth hard. He looked at the two men who were waiting for him to speak, and he finally said, "Get dressed, Juan. I want every man we can get to meet at Three Pines by daybreak."

"What'll I tell 'em?" Juan asked as he pulled his boots on.

Reno said softly but with a bleakness that cut like a knife, "Tell them to bring their guns, Juan!"

TWELVE
War Council

Swenson's barn was packed from floor to ceiling with hay, but the men that crowded into the open space on the first floor were glad to escape the biting cold outside. Ole Swenson carefully lit a lantern, and after hanging it on a nail, said, "Be careful of this lamp—and no smoking. This place would burn like a torch."

Banks of fragrant hay muffled the piercing whistle of the wind that rasped at the door, and there was a tomblike silence broken only by the heavy breathing of the men. The single lantern flickered weakly, breaking up the darkness, highlighting their faces so that there was a lean, hollow-eyed look about them.

Already it was the shank end of the day, with an early darkness falling, and Reno realized this was a factor that worked against the need for action. During the war he had learned that early morning was the time to get men inspired; by late afternoon they were sluggish, already tired and thinking about food and sleep.

But it had taken most of the day for word to spread, and

they had come filtering into Swenson's place by twos and threes. All day they had talked and argued, and as usual the more faithless had succeeded in dampening the spirits of those who might have been ready to act. Reno had said little, spending most of the day with Barney.

Catherine had come with them. She and Billy Sixkiller's wife, Annie, along with Swenson's wife, had done what little nursing they could.

Doc Moody came at noon, half-frozen by the falling temperatures and the freezing winds. While he was tending to Barney, Catherine came to stand beside Reno. She had observed the expression that lay thinly veiled in his dark eyes, and she knew him well enough to realize that his silence covered an anger that he was keeping a tight hold on.

She took his hand and said, "He'll be all right, Jim."

Reno forced a smile that did not touch his eyes. "My fault. Shouldn't have let him do it."

"Why, you can't live other people's lives for them. We have to do some things even if we risk getting hurt."

"Guess I ought to know that better than most." A thin trace of humor moved in his dark face, and he added, "I'm thinking how many times Lige Stevens tried to save me from getting hurt. And I'm remembering how few times I ever listened to him."

"He'll be all right," she said gently. "God will take care of him."

Reno had been gazing out the window at the far-off hills, but her words struck a chord in him, and he turned to look directly into her face. He searched her clear eyes seeming to be memorizing her features, and there was a wonder in his voice when he said, "You really believe that, don't you, Catherine—that the good will come out of things."

"Yes, I do."

"Why is that, I wonder?"

"Why, I suppose because to believe anything else would take all the meaning out of life," she answered. Then she smiled and said, "You thought that once, didn't you, Jim."

He slowly nodded and some old memory flowed through his mind. It softened the hard planes of his face, making him look younger.

She sobered and then her eyes grew warm as she said, "I believe you'll think that way again. You've seen so much that's bad, but deep down you know that there are people who are really good."

"I know you, Catherine."

"I—I didn't mean—" She broke off, and the color that touched her cheeks made her more attractive. "I meant men like your stepfather."

"I've seen a few—but they sure didn't inherit the earth. Most of them died poor."

"But, Jim, the story doesn't end with death!" She smiled. "If we know Jesus Christ, we've got forever."

He considered that, and his face was a study, as if he were hearing something too good to be true, something he wanted to hang on to but was afraid of.

He had finally said as he left her to go meet with the others in the barn, "Catherine, most of the things I've seen have been pretty hard. Most of it makes me pretty skeptical, I guess, about God and the Bible. But then I see someone every now and then . . ." He laid his hand on her shoulder, and there was a gentle wonder in his voice. "Why, I get downright skeptical about all the things I see in this world!"

He had left the house to join the rest of the men who

were filing out to the barn, but even while the talk ran back and forth, and tension filled the group, he kept thinking about the faith of Catherine, realizing that for the first time since he'd left home as a very young man, he was being compelled to think about his life and what it meant.

A thread of talk ran raggedly from man to man, some men so angry that they shouted and were ready to ride out against Skull at once. Others were held back by the fear of what such a course would bring. Reno leaned back against a wall of hay, listening, but taking no part. His mind was still taken up with Catherine's words and the calm certainty on her face. A restlessness gnawed at him, and he wrenched his mind back to pay attention to Thad who had shouted them down and was urging them to move together.

"We have to stick together or we're lost. And I know that's not easy." He glanced around at the faces framed in the darkness by the flickering light of the lantern. "For skull, it's easy— they all work for one man on one ranch. When they move, it's at his word and that's it."

"We can't match a bunch of fighting men, Thad." Bert Prewitt argued. He was a small man with gentle eyes and a large family. He was a deacon in the church and nothing wa more difficult than to think of him as a fighting man.

"What holds the Skull crew together, Bert?" Thad shot the question at him suddenly.

"Why, I don't know . . ."

"They're just hired hands," John Malon broke in. "I see what you mean, Thad."

"Right! Bert, don't you think the things we—all of us in this barn—have in common mean more than wages?"

Prewitt slowly nodded, saying, "Yes, I can see that. We're family men and these are our homes we're talking about."

"Right!" Thad said, and he began to talk earnestly, his face alive with determination. "Sure, they have more men, and some of them are fighting men. But there's one thing that we have going for us that Skull doesn't—and that is that we're *right!*"

"That's what I say," Ray Catlin interjected suddenly. "We're doing what men ought to do—working, making a living for our families, building up a land." Catlin dropped his head, and there was a strange reticence about him as he finally said, "I—I have to say that some of my life, well, it won't do to talk about, because it was no good." He struggled to go on, and they all knew that Ray had not always been on the right side of the law during his youth. But he looked up with a light in his eyes and said firmly, "But a few years ago my life changed. I've tried to be a man of God since then and that's what I think I'm trying to do now."

Then Roy Cooper, a short, balding man with his upper body shaped by his years at a forge, said, "Well, I appreciate that, Ray, but I got to say that I don't agree. I call myself a Christian, too, and the thing that bothers me is, how am I going to take a gun to a man? I keep thinking of the verse in the Bible that says, 'Thou shalt not kill.'"

Every eye turned to Thad, and Reno saw the pressure build up in his face. "All right, Roy, I guess you've put your finger on the thing we've all been thinking about. So we've got to settle that—or else leave the country."

"Amen!" exclaimed Josh Jordan, who had no more religion than a gopher. "I ain't no Christian, but dumb as I am, I know you can't kill a feller in a nice Christian way."

A murmur of assent ran around the room. It was, Reno recognized at once, the turning point for these men, and he fixed his eyes on Thad. If he failed to satisfy the group on this point, all was lost.

Thad dropped his head for a few seconds, and then looked up. "All of you have heard me preaching in a pulpit, but I'm not going to preach now." His voice was low, an intimate tone not at all like the resonant pitch Reno had heard him use. "I'm not a preacher, anyway—I'm just a man trying to get by like the rest of you. And I know exactly what Roy is talking about. I've stayed awake many a night trying to get a handle on the same thing."

Thad looked across the room, taking in the faces framed in the darkness: the round, serious face of Ole Swenson, flanked by his two grown sons; Andy MacIntosh, a dour man always, but now with his face even more stern as he stood close to the lantern which put golden glints in his red beard; John Malon stood next to Fred Flemming, the two being best friends, and on the face of each man Thad saw the struggle as yet unresolved; Billy Sixkiller's sardonic features were almost hidden by the hat he habitually kept pulled over his face, but his obsidian eyes glinted with a deadly purpose, and Thad knew that Billy, at least, had already declared war on Skull.

Dave Melton, still moving carefully as he nursed the wound he had received, leaned against a post, staring at Thad. There was a bleak expression in his youthful face that had not been there before the shooting.

At the edge of the circle stood Mose Hackett. He was the oldest man in the room, but his bent shoulders and snow white hair that escaped the old black hat were offset by a pair of youthful blue eyes. His three hulking sons, Jim Bob, Custer, and Maylon, flanked him, and they were silent as usual. The Hacketts, who came from Arkansas, were a clannish people, tied to the death to family and suspicious of all outsiders. All three of the boys had come through the Civil War alive, a thing unheard of as far as Reno knew.

Billy Sixkiller's two cousins, Jay and Toddy, were young men, and though they had no land as yet, they had ideas in that direction. They were pretty hard boys, much like Billy, and Thad knew that in a fight they would be worth their weight in gold.

Josh Jordan owned nothing, and never would, having a wild free spirit that most old mountain men possessed. But he had a fierce loyalty to Thad and there was no doubt of his feeling. He stood next to Juan and a hired hand of MacIntosh named Masters.

"I'm no theologian," Thad admitted, "but I heard a preacher who once said that the world *kill* in the Scripture you mention, Roy—'Thou shalt not kill'—he said it meant 'Thou shalt not *murder'* And I guess I can see a difference in the two. Roy, what would you do if a man broke into your house and was about to harm your wife and kids?"

Roy Cooper's square face was steady as he said, "Why, you know the answer to that, Thad. I'd shoot him, do anything I had to."

"Sure, so would all of us. And do you think that would be a wrong thing?"

"No! I think any man who would let somebody hurt his family and not lift a hand . . ." Suddenly Cooper paused, struck by the logic of the thing, and he went on with strong conviction, ". . . Why, I see what you mean, Thad. God wants us to take care of our families!"

A murmur ran around the room, but MacIntosh, who had learned his theology at the feet of dour Scottish ministers in

Glasgow, asked sharply, "Aye, but what about the verse that says, 'Turn the other cheek'?" He shook his bearded face vigorously. "Ye'll have trouble gettin' around that one, Thad."

Stevens looked at the fierce face of MacIntosh, and thought for so long that the silence ran thick. Finally he shook his head.

"I'll be honest with you, Andy—I just don't know! Sure, there are lots of sayings like that. If there weren't, we wouldn't be here arguing about it. I don't guess any of us got through the war without the agony of wondering if we were doing the right thing."

"Then, how can we decide, Thad?" Roy asked quietly.

Thad shrugged his shoulders, and there was fatigue and grief on his face as he said, "I've already decided, Roy. The choice is this simple: either I give up my place and my dreams of a good life—and that includes a family, which I don't have, but most of you do—or I fight for the freedom to live the kind of life that I think God wants me to have."

"Ain't no doubt in my mind," Billy said softly. "I guess I ain't much of a Christian anyway, but I know God expects me to take care of my family."

Ole Swenson slowly nodded his head and glanced at his grown boys. "I ain't never lifted my hand to a man in anger—but me and my boys, we'll do what you say, Thad."

"Goes for me, too, Thad," Malon agreed, and Flemming nodded silently.

Old Mose Hackett had not spoken a word, but he glanced around the room and there was no doubt in his bright blue eyes. "I didn't come here to talk. Me and my boys, we done decided that we done fit one war to keep folks from tellin' us how to live. I guess I ain't too old to do it one more time."

Then there was a sudden wave of comradeship that swept
the room, drawing the men together in a way that Reno had
experienced often during the war. Everyone was talking and
there was an air of relaxation that replaced the tense strain
that had prevailed.

Finally Thad said, "All right. I'm glad we've agreed, and
I'm not talking preacher talk when I say that I believe God will
be with us—but we've got to talk about how we're going to
move."

"Right!" Josh spat out a gob of tobacco juice, and added,
"Good intentions is fine, but I've seen some mighty good men
get killed on account of 'em."

"Jim, I guess this is where you come in," Thad said, and
there was a strange smile on his broad lips as he added, "You
know more about this kind of thing than the rest of us put
together. I'm expecting you to lead us."

"You got to do it, Jim," Josh said. "I don't mind dyin'—but
I got no intentions of throwin' my hide away foolish-like."

Sixkiller asked, "You in, Jim?" and waited tensely for an
answer.

They were all, Reno saw, waiting for him to agree, but he
hesitated. It would all be on his head; every man that fell
would be, to some degree, a weight on him as long as he lived.
He still carried a weight like that from the old battles.

He waited so long that Ray Catlin said, "Jim, I'm no man
to beg—but I'd take it as a favor if you could see your way
clear to helping us out."

Reno looked around the circle, sighed heavily, and made
his decision.

"I'm with you all the way." It brought a lift to the room,
and he saw relief in Thad's face, but he went on, raising his

voice over the talk. "But I got something to say." He waited for silence, then asked, "Mose, which Yankee you hate the worst?"

"Sherman!" the old man shot back instantly, and his eyes turned fierce with the thought of the man.

"How about the rest of you?" The name *Sherman* went around the room, and Reno asked, "You don't feel that way about Grant or McClellan?"

"No!" Hackett spat out. "They wuz *soldiers!*"

Reno stated, "I aim to fight Skull the same way Sherman fought." He saw the shock in their faces, and smiled grimly. "Sherman did one thing that no other Yankee did, not even Grant. He made total war. Wiped out everything in his path. And that's what we'll have to do if we're to come out of this thing alive."

"But, Jim," Thad asked quickly, "do you mean we . . ."

Reno cut him off instantly. "There's no 'nice' way to fight! I wish there was. But let's have it out in the open right now!" His voice was as cold as the wind that nibbled at the barn and there was an iron, unyielding set to his chiseled face that wiped away all the warmth and humor they had learned to recognize. This was Reno in a fight, out to kill or be killed, and it sobered the crowd instantly.

Sixkiller nodded. "You're right, Jim."

"The rest of you understand what I'm saying? We have no war on women and children—but anything that draws breath, man or beast, that is Skull is under the gun!"

"All right, Jim," Thad said after a slight hesitation. "You tell us what to do." He had a sad look on his face, and he added, "I reckon I'll have a lot of repenting to do if I live through this."

Reno's face broke and he said in a soft voice, "Why, I

guess we'll all have that chore, Thad. I know I will." There was
an air of profound regret on his face, but he shook it off at
once, saying, "All right, we hit Skull hard. Billy, I want you to
check guns and ammunition."

"How much you figure we ought to take, Jim?"

"All we can carry. Josh, you get enough grub ready for
three days' rations. Ray, you see to the horses—and I want an
extra for every man, and all of them in first-class shape." He
handed out instructions crisply, checking off details that none
of them would have remembered.

"When we going to hit 'em, Jim?" Ray asked.

Reno's smile was a quick, grim flash in the flickering darkness. "When they least expect it. Grab some sleep if you can,
and I want a good breakfast, Josh. We'll pull out at midnight."

"Going to be snowing by then," Josh complained.

"That gonna spoil your holiday, Josh?" Malon asked.
"Maybe you better stay here with the women and kids."

They laughed at Josh who let fall a few choice bits of pro-
fanity, and Jim winked at Thad, approving of high spirits. They
would need a little lightness before the smoke cleared.

"I'm going to check on Barney," Reno said, and as he
stepped out the door, a blast of freezing wind with tiny grains
of snow whipped around his face. He blinked his eyes and trot-
ted to the house. Doc Moody was drinking a cup of coffee by
the kitchen table, his droopy moustache dripping at the ends.

"How's the boy?" Reno asked.

"He'll live." The doctor's cynical mask slipped momentar-
ily, a flash of raw anger glinting in his rheumy eyes. "Don't
think his right eye's going to do him much good. Have to see."
He took a sip of scalding coffee and enumerated Barney's inju-
ries: "Left arm broke in two places, some ribs busted—can't

tell how many yet. Mouth in bad shape, some teeth broken off. That's going to hurt him. Worst thing is, he's hurt inside. Have to watch him real close, Jim. He's going to have trouble accepting that eye, I reckon."

A fire was burning in Reno's eyes, but he only nodded. "Is he awake?"

"Yes, but I just dosed him good with laudanum. You might have just a word with him. He sure thinks the world of you."

Reno slipped across the room and entered to find Catherine sitting beside Barney. She got up and he slipped into the chair.

Barney's face was so swollen Jim almost failed to recognize him. His lips were swollen into huge sausages and he breathed noisily through his mouth. Bandages covered his head and one eye, but the other opened as Jim laid a hand on the arm that wasn't bandaged.

"Jim?"

"Take it easy, Barney."

"Jim? I tried to stop them, but . . ." The single eye fluttered and a thickness filled Reno's throat as he saw pain trace its way across the boy's face. "I couldn't."

"Don't worry, Barney," Reno assured him. "It's going to be all right."

"They—killed all my cows, Jim!" Barney's thin frame twisted helplessly and he tried to raise up. "Why'd they shoot my stock, Jim?"

"Barney, we'll get it all back," Reno said. "You'll be back at your place and you'll have that stock back. It'll be just like you wanted, Barney."

"But, Jim . . ."

"I promise you, kid! You can bet on it!" There was an iron quality in Reno's voice, and Barney looked at him and smiled. Then his good eye fluttered and he dropped off.

Getting to his feet, Reno led Catherine outside and said, "Don't go back to the ranch. Stay here and help with Barney."

As he turned to go, she said quietly, "You be careful, Jim."

He nodded, then he came to her and she put her arms out, ready for his embrace. He took her, and there was a strange sense of peace in Catherine as his lips fell on hers, and when he left, she went back into the sick man's room with a serene light in her eyes.

Josh commandeered the Swensons' kitchen, and when the men got up in the cold darkness, they stumbled in to sit down to a steaming table piled high with eggs, biscuits, sausage, ham, grits, and sawmill gravy. They fell on the food, washing it down with huge draughts of staunch black coffee. Finally they finished, and Reno led them to the horses that were saddled. The extra horses were loaded with food, bedding, and ammunition.

"Got everything set, Jim," Billy reported. "What's the plan?"

"We gonna hit the big ranch?" Mose Hackett asked. His breath made a silver haze in the freezing air, and there was an eager light in the old man's eyes.

"Guess they'd like that, don't you reckon, Mose?" Reno asked. "What you think Ranger John Mosby would do in a situation like this?"

The old man rubbed his chin, then said, "Why, he'd hit 'em where they wasn't looking, Jim."

"That's what we'll have to do. It'll be snowing hard by the

time we get to that line house over by the river. Billy says that's where Skull keeps the best of its stock. How many you figure, Billy?"

"Maybe two hundred head—maybe more. They'll be shipping 'em soon now."

"No, they won't," Reno said flatly, and they looked at each other surprised at the statement. "Skull killed all of Barney's stock. I figure this bunch will be a good down payment on what they owe him."

"We gonna take the cows, Jim?" Josh asked in surprise.

"No, It's going to be an eye for an eye, a tooth for a tooth."

Andy MacIntosh stirred restlessly, then demanded, "You want to kill those cows?"

"Every one of them," Reno said. "Then we burn the house to the ground."

"What about the hands, Jim?" Sixkiller asked. "They'll have eight or ten men at the house."

Reno raised Duke's bridle and just before he led off, he said, "They'll have to decide."

"Decide what?"

"If it's a good day to die!"

They left the yard, the steel shoes ringing on the frozen ground, and Catherine, who was staring out of the window watching them leave, wondered how many would not come back.

The storm had caught Boone off guard, and he had scattered his men in several directions, trying to get the strays into the spots where they could be held until the storm broke.

He came into the house a little after ten, his head white with snow. Stomping his feet clear of the slush, he took the cof-

fee that the cook handed him and sat down to eat a late breakfast.

Aaron came in a few minutes later, his face drawn with
the cold. "This is bad! We have to move every head as close to
the shelters as quick as we can."

"Crew's doing that now." Boone ate slowly, chewing carefully, his newly mended jaw still tender.

Stacy and her mother came in, and Lee was complaining
about the cold.

"Shut up, Lee," Boone snapped. "We got enough trouble
without a bellyacher like you."

Lee flared out, "Boone, if you don't like the way I talk, do
something about it!"

Their nerves were all tight, but Aaron ordered, "Both of
you shut!" He stared at them, and Boone fell to his food, while
Lee glared at him.

"It's pretty bad, isn't it, Dad?" Stacy asked.

Aaron Carr nodded. "Bad as anything I've seen this time
of year. We're going to lose some stock, no doubt about that!"

They ate silently, and were almost finished as feet
drummed across the porch outside and the door burst open,
admitting Conboy and a puncher named Riley.

Conboy had shock on his brutal face, but could not seem
to get a word out. Riley was covered with snow that trailed off
on the floor, and there was a fresh cut on his left hand, the
blood frozen.

"What's wrong!" All of the Carrs got to their feet, and
Boone's voice was ragged as he asked, "What's happened?"

"Tell 'em, Riley!" Conboy groaned, and he slammed his
fist into his hand. "I *told* you we should have gotten Reno outta
the way!"

"Riley, tell it!" Aaron Carr demanded.

"We got wiped out, Mr. Carr!" the tall puncher said. His lips were white with cold, and there was on his face the shock that comes to a man who has almost had a fatal accident. "We were all asleep, and then about three this morning, we heard shooting. All of us jumped up and pulled our clothes on, then we grabbed our guns and went outside. It was dark, and we could see the flashes of guns over where the herd was, so we started to get our horses and get whoever it was." He stopped and there was a droop in his thin shoulders.

"Well, what happened, Riley?" Boone demanded.

"Just as we got to the barn, somebody shot over our heads and told us to hold it. Fred went for his gun and got dropped right there."

"They shot him?" Aaron asked. "What about the rest of you?"

"Nothing we could do, Mr. Carr. They was on all sides of us with rifles, and they just shucked off our guns and told us to get our horses and git!"

"It was Reno, wasn't it, Riley?" Boone guessed, and he looked insane as he spoke.

"Him and a bunch more. I don't know how many, but a good-sized bunch."

"What then?"

"I asked if we could get our stuff outta the house, and Reno said no. Then—" Riley swallowed and shook his head. "I hate to tell you this. He told some of the men to fire the house—and that's what they done. We had to ride back in our shirtsleeves."

"All right, Riley," Aaron said calmly. "Nothing you could have done."

"Well, that ain't all, Mr. Carr," Riley said and gave a strange look at the owner. "All that shootin' we heard?"

"Yes?"

"Well, they was killing the stock, Mr. Carr!"

"Killing my cattle!"

"Yes, sir, and it was—well, it was bad. The cows was too cold to be spooked, and they was just shooting them with rifles, like it was just another chore." Riley shivered. "I thought I was pretty tough, but this Reno . . ." The thin rider gave Carr a steady look.

Boone moved toward the door, yelling, "All right, let's get after them! They're asking for war, and I'll see every man of them hanging from a tree!"

"Wait a minute, Boone," Aaron said, and he looked ravaged, his age revealed by the deep lines in his face. "What you planning?"

"Why, I'm gonna get those two-bit nesters!"

"What about the ranch, Boone? Who's going to save the stock while you're chasing after them?"

"Why . . ." Boone paused, and his heavy face stirred with impatience as he said, "If we don't get 'em, what's to stop them from killing more of our cattle?"

"No!" Aaron snapped. "We've got to send as many small bunches of guards as we can everywhere we've got stock."

"I say we get every man we got and wipe the Valley clean of every bit of scum!" Boone snarled.

"You're not thinking straight, Boone," Aaron said impatiently. "In the first place, where would you find them in this storm? If you did find them, it'd probably be because they wanted you to."

Boone snorted, "They ain't got sense enough to set a trap for us—nor the guts, either."

"Wrong! I thought you had more sense, Boone, but since you can't figure it out, let me tell you that nobody is leading our crew into a war—not now. Later, we'll see."

Boone stared at his father, and it appeared that he would argue. Then he said lamely, "All right," and added, "Conboy, come with me. We've got work to do. Lee, you come, too."

"What do you think set it off, Dad?" Lee asked as he got up to leave.

"Had to come, Lee," the old man said. "Didn't need a reason."

"I don't think that's right, Dad," Stacy said slowly. "Men like Fred Flemming and John Malon wouldn't do a thing like this—not unless they were pushed into it."

"Too late to argue about it, Stacy," he replied. He looked around the room, and when his old eyes came to rest on her he said in a voice softer than any she'd ever heard from him, "Things are breaking up, girl. Things I hoped would never change are being smashed."

She took his hand and assured him, "We'll find a way, Dad."

If she had heard what Boone was saying to the men he was about to lead out of the ranch, she might not have been so certain.

"Go get every hand we got and have them at the old Brent place as soon as you can."

Lee frowned. "And leave the stock? That doesn't make sense, Boone!"

"We'll get this chore done and then we can take care of the cattle," Boone said harshly. "The old man ain't no good, Lee. He'd never have let this happen when he was young. If we don't stop that bunch, they'll wipe us out."

"You're right, Boone," Conboy said. "We gotta split them up, break their back—then we can fight the winter."

"But Dad said . . . ," Lee began, but Boone slashed at his horse, driving him out into the blast of icy sleet, yelling, "Mind me, Lee! We're gonna stop Reno's clock tonight! And as many of his friends as we can catch. Now, let's go!"

THIRTEEN
No Quarter

"You know Skull ain't gonna sit still, Jim." Josh turned his back to the fire crackling in the fireplace, sighing with the comfort of it. The whole bunch had crowded into Ray Catlin's place after they left the field of slaughter, except for Billy, Custer Hackett, Flemming, and Juan. Reno had sent these off as scouts, with instructions to bring word back to the rest as soon as Skull moved.

Reno poked at the fire with a stick. He had not liked killing the cattle, but when MacIntosh had protested the action, he had cut him off, saying bluntly, "Better cows than men, Andy. Skull has to know we can hurt them bad, and that means their stock."

Now he answered Josh with a frown on his forehead. "They'll come after us right, Josh. But how? With a blizzard looking them in the face, they just have to be thinking of the cattle that'll die if they don't take care of them."

"They might not come after us, then?" Dave Melton asked.

"No way to tell. Offhand I'd say if the old man calls the shots, they'll go for the stock—but Boone won't do that."

"No, he'll come to wipe us out."

"That's why I sent the scouts out, Dave. With this snow piling up the Carrs will have to stick to the few open ways, because the passes will be in drifts. We'll wait here until tonight, maybe even tomorrow. By that time we'll know if they are coming after us."

Thad came to stand by Reno. He looked haggard, but there was no weakness in the line of his jaw as he said, "Jim, you realize our own cattle are going to need care? If we stay here and they all die, why, I guess most of us will be finished just as sure as if Skull ran us out."

Reno nodded. "I know, Thad. We could wait until morning; then if we don't get any word about a bunch hunting us, we could split up and take care of our own stuff."

Thad looked around, and there was an air of agreement. "Guess a few hours won't make much difference. Skull and the other big outfits stand to lose the most. We've got such small herds that we can crowd them into corrals and keep them from wandering off to freeze or starve."

"You have hay put up, too," Reno added. "That's going to make a big difference. Bit outfits don't ever have enough feed for a situation like this."

For awhile they were all tense, every noise taking their eyes to the horizon. The snow was coming down so thick now that it was impossible to see over twenty feet ahead, but the thought of a Skull crew sneaking up on them was never far from their minds.

Finally, they got their blankets and tried to sleep, but Reno kept watch, his eyes alert and a tension in his face. Not for a second did he think that Boone would give up the trail, but he knew he could not hold the men much longer when their cattle and their families were being threatened by the storm.

They ate a cold breakfast, and one by one the scouts came in, all except Billy Sixkiller. None of them had seen a thing.

"I guess we better see to our families, Jim," Fred Flemming said slowly. "We can meet again when Skull makes a move."

"All right, Fred," Reno consented, but he knew that there would not be time to gather a force when Skull came riding out of the storm.

All of them left except the Hacketts and Josh. Reno got extra supplies from those who were leaving, including most of their ammunition.

"We'll get together when this blows over, Jim," John Malon shouted over the rising howl of the wind.

"Sure, John. Don't get lost."

"No, that wouldn't be good. Temperature's falling like a rock. The whole valley will be frozen by tomorrow morning."

After he and the others left, the rest sat down and waited for Billy. He arrived an hour later, and when his horse came at a clumsy gallop over the icy ground, his wind broken by the furious pace he'd been forced to, they all knew it was trouble.

Billy slid from the back of the exhausted horse, his clothes iced and his breath in short spurts.

"They're comin'—must be nearly the whole crew."

"Which way, Billy?" Reno demanded.

"I seen 'em at that high butte near where Eleven-point turns south." He looked around and asked in surprise, "Where's the bunch?"

"Pulled out," Josh snorted in disgust. "We won't never get 'em collected now!"

Reno thought over the contour of the country, and he said slowly, "They're headed for Circle M."

"Way I figured it," Billy said. He seized a plate and filled it with cold beans, then sat down and began stuffing them into his mouth hungrily. He stopped long enough to ask, "What's the ticket, Jim?"

Reno looked at the Hacketts and said, "Mose, what you think?"

The old man grasped his meaning at once. He grinned, exposing yellow fangs, and snorted, "Son, I was one of Stonewall Jackson's boys. You think they's anything in the world I'd back off from after what I went through with that man? Me and my boys, we didn't come here lookin' for no church picnic. Turn your wolf loose, son, and let 'im howl!"

Reno laughed. "All right, Mose. Now here's what I got figured." He drew a battle plan on the top of the table with a charred stick, his eyes intent on the men's faces. There was no way he could tell these men that what he proposed was anything but a fine chance to get shot, but there was no fear in any of them, and when he had finished, Billy Sixkiller wiped his mouth, got up, and said, "Let me get a saddle on my good hoss."

They pulled their gear together and rode out into the storm, Josh leading. The old man knew every cactus and gopher hole, and they needed to make good time if they were to get to the ranch before Skull.

Before they had gone half a mile Reno's hands were numb, and he had trouble framing words in his stiff lips. The blood flowed sluggishly through his body, and he slapped his arms against his sides from time to time to keep it flowing.

Nobody complained, and as time ran on the cold became

bearable. "Hope the horses' lungs don't freeze," Ray commented, his voice sounding thin in the wind.

"I hope *mine* don't free!" Maylon Hackett retorted.

After what seemed like days, Josh pulled up and said, "There's the ranch."

They were on a rise to the east, and there was just enough of dawn's feeble light to see the house at Circle M. The house looked empty and desolate in the morning chill. Catherine was not there, for she was helping to care for the wounded Barney at Swenson's.

"We beat 'em, I reckon," Mose said. "Now what?"

Reno had made a new plan on the long ride. "Mose, I want you to take one of your boys over to where the road goes toward town. Send the other two west, over to the old trail that goes to the mountains. Josh, you go along with them."

"What!" Thad sat straight up in his saddle. "Jim, there's only nine of us against the whole Skull outfit—and you want to split us in half?"

"What's in your head, Jim?" Josh asked. He had great confidence in Reno, but this move seemed foolish.

"We're going to have to gamble," Reno said. He stared at them and there was a stubbornness about him that told them his mind was made up.

"They've got to come at the ranch down that road, the one you'll be on, Mose. When they get here, we'll have to catch them off guard. Ray and I will get up in that draw. It's got a little bunch of rocks that'll give us all the cover we need. Billy, you and Thad will get cover, one in the left of the barn, maybe, the other close to the house. When they ride in, it'll look deserted. I think after they make up their mind to that, they'll be off guard. Then what I propose is to get them loose, then wipe them out."

"But Jim, they may send in a man, or they may not all come in," Ray protested.

"They we'll be the ones in a trap!" Thad argued.

"That's right." Reno shrugged. "But with only nine of us, we don't have any other choice that I can see."

"I don't like it, Jim," Sixkiller said. "Why you sending some of us out on the roads?"

"When they leave here on the run," Reno said, "I want them to run right into another ambush." He turned to the Hacketts. "Don't waste any lead in warning shots, Mose."

The old man stared at him for a long time, then replied, "Ole Stonewall would've been glad to have had you fer one of his captains, Reno. He surely would."

Thad stirred restlessly, his face troubled. "It's—it's pretty tough, Jim."

"Killing always is," Reno said evenly. "This is what you've been agitating for, Thad. If your faith won't let you do it, now's the time to say so."

They all watched Stevens' face, and it was obvious that he was struggling, trying to find a way to avoid the ambush. Finally he succumbed. "All right, Jim. Let's get at it, and God have mercy on us all."

Reno stared at him and then said in a soft voice, "And on them, too, Thad."

Then he said, "They'll be here soon. Mose, get moving." He watched the four men move out, calling after them, "We'll meet at the old bridge below Swenson's if something goes wrong." Addressing the rest, he said, "Let's take our positions. Wait for my shot, all of you, and when you hear it, open up with everything you've got."

Billy took the horses out over a ridge behind the house,

and by the time he got into position in the branches of a huge walnut tree, light was pouring over the edge of the horizon. The snow had stopped, and Reno hoped that Skull didn't cross any of their tracks.

It was half an hour later that Ray called out quietly from his post, "Here they come, Jim!"

"I see them, Ray—no more talking."

A single horseman crested the rise, a sudden blob of darkness against the blinding whiteness of the snowy ground. He drew his horse up, and sat there sweeping the ground with a careful gaze. *A scout,* Reno thought, and for one long moment he froze, but then the rider moved his arm and a column of men rode over the top of the hill, winding a serpentine pathway down the slope toward the house.

Boone was in front, with Conboy right beside him, leading what looked like about twenty-five riders, all of them carrying rifles.

Reno eased the safety off the carbine, and slowly laid the barrel on the slab of rock in front of him. The snow was packed, frozen like iron, and he checked the other fully loaded rifle he had brought. The others each had one, and with a six-gun it was a formidable bit of firepower. But only if they caught the crew off guard. If they scattered and found cover, they would hunt the four men down like rabbits, and there was no hiding in the unspoiled whiteness of the snow.

They came on slowly, eyes searching everything that might contain danger. Reno heard the sound of safety catches being released, the snow carrying the sound across the earth.

Suddenly Reno remembered how at Shiloh he had lain in a ditch waiting for a line of blue-clad Yanks. The sun had been shining and there had been the hum of bees in the peach trees over his head; but the feeling he'd had in his throat had been the same as now—the same as it always was before he fell into the rage of battle.

A breathlessness came over him as the file of men came up to the yard, and his throat closed on him. This was nothing new, but the feeling he had when he placed his hand on the trigger and caught Conboy in his sight was. Suddenly a tremor shook his arm and the sight wavered, and he knew that unless he shot quickly and accurately all of his men would be killed.

He wasn't afraid—no more so than he'd been at other times like this—but there was a fullness in his throat and something pulled at him inside that made him suddenly put his head down on his rifle, eyes closed. He did not move, and the sound of the horses moving toward the house was clear in his ears. Then he did something he had not done since he had left home. He did not move his lips, but the words, *Lord, forgive me! I don't know anything else to do to help these people. I'm so sick of things like this! Help me, God!* passed through his mind.

That was all. But all at once he experienced a calmness. The tightness left his throat, and he looked up to see a man getting off his horse. He had a can in his hand and he scattered clear liquid all over the front porch, then looked at the crew and grinned. "Anybody got a match?" he asked.

"Burn it, Jerry," Boone said, reaching into his pocket for a match.

A quick look showed Reno that the entire crew was sitting easily in the saddle. Most of them had put their rifles back into the saddle holsters, and he knew that they were feeling good that there would be no fight. It was always like that when a fight failed to materialize, Reno knew from experience.

He put his cheek on the smooth butt of the carbine and

drew a bead on Conboy. He wanted Boone, but the big man was concealed from him by the bulky body of the foreman.

The carbine spoke with a sharp cracking sound and Conboy was knocked out of the saddle as if struck by a giant hand.

Instantly a fierce wave of fire swept the yard as the four men poured a hail of lead toward Skull's crew.

The horses went wild, and this saved the lives of some, including Boone. The big man was half-thrown, and he slipped to the ground, finding safety behind a thick oak watering trough. "Take cover!" he was shouting, and then he said, "Hold on to those horses! Take them to the rear!"

He was, Reno realized, a cool customer, for without horses they would be pinned down.

Three men were down, and one man leading the horses went down in that terrible motion that goes with sudden death. Another man took his place, and Reno slowed his fire. He knew he had wounded at least two others, but there were at least twenty fighting men, and if they played their cards right, no four men could keep them pinned down.

"There's one up in that tree!" Reno heard Williams shout, and half a dozen guns began taking the big walnut tree where Sixkiller was peppering away at the men on the ground. It got too hot for Billy, and Reno saw him slip to the ground and take position behind a pile of split rail posts. But Skull had seen him, and he was in a bad situation.

Reno saw a man lean out the window to get a shot at Billy, and with a single shot Reno rolled the man inside to fall with a crash on the floor.

But Boone had seen the flash of his rifle, and as Reno threw a shot toward where Boone was covered by the trough, a hail of lead knocked up snow in front of him, blinding him as small crystals were driven into his eyes.

Throwing one rifle down, he grabbed the loaded one and began rolling to his left. He fell and twisted toward a line of scrub oaks, and by the time he got a little cover he saw that Boone was organizing a charge. Ray, he realized, had been spotted too, for he was under fire from several points.

Halfway up the hill was a draw, and if Boone could get there with a couple of men, there would be nothing to stop them from pinning Billy and Ray down.

Reno tried to lever a shell into the chamber, only to discover the rifle was jammed. Feverishly he worked, watching as Boone accompanied by four others leaped out of the shelter and made a dash for the draw.

The other Skull riders were pouring such a terrible fire against Billy and Ray, they had no choice but to draw back out of danger.

Boone and the others were almost to the draw, and Reno acted without thinking. They had to be stopped! Drawing his .38 he stood up and turning his body sideways he threw his arm forward into the classic dueling position. He knocked one man off his feet, but instantly he was sighted.

"There he is!" Boone shouted savagely. "Gun him down!"

A bullet whistled by Reno's ear, and another plucked at his boot. He drew down on Boone, but the big man was weaving from side to side, shooting from the hip, and he missed.

He missed with the next, then a bullet raked his side, throwing his next shot off. He ignored it and sent a bullet toward the short, husky rider who was leading the rush. The man grabbed his throat and fell gurgling to the ground.

Then Reno's gun snapped on an empty, and Boone Carr's face glowed as he hollered, "He's empty, boys! Get him!"

Reno let his arm drop. There was no place to run, and he simply waited for a bullet to knock the life out of him.

Then there was a sudden wave of firing that caught Skull off guard, coming from a position they had not seen. One of them staggered, another had his hat snatched off, and then a slug touched Boone on the cheek leaving a raw red streak. He flinched and fired at the unseen marksman, then called out, "It's too hot, boys—let's get outta here!"

There was a scramble as Boone led back to the house the three men who could walk, and they ran to the horses, mounted up, and using the house itself as a shield, drove wildly out of the yard and headed down the road.

Reno hurried down the slope in time to see Thad come out of the timber. He had been the one who had driven off the rush and there was a strange look on his face as Reno caught up to him.

"Well, Thad, you saved our bacon for sure. If they'd gotten up to that point, they'd have wiped us all out."

Thad stared at Reno, and there was a look of strain on his face. He was pale and there was a slight tic at the corner of his left eye, but when he spoke his voice was steady. "Jim, it's funny! I mean, it's really . . ." He stammered then and a faint smile touched his lips. "All my life I've envied you, because you could do things. And I guess I always was wondering if I had any guts. If I could stand fire."

Reno smiled and put his arm around Thad's shoulder. "Well, brother, now you know. If you hadn't left your position and risked your life, I'd be dead right now. I owe you for that."

Thad flushed, but there was a look of strength and confidence in the man that had been lacking. Becoming a man, Reno had often noticed, was not a matter of so many birthdays.

Billy was coming down from the hill, and there was a bitter look on his face. "Ray's dead. Hit plumb center."

They took it hard, all of them. The man's ready courage and cheerful attitude had been something all of them valued, and they knew that no matter what happened, the price had been high.

Suddenly a crescendo of gunfire broke the silence, and Thad said, "They ran into the others!"

They stood there, hearing Josh firing with monotonous regularity, and the chattering of the smaller caliber guns beat a tattoo that reached their ears in a way that seemed muffled and slow.

Then it was over.

"What now, Jim? We going back to Swenson's?"

Reno stared at him. "Swenson's? No, Thad. We're going to Skull."

Thad opened his mouth, then shut it with a snap. "Right! Let's go all the way."

Sixkiller smiled, and said in a tired voice, "You done ruined a good preacher, Jim."

Reno shook his head. "Don't agree, Billy. I sort of think this business will give him a little more idea of the frailty of us poor human beings." He added, "We'll put Ray inside."

Later they picked up Josh and the Hacketts, who were on their way in.

"Anybody killed?" Billy asked.

"Not any of *us,*" Mose said. "We got some of them, though." He shook his head and there was a sad look on his worn face. "I didn't know I had any pity left in me, but when them boys ran smack into our guns after bein' cut to pieces by you fellers, why, I got to admit it got to me some."

"I guess you're a better man for feeling that way, Mose," Thad said. "If it ever got so you could feel good about a thing like this . . ." He shook his head, then turned to Reno. "I guess we're ready, Jim. You want to pick up some more men before we go to Skull?"

"Yes," Reno replied. "I don't want any man ever forgetting what it cost to do this. Go get every man you can find and we'll meet at that big old pine by Len Dawson's place. Get to it."

They agreed on the plan and hurried off to gather the others. Reno and Thad sat there, and finally Thad said, "Jim, I hope we never have to do anything like this again as long as we live."

"You thinking we did wrong?"

"No, we did what we had to do, and I guess we'll do some more of it before it's over." He stared at Reno and asked with a slight hesitation, "How about you? I've guessed this is just the sort of thing you were running to the coast to get away from."

Reno turned to face Thad and said slowly, "Sure, I was trying to run away from what I'd been."

"And now you've been pushed right back into it!"

"I don't figure it that way," Reno said. "Hard to put into words, Thad, but I feel—well, I guess you'd have to say I feel like my life has really meant something here in the Valley."

"You're right there. If you hadn't come, we wouldn't have had a chance."

"Not sure about that, Thad," Reno said. "The days of the open range are over. Sooner or later Carr and the others are going to have to give way."

"Maybe. But not in our time." Thad shook his head stubbornly.

"Something else, Thad, and don't make too much of it."

"What?"

Reno stared off at the white horizon, shifted in the saddle, and said, "I've been thinking a lot lately about Lige."

"About Dad?" Thad asked quickly.

"He was about the best man I ever knew," Jim mused, "and no matter where I've been or what I've done, I've never gotten away from those Bible verses he used to say over and over again."

Thad opened his mouth, then closed it at once. Reno caught the motion, smiled, and asked, "Aren't you going to preach at me, Thad?"

"No, I'm not. Don't figure you need it, Jim." A smile broke up the gloom on Stevens' face as he continued, "I've always thought that God was a lot better preacher than anybody else. I figure, Jim, he's going to hand you whatever preaching you need, then you can take up the matter of your life with him."

Reno said nothing for a long time, then he grinned wryly. "I never thought God cared."

Thad smiled confidently. "Oh, he cares, Jim! He always has!"

Benny Lyons took the money from Aaron Carr, and tried to explain to the old man how it was.

"Mr. Carr, I hate to leave, 'cause you been good to me. But when I came to work at Skull, I hired on to work cattle, and you got to admit I done that, ain't you?"

Aaron Carr's face was pale. It had been since Boone had ridden in with men shot to rags, some of them dead, others wounded, and all of them sick from the ambush.

"You've been a good hand, Lyons, but when I rode for a man, I always figured I owed him some loyalty."

"Mr. Carr, you always had the best I had in me!" Benny protested. "And if it was just a matter of your not bein' able to pay me, or if it was *anything* but this, I'd stay, you bet." He put his head back and looked Aaron Carr right in the eyes. "I just ain't no fighter, Mr. Carr. Never claimed to be." He turned and walked out of the room. Stacy, who was standing next to the wall watching, came to her father.

"Don't blame Benny, Dad," she said. "It's not his fault."

"Only seven men left!" the old man said softly. "The rest either shot up or running! I can't believe it."

"We'll make out, Dad," she said. "Skull has had hard times before."

"Not like this," Aaron replied, and he looked a hundred years old, she thought. There was a tremble in his hands that had not been there a month earlier. "Why, we don't have enough hands to take care of those cattle that are starving in this blizzard!"

"We'll hire some hands!"

"Who? If men we've kept on for years won't stay and face that mob, what makes you think anybody else will?"

"We'll make it, Dad!" Stacy insisted. She spent the next hour going over plans with him, and none of them made much sense, but at least he was coming out of the trance he had gone into when Boone had brought the crew back.

Lee came storming in. "We have to do something! If we don't get those cows into some kind of shelter, we won't have a head left! Where's Boone?"

"I don't know," Stacy said. "He rode off to town—to get drunk, I suppose."

"He should! You can take this or leave it, Dad, but Boone's gone crazy!" There was a fixed look of anger on Lee's face. He had said little about the raid on Circle M, but he had changed. Both Stacy and Aaron were shocked and glad when he added, "I'm going to get some help and save those cows if I have to drag them here."

"I'll help, Lee!" Stacy said at once. "Saddle my horse while I get my coat. . . ."

There was a sudden chill in all three of them as someone outside yelled, "Mr. Carr! Mr. Carr! They're coming!"

Lee rushed to get his gun, but Stacy said, "Don't be a fool!" Then she turned to her father. "You'll have to talk to them, Dad."

"Yes! I will!" Aaron led them out on the porch and there in a long line was the solid strength of the settlers and the small ranchers of the Valley. They all had rifles, and as the Carrs looked down the line they saw faces pinched with cold and hunger, but all bearing the iron determination to have their own will.

"What do you want?" Aaron Carr asked, stepping to the front. "Have you come to kill us like you did the rest of the crew?"

Thad stepped off his horse, and he faced the man he had been afraid of for years. He marveled now at how feeble the old man looked.

"The trouble was not of our making, Aaron," he said calmly. "Skull raided Barney Purtle's little place. They killed all his stock, and they tried their best to kill him."

"I—I never sent Skull men to do that!"

"Your responsibility, Aaron," Thad replied in a hard voice. "And Skull raided Circle M. Tried to set fire to the place. What would you do if men rode up here and set fire to Skull Ranch?"

"Which we may see, Carr," Billy Sixkiller said. "Ray Catlin

is dead, and it might help me a little to see this whole place go up in smoke." A swell of agreement went along the line, and it would take only a word, they all realized, to touch off a house-burning.

"I ordered my men to work the cattle, Stevens," Aaron faltered. "If they raided any ranch, it was not by my orders!"

"That's right, Thad," Stacy interjected, and she came to stand by her father, a steady light in her fine eyes. "You can't really believe that Dad is a murderer. Whatever else you might think about him, you know he's not a liar!"

Thad gave Stacy a compassionate look, wishing he could spare her the pain that was lining her face, but he knew there was no way.

"That's true, Stacy," he said, "but he put Boone and Conboy in charge of Skull. He knew what was going on, so he has to stand to it."

"I've always stood behind my actions, Stevens," Aaron said in a steady voice. He stood tall at that moment, and even those men who had felt his rough hand were forced to admire the courage of the old man as he looked them right in the eye. "I built this ranch out of my sweat and my blood. I held it against outlaws, thieves, and Indians. I went through droughts, blizzards, Texas fever. And . . ." Aaron Carr's face changed slightly and his voice, still rough, carried a tone which came closer to humility than anything his family had ever heard. "I came up rough. I've seen little mercy in the world. Maybe there was more to see than I looked for, and maybe I should have listened to those who tried to tell me about it." He paused then and started to say more, but changed his mind. He gave a fatalistic shrug and stood there waiting for whatever was to come.

"I say burn him out!" one of the men shouted. He was a skinny man dressed in a dirty buffalo coat. He had not joined the others when it looked like a fight, but as soon as the trouble was over, he had ridden in and done nothing but talk of what ought to be done to the Carrs.

"Shut up, Ollie!" Billy ordered with a glance that stilled the man. Then he asked, "What's next, Thad?"

Reno sat on his horse, and he was quick to see that no longer did the settlers look to him. When there was bloody fighting to be done, he had been the first they'd look to. But now that the battle was practically won, the men instinctively turned from him to Thad. And Reno knew that somehow Thad had grown up in the raging fire of battle, that he knew his courage, and not doubting it, would be free not to worry about it again. This was, Reno understood, the test of a courageous man. Those men who went around feeling compelled to test their strength against others in some sort of contest, had no real confidence; that was why they had to constantly reaffirm it.

But Thad had matured, and Reno saw the light of wonder in Stacy's eyes as she watched Thad easily take over the will of the crowd.

"The next thing is to come to an agreement that will let all of us live together—and that means the large ranchers as well as the small."

Aaron Carr was staring at Thad as if he'd never seen him before. He lost a little of his stony anger and said with a little of the old bite in his voice, "You're going to let Skull exist, Stevens? Mighty good of you!"

"You're going to have to change your ways, Aaron," Thad said with a ringing note of authority. "The open range won't last five years, and you're going to have to accept that. Just like you accepted the Indians and the rustlers as a problem to deal with and to whip, you're going to have to find a way to raise your herds under controlled conditions." He smiled briefly and said, "Better talk to Frank. He's got some ideas in that direction."

"He left Skull."

"Oh, I think he might want to come back—if he had a free hand to try out some of his ideas about registered stock and controlled breeding."

A thought flashed across Aaron's face, and Stacy reached out to take his hand, her mother taking the other, while Lee urged, "I think that would be good, Dad."

They made a pretty picture there, Reno thought, the Carr family, and he had an idea that Aaron Carr beneath all the bluster had too much hard-rock sense to go down to defeat because of bull stubbornness.

Carr finally said, "Well, we can't stand out here all day freezing our tails off. All of you come in. Mother, make some coffee."

A shock ran along the line of men holding the rifles, and Reno grinned at it. He saw Swenson whisper something to Flemming, and the two slid down and walked toward the door; then one at a time all the men dismounted and followed them inside.

"Kind of like a happy ending in a story book, ain't it, Jim?" Josh grinned as they waited to get inside.

Reno smiled. "Sure is. Don't guess they'll need any old fire-eaters like us."

Andy MacIntosh heard this and turned a stern face on them, his voice thick with the dour Calvinism he had taken in with his mother's milk. "Don't be thinking this is the end of it," he warned. "It's just a wee beginning, and no matter how nice and tidy it seems right now, every man's got to eat his peck o' dirt! Man is born to trouble, and we'll go to our graves with the scars!"

"Wal, now, Andy," Josh said with a mock-serious look, "I reckon I can make it through the worst as long as I got you on hand to cheer me up with your happy face and cheerful sayings!"

Andy did not blink as he replied in a hard voice, "You can laugh if you like, Jordan, but we're a long way from home."

Reno stared at Andy, and he thought of something Lige Stevens had once said when things were bad at home and there was little hope. He had put his hand on Jim's shoulder and said, "Things look pretty bleak, don't they, son? We're a long way from home, but we've got a mighty good guide to see us there!"

As he went inside, it came to him that Lige's saying was potent enough for this situation, but the dark streak of pessimism in his blood was not so grim; and as he saw men who would gladly have drawn a bead on Aaron Carr sitting around, drinking coffee and listening as the leaders argued their case with the old man, it made him wonder if there wasn't something in Catherine's firm belief that the good will inherit the earth.

FOURTEEN
The Last Bullet

For years afterward they called it The Blizzard, as if it were the only one that had ever struck the Valley, or at least as if all the others were not worth keeping track of.

For three days the sky was filled with swirling gusts of brittle flakes—not downy and light, but heavy and rough like chunks of ice. As the temperature fell like lead, it froze the trees and there was a constant cracking as the big oaks split and crashed to the frozen ground, like giants brought to earth.

Men drove their horses through the scudding drifts until their legs froze to the saddles. On the third day the snow stopped falling, but the cold gripped the Valley like a vise.

"Ain't natural, Jim," Josh said slowly. His lips were nearly frozen, and he had to say every word carefully, like a drunk. "Look at this." He spat toward the ground and there was a sudden sharp crackle of sound. "That spit froze!" he declared, shaking his head.

"Come on—we got to get thawed out," Reno answered. "I reckon we got all we can handle anyway."

They drove the strays toward Arrow, stopping several

times to let the feeble young animals rest. By the time they reached the shelter where Thad had penned up all his stock, each of them was carrying a calf across the front of his saddle.

Thad met them, opened the gate, and then closed it as the cattle filtered weakly into the enclosure.

"That all you could find?" he asked.

Reno slid out of the saddle stiffly and put his calf on the ground. There was an ingrained weariness in his face as he nodded. "Ran across a few who didn't make it."

Thad nodded back and said, "You did well, Jim. I reckon we've about got all the stuff put up on this end of the Valley, and Flemming came by a while ago and said they'd all pretty well got their stock sheltered."

Reno had worked around the clock for the best part of three days, but so had every other man. Now as he followed Thad into the house, weariness flowed over him.

He sat down at the table with Josh, Juan, and Thad, too tired to eat much. Finally he said, "I've got to get back to Circle M."

"Rest up first, Jim," Thad urged.

"No. I don't like to leave Catherine alone. Ready, Juan?"

"Sure, Jim."

Thad followed them out to their horses, saying as they were gathering the reins, "Soon as we can, Jim, I want everybody to come to the church for a sort of early Thanksgiving service. We came out of this pretty well."

Reno nodded. "Catherine will want to come. I'll see she gets there."

Reno slept around the clock, and when he woke up and came to fill up on one of Catherine's breakfasts, she sat him down saying, "We're going to church this morning."

"Today?" Reno stared out the window and asked, "Still freezing?"

"The cold started breaking a few hours ago. The ice isn't melting, but it's not bad. Anyway, the roads aren't frozen too bad, so most everyone can travel. Now eat and go clean up." ,

He grinned around a mouthful of pancakes. "What if I say no?"

"I'll hit you with a stick," she said playfully, and there was a sudden sense of ease in the room that both of them felt. As she refilled his coffee cup she put her hand on his shoulder, and it was done so naturally that neither of them noticed it. Sitting down and sipping her own coffee, she smiled and asked, "Lige ever read you the verse out of the Bible that says, 'All things work together for good to them that love God'?"

"Lots of times. Never did see how it worked out, though."

"I think it takes something like this to make us see it. This blizzard made us all pull together, made us act like neighbors."

Reno had to smile. "Too bad it takes a blizzard to make people act right."

"Yes. I guess the church's best hour is when someone's house burns down. Then we all forget to fight and be envious and do all the terrible things we do—and we act like Christians."

He sat there soaking up the warmth from the stove, enjoying the food, and realized with a jolt that this was something he had always lacked. A place, a woman, a sense of time that made life meaningful.

She noticed that he was saying little, and finally when he finished she got up, washed the dishes, and put her coat. "I told Juan to harness the team. Let's go."

"Lige always said the ruination of the world was bobbed hair, bossy wives, and women preachers."

She flashed him a merry smile, and pulled him to his feet. "Well, I don't have bobbed hair anyway!"

They got into the buggy and the ride to the church was fun. They sat together, Juan, Reno, and Catherine, under warm buffalo robes, and were amazed by the countryside.

Snow had turned the whole face of the land into one smooth brow, and the featureless horizon glittered like a field of diamonds as the sun fell on it. All the stalks and stumps were veiled in delicate rounded curves, and decorations of frozen ice and snow were draped like Queen Anne's lace along the tree boughs.

"Beautiful!" Catherine said as they passed a pile of stones that were covered with ice. "They look like diamonds, don't they?"

"Oh, it's all pretty enough, I know," Reno agreed. "But lots of cattle died, and the deer are having a hard time."

"I know, Jim," Catherine said gently. "But we have to take what God gives us. And I've always liked that verse that says he makes everything beautiful in its time."

"Well . . ." He smiled, and gave her a deliberate look that brought a flush to her face. "I will admit that he sure made some things beautiful."

She dipped her head at the compliment, and they drove on to the church, making good time along the frozen road. There was enough thaw that the ice was slushed on top giving the wagon wheels a grip, and when the three pulled into the churchyard there were quite a number of wagons, buggies, and saddle horses outside.

"Guess we're late," Catherine said, and they hurried inside to find the little church packed.

"Been waiting for you," Thad said with a smile. "Now we can start."

Reno sat down with Catherine on one of the hard benches, and for the next hour he was in the middle of the singing and the preaching. It took him back, and he was amazed to discover that he knew by heart the words to almost all the songs. Words he thought were washed away by time rose to his lips, and although he was self-conscious at first, he finally entered into the singing with gusto.

Then there was a testimony service, with men and women rising to declare what God had done for them. Most of the testimonies had to do with the fact that some folks had been able to save their stock, and Reno had the feeling that these were much more fervent than the twenty-year-old testimonies many of the congregation had delivered by rote.

Finally Thad spoke, and it was a good sermon. Reno was taken off guard, for it brought Lige Stevens right before him. Although Thad was a much larger man than his father had been, he had the same voice, the same mannerisms that Reno remembered, and he sat there quietly, marveling that in some strange way Lige Stevens was still alive in the person of his son.

Thad said firmly, "Everybody here has been blessed. Nobody was left out. And I've heard all of you say how grateful you are. Amen?"

"Amen, brother!" came the echo from every throat.

Then Thad paused, and there was something in his face that brought an air of tension into the crowded church. Ordinarily, they knew, he would have closed with a prayer, but he did not do so. He stood there, looking over the crowd, weighing them in his mind, and finally said, "I wonder if we really *are* all that grateful to God?"

"Why, I think we are, Thad," John Malon said. "What makes you say a thing like that?"

Thad let his eyes fall on Malon and said, "I talked to Lee Carr this morning. He said that Skull is about to go under. Most of their hands quit. They don't have but two or three riders left, and no hay to feed what cows they can get to shelter."

Malon stared at Thad. "Well, that's too bad. Hate to hear it, Thad."

"Do you, John?" Thad asked with a tight smile. "If it was me who was about to go under, or Andy there—or any of us in this room—what would you do?"

"Why . . ." Malon's face reddened and his voice got hard as he answered, "You're putting it wrong, Thad. . . ."

"I don't think so," Thad insisted firmly. "Show me in the Book where it says we aren't supposed to help our neighbors when they're in trouble!"

"Well, now, Reverend," Andy MacIntosh said with a slow smile breaking through his bleak features. "I think you've got us there!" He turned to Malon, adding, "I think you know the part that goes 'Love your enemies,' don't you, John?"

"What are you saying, Thad?" Catherine asked. "That we should go help the Carrs?"

"I'm going—that's the way I see it," Thad said. "What I think is if our religion means more than just something we do on Sunday, every one of us ought to go help Aaron Carr."

"But he's been rotten to us!"

"That's *his* problem!" Thad shot back. "What Aaron does is his business—what I do is God's business. Now, who'll go with me?"

"I'll go, Thad," Billy Sixkiller volunteered, rising up. He had not been to church ever to anyone's memory, but there was a broad smile on his face now. "I know one verse I learned in mission school, about how if you do good for people who don't like you, you pour burning coals of fire on their heads. That's what I am to do to Aaron Carr—and burn his brains out!"

It caught the fancy of the crowd, and one by one they began falling in line, until finally even Ollie Yates, who had never been caught doing a good deed for anyone, volunteered with a little pressure from his wife.

As they were making plans to get to Skull, Reno said shaking his head, "Thad, I'm afraid you've wound up being a preacher. Can't imagine anyone else getting this bunch to go over and do a good deed for a man like Aaron Carr."

Thad was embarrassed at the speech. "He'll probably set the dogs on us, Jim."

"I remember one verse your dad quoted pretty often. Maybe I ought to lay it on you now."

"What's that?"

Reno said without a trace of a smile, "He that findeth a wife findeth a good thing." He saw it rattled Thad, and laughed as they left the church.

Lee had dredged up a crew of sorts, mostly shiftless railbirds from the saloons. Only by paying them four times the going rate for riders could he get them to Skull, and it proved to be a futile effort for the most part. They had to be driven into the storm, and if no one watched them, they would take refuge in the warmest spot they could find, tanking up on the pints of whiskey they all carried.

"I ought to shoot the whole bunch of trash!" Lee raged as he stormed into the house for a quick meal. "But they're not worth the powder it'd take to blow them up!"

Stacy put a plate of beef in front of him, laid her hand on his shoulder, and said, "You've done so well, Lee. I'm proud of you."

He flushed, and there was a new air of confidence in his face. Boone had come back nursing a hangover, accompanied by Williams and Kincaid. The three had been drinking steadily, going through the motions of work, but spending more time in the bunkhouse than they did trying to save the dying cattle.

Aaron came in, coated to the eyebrows with ice, and Stacy ran to help him off with his coat. "Sit down by the fire, Dad," she suggested. He looked as if he might have a fever, for there was a red spot in the center of his pale cheeks.

"Boone get those strays over by Three Pines?" he asked wearily.

"I—don't think so," Stacy said with a look at Lee.

"No, he's been tanking up with Williams and Kincaid all morning." Lee slammed his cup down on the table shouting angrily, "What's *wrong* with him? Can't he see the ranch is going down? I can't get any sense out of him!"

"I'll talk to him, Lee," Aaron soothed. He looked across the room at his youngest son and there was a warm light in his blue eyes when he said, "You've done a fine job, son. Nobody could have done better."

"Well . . ." Lee's face was filled with pride. It was the first time he could ever remember Aaron saying anything like that, and he smiled at him, saying, "Glad you think so, Dad. But it's going to take a miracle to save Skull."

"I know, Lee. I know."

There was such a defeated note in his voice that both Lee and Stacy glanced at each other. They had never seen him so tired; he had been the one who had held things together, and now, they realized, he had been pushed to the limits of his endurance.

"How about Abe Frazier—or maybe T. R. Smith over at the Flying R?" Lee asked. "Maybe they could spare some men to help us out."

"They've got the same problems we have. Too many cows spread out over too big a space."

Footsteps hit the porch, and when the door swung open, Frank walked in. He stamped his feet free of ice, then walked over to where they were staring at him.

He pulled his hat off, grinned at Aaron, and asked, "Need a good hand, Mr. Carr? I sure do need the work."

Aaron stared at this big son of his, realizing how hard it had been for Frank to come like this, and some of the defeat that etched his worn face faded. He tried not to show any emotion, but he could not keep his voice from revealing how he had missed this son.

"I—I couldn't ask you to do that, Frank." He swallowed and shook his head, then said, "It means a lot, I tell you. I guess I wanted you here more than I've been able to say. But you've got your own place."

Frank shrugged and a smile flashed across his broad face. "Are you trying to break it to me that you've cut me out of the will, Dad?"

"No! But you've got your own place now. . . ."

"Well, it's not all that much of a place." Frank grimaced, and with a wry smile he said, "If you'll let me come back, I think I can take care of that little spread in my spare time. What do you say?"

Aaron Carr's smile was a good thing to see, and Lee let

out a yelp and ran to pound Frank on the shoulder, crying, "Now we can get something done!" Stacy said nothing, but she pulled Frank's head down and kissed him soundly.

"Boy, I'm *glad*—but even with your help, it may not be enough. We got a lot of dead cows, and the rest are in bad shape, but we'll try!" There was a sparkle in the old man's eyes that had been missing, and he slapped his thigh, saying in a lively voice, "We'll do what we can!"

"Well, Dad, I didn't come alone," Frank said. Nodding toward the outside, he explained, "I picked up a crew—well, to tell the truth, they picked *me* up."

"A crew?" Aaron exclaimed. "Where in the world did you find a crew?"

"Like I said, they found me. Come on and meet your new hands."

Aaron cast a mystified look at Lee and Stacy, then the three of them followed Frank out onto the porch.

"What in . . . ," Aaron gasped, and all of them stood there staring at the wagons and riders drawn up in the yard.

"Sorry-lookin' bunch, Dad," Frank said with a grin, "but I reckon we can use 'em."

The yard was filled with at least ten wagons loaded with hay, and Ole Swenson waved a gloved hand at Aaron, a wide grin on his lips. "Where you want this feed, boss?" he hollered.

John Malon called out from his wagon perch, "Wake up, Aaron! We got work to do!"

They were all there. Andy MacIntosh, Fred Flemming, Dave Melton, Mose Hackett, and others grinned from their wagons at the stunned expressions on the Carrs' faces.

Reno sat on his horse, along with Josh, Billy Sixkiller, the Hackett boys, and seven other riders. Thad got off his horse and walked up on the porch to say, "Well, let's get at it, Aaron. You got a crew that needs some orders."

Aaron Carr stood there, and there was a painful silence as he tried to take it in. His gaze ran over the yard, picking out men he'd had hard words with, some he'd done his best to run out of the Valley.

Reno saw it was hard for Carr, harder in one way than the bullets he'd taken to build the ranch. Fighting was one thing the old man knew and understood, but as he stood there trying to swallow, trying to think what it all meant, Reno knew that no matter what happened in the future, Aaron Carr would never again be the same.

"Thad—I don't understand," he faltered.

Thad grinned and said, "To tell the truth, Aaron, I don't understand it myself. What I think has happened is that some of us who've gone around calling ourselves *Christians* for a long time—well, I think we're *acting* like it for a change."

Stacy stepped forward, her face aglow with pleasure he had longed to see. She put her hand on his arm and there was a promise in her voice as she said, "Thad—thank you!"

Looking at her, Thad suddenly turned to face Aaron. "Looks like we might be seeing a lot of each other, Aaron—as neighbors , of course," he added quickly with a smile at Stacy.

"Let's git movin!" Josh Jordan shouted. "Whar we need to put this here feed?"

Aaron put his head up, stared out at the crowd, and said, "I've never been much of a one for talk. Heard too many promises, I guess, that didn't hold up." He continued in a ringing tone, "But I thank you for this—and I'm asking you to give me a chance to be a different kind of man than I have been!" Then turning, he said, "Frank, you and Lee tell us what to do."

It was, they all realized, an abdication. Aaron was stepping down, and these men had learned enough of Frank Carr to know that Skull would never again be a threat to them. A cheer went up, and there was a carnival air in the yard as Frank and Lee began to tell the riders where to find the cattle that were most desperate.

Catherine climbed down from her wagon, handing the reins to Juan. She went to Stacy and said, "Maybe I can help you cook for this bunch. They'll probably eat you out of house and home."

Stacy smiled at her, then the two women embraced, and there was a smile on Stacy's face as she drew back. She glanced at Reno who was now dismounted and leading a team toward the barn. "I think you're a lucky woman, Catherine."

Catherine flushed, then laughed and said, "And so are you, Stacy!" They laughed together then, and started into the house to begin preparing the huge meal that the crew would require.

Horses were milling around the yard, and talk filled the air as the riders got their instructions, when over all there, loud and harsh, came the voice of Boone Carr, cutting off all talk and causing Stacy and Catherine to wheel and return to the porch.

"Reno! You ain't gonna get away this time!"

Boone had come out of the bunkhouse which was to the south of the Carrs' home, and he was flanked by Red Williams and Bob Kincaid. They were moving steadily toward the yard, and at once it was clear that they were gunning for Jim Reno.

Like a wave, the crowd broke, wagons wheeling to one side and men on foot and in the saddle swinging aside to leave a wide open space in the yard.

Boone was in the center, but less than a step behind him to his right was Kincaid, who was hatless. Williams was to Boone's left, a hungry smile on his thin face and his hand brushing the handle of his fancy gun.

"You killed Skull men, Reno!" Boone broke out in a wild voice. "You ain't gonna get out of this place alive!"

"Boone!" Aaron Carr lifted up his voice toward the three. "You've gone crazy! You and those two get out of here and sober up!"

Not a flicker on Boone's face revealed that he had heard his father, and he came straight on, death in his eyes.

A hush fell over the yard, and Reno turned slowly to face the three who had stopped about forty feet away. He had known deep down that sooner or later this moment would come. Dimly he was aware of movement behind him as Frank Carr moved to shield Catherine and Stacy with his body, and he sensed that Billy Sixkiller was sliding away from the crowd to take up station to his right.

But as always at times like this, sounds were muffled to his ears, and the sweep of his vision narrowed until he saw clearly the three men crouched with their hands hovering over their guns—all else faded. It was as if he were looking down a long tunnel at Boone, Kincaid, and Williams, as if all else had ceased to exist for this moment in time.

Far off in the distance he saw a group of alders sheathed in ice, held in place by the embrace of the cold, and the three men who stood before him seemed, for that moment, to be frozen as well.

Aaron and Frank were calling out to Boone, but there was no reason in the face of the big man who stood poised like a hawk about to fall upon his prey. Boone was cursing monotonously, and as soon as he worked himself up to the killing point he would go for the gun beneath his hand.

Perhaps he would, but suddenly Kincaid stepped forward, placing himself squarely toward Reno, his arms crooked, hands like huge claws. He was smiling and there was a burning light in his smoky eyes as he addressed himself to Reno.

"You always had luck, Reno," he said in a voice edged with hate. "You never saw the day you could beat me! Always made me want to puke the way some curled up their toes and went yellow when they tried to face up to you." He lifted his hands away from his guns and his voice was a high thin cry as he yelled, "I don't need anybody's help to take you! Now—go for your iron!"

Reno had not moved, except to turn his body slightly to the left. He realized that Kincaid would draw soon, but he felt a sickness deep down as he stood there, and he knew it was a flaw which would kill him. Yet he could not avoid the repulsion that gripped him as he felt the moment rushing toward him when he must pull a trigger, for he was sick to the death of death itself.

His face was pale, and he said softly in a voice that scarcely carried across to Kincaid, "I won't draw on you, Bob."

Kincaid's eyes flew open, and then narrowed like a cat's, and his hands dropped to his guns.

He was a faster man than Reno had ever faced, his guns leaping from the holsters, sweeping up level as he dropped into a fighting crouch.

Reno's hand dipped smoothly toward his gun, and there was no jerking or yanking in the act. As Kincaid's guns swung up level, Reno's cleared leather, and in that practiced motion of turning sideways to give the least possible target to Kincaid, his arm swept up in a rigid line.

He was a fraction slower, and as his arm swept up,
Kincaid threw a shot from one gun that kissed the air beside
Reno's right cheek, then two shots echoed so close together
that they sounded like one explosion. One of them hit the dirt
in front of Reno's left boot, and the other raked across his side
just over his belt. The pain was like a hot iron, but Reno
ignored it. Getting shot at was something he had learned in
the army, and he had accepted the fact that he would get hit.

It stood him in good stead. Kincaid loosed two more
shots, again brushing close to Reno's head. Then the broad
chest of the gunfighter was targeted clearly as Reno stared
down his arm across the sight which was fixed in a rocklike
grip.

In that fraction of time, as he held steady on the gray
bone button on the gunfighter's shirt, Reno hesitated, and he
was conscious of a vast sense of waste as he pulled the trigger.

The slug struck Kincaid one inch below the button, the
force of it knocking the wind out of his lungs with a whooshing
sound, and there was a look of shock and anger on his face as
he fell backward. But his eyes were beginning to cloud as he
pulled the trigger on one gun, sending a slug into the snow as
he fell, arching his back, digging his heels into the snow, then
slowly relaxing in that terrible way that Reno had seen so often.

Reno took one step forward, but a flicker of a movement
caught his eye, and the roar of Williams' Colt shook the air. A
blow struck him like a huge hand, turning him around, and
then he saw the red wink of fire from the muzzle of the gun
and felt something tug at a lock of his hair. His gun seemed
very heavy as he raised it to fire, and he saw William's mouth
spring open with fear as Reno's weapon trained itself steadily
on him.

Wildly the gunman began to fire, and there was a sense-less cry of despair rising from his throat when Reno's bullet drove the life out of him. He sprawled bonelessly into the snow and did not move.

Then the world was spinning and Reno could not hold the gun upright. He slipped to his knees, and there was something he ought to do, but he could not think what.

Boone's face was contorted with rage, and he was stalk-ing toward Reno kneeling in the snow trying to lift his gun.

It was like moving underwater, and Reno fought his way free from a curtain of red mist that kept blinding him. He lifted his eyes to see Boone taking short steps toward him, firing a shot each time his heel jarred the ground.

Reno lifted his gun, fixed it on Boone's face, but did not fire. Twice, three times, Boone fired, and still Reno held his fire. Someone was shouting, "Shoot him!" and he thought it was Catherine, but could not tell. He was in a cave, where hollow echoes rang and lights flashed, but he could not pull the trigger; then he knew he had been pushed one inch too far, that he had fought too many battles and that he could not shoot this man.

He lowered his gun, and Boone, seeing this, cursed wildly and stopped abruptly. He took his gun in both hands and deliberately brought it to bear on the helpless man before him. The muzzle of his gun looked enormous, and there was a strange surrender in Reno as he waited for the end.

Then, from behind him came a single shot, and Boone's head snapped backward. Boone fell like a huge tree full-length on his back and there was only a twitch in his body once, twice, then he lay still.

Hands were pulling at Reno, and Catherine's voice was whispering in his ear, "Oh, my dear! My dear man!"

"Get him inside," he heard her say, and the red curtain fell at once over his eyes, and there was a great roaring in his ears as he fell into a dark, cool space where there was no sound and no light.

Duke tried to Buck as Reno settled himself carefully into the saddle for the first time in two weeks. Reno's face was pale and he grunted with the dull pain the pitching of the horse sent into the barely-healed wounds.

"Stop that, you fool horse!" Catherine said instantly, and from her horse close to Duke, she leaned forward and struck him a solid blow between the ears that made a solid thud. Duke shook his head, and instantly stopped his foolishness.

Reno grinned at her, and asked in a teasing voice, "That's what I can look for when I cut up a little, Catherine?"

She gave him a stern look, but could not conceal the light of humor in her eyes. "I declare, it's what you need, Jim Reno! You don't have any business on a horse as sick as you've been."

Reno thought over the past days, how he had been in a fog that lifted from time to time, and always she had been there, whispering hope and lifting him out of the darkness time and time again.

"Can't be an invalid forever," he said. He looked around as they walked the horses out of the yard, breathing in the fresh air, his eyes drinking in the world.

He stole a glance at her, marveling at the beauty of her expression, and said, "Fellow told me about a funny thing once."

"What was that?"

"He'd been a sailor, and he said that in one of those islands he went to, whenever somebody saved your life, he was made responsible for you."

"Responsible?" Catherine asked. "In what way?"

"Way I understand it," Reno mused, "the life that was saved was a new one—that's what the heathen thought, you see?" He was not looking at her as she studied his face; in fact, he seemed not at all interested in his own tale. "Well, if he was a new life, so to speak, somebody had to be in charge of him, just like he was a baby."

They rode on, and Reno said nothing more until he nodded at some cows nibbling at some dead grass sticking out of the thin crust of snow. "Cattle look good," he commented.

"Well!" she demanded. "You want me to use this quirt on *you*, Jim?"

He laughed and turned to face her, a warm light in his black eyes making him look younger. He took her hand and said, "Well, I thought you were smart enough to catch the moral of that little story."

She shook her head, saying, "I guess I've not got much sense left, Jim. After that day Boone died, I think we all sort of blocked everything out of our minds except saving the cattle."

"Ever find who shot Boone?" Reno asked.

She shook her head. "None of us wanted to know—but my guess is that it was Billy Sixkiller."

"Wouldn't be surprised."

"But, Jim," she said, suddenly stopping her horse, *"you* didn't do it! And you could have; we all saw that." She moved her horse closer to him and touched his face in a sudden gesture of trust. "Why not, Jim? Why didn't you shoot?"

Reno put his hand over hers, holding it tight against his face, and as he relived that moment when he had stayed his hand, there was a glad light in his face.

"I couldn't do it, Catherine, and it made me glad! I've seen so many who killed until it meant nothing, and I guess I was running away because I was turning into that sort—but now I know I'm not."

"The last bullet's been fired, Jim?"

He shrugged, saying, "As to that, I can't say. But I know it's going to take something big to make me pick up a gun ever again!"

She stared at him, and then there was a smile on her lips. "Tell me what the story means, Jim."

"About being responsible for anybody whose life you save?" Jim pulled Duke around so that they were side by side. Then he put his arm around her waist. "I'm feeling faint, Catherine—I'd better hang on for support. I've been sick, you know!"

She smiled. "Just tell me, Jim."

He looked at her, wondering how such a small body could hold such vitality, knowing that for him she had everything.

"I guess since you saved my life, you've got to be responsible for me, Catherine," he said. There was a husky note in his voice that moved her. He kissed her, pulling her toward him so roughly that she gasped. She resisted, then gave her lips to him, and there was never any ending to the kiss, it seemed; but finally she drew back.

Lights danced in her eyes as she said, "All right, Jim, I'll keep you—and you keep me."

Reno gave a sudden sweep of his arm, and there was a happiness released in him that overflowed into a beaming smile and made her take his hand in both of hers.

"Lige said once that there were times when we were pretty far from home, but you know, I think you and I are pretty close to home! Come on, Catherine," he said, and waved his arm toward the horizon. "Let's see what's over the hill."

"All right, Jim," she said, and they moved on together so close that they cast a single shadow on the ground.

RIMROCK

One

Stage to Rimrock

There was no escape from the fine dust that seemed to surround the rolling stage like a dense cloud. Ada Lindsey dabbed at her face, stared at the grimy results, then forced herself to maintain the ramrod posture she had maintained ever since the stage had left Dallas.

Three nights spent in wretched stage stations with greasy meals and dirty beds crawling with insects had etched fine lines in her face, but at the age of fifty-five she had endured the discomfort better than might be expected. She was a small woman, the delicate bone structure of her face and hands revealing her patrician heritage. Small ears almost hidden beneath the brown hair lost nothing by the silver sheen that tipped the ends. Her arched nose above firm lips betrayed the iron will that lay beneath the surface. Dark blue eyes deep-set over high cheekbones made no attempt to avoid direct contact with the men who sat across from her on the hard leather seat.

"Have a little water, Mother." The tall, lean young man who sat next to her pulled a limp leather flask from a space beneath his feet, but before he could remove the brass cap, Ada shook her head and straightened her back a fraction.

"No." Nothing other than this, but there was a studied rebuke in the word which stung the young man. He hesitated, then flung the water bottle behind his feet with more violence than was necessary.

The whale-fat whiskey drummer who sat directly across from him grinned broadly. He almost said, "Mama spanked the baby!" but something about the lean chin and a restless look in the eyes of the young man restrained him. A dude, all right, but looks like he might be a handful if he ever cut the apron strings, he thought.

They were mother and son; both had the same sharp facial planes which were somehow not Western. The young man's jaw and cheekbones were pronounced as were the woman's, but in the man they were sculptured into an intense masculinity, augmented by the craggy brows that shaded dark blue eyes. He was lean, but the wiry cast of his torso gave promise of considerable strength which would increase with age.

The drummer, whose name was Smith, searched for a flaw in the young man. It was his theory that every man had one, and usually he prided himself on being astute enough to discover a trace of it in the face. As the stage rocked and swayed across the monotonous Kansas landscape, he studied the young man who had leaned back and closed his eyes. Finally he had it: The mouth—that's it! Despite all them fine looks and high-falutin' ways, he's got a pout like a kid who's had his candy took away from him! There was a pronounced fullness to the mouth, especially the lower lip, which gave the face a vulnerable look despite the masculine good looks. But it was not youth, Smith decided. He had seen the knife-edged lips of Billy Bonny when the Kid was younger than this one.

He jist ain't pulled away from Mama's apron string yet. Smith grinned, and diagnosing the young man's character made him feel so good he pulled a full bottle of whiskey from a black leather bag beneath his feet, uncapped it, and almost took a drink. A wicked light appeared in his eye, and he leaned forward and held the bottle out to the woman.

"Have a snort, ma'am?"

As he had expected, the woman looked at him as if he had crawled out from under a rock, her blue eyes icy with contempt. It was what he wanted, and he thought, Reckon you're one of them purse-poor Southern gals whose feet never touched the ground before the war. Expect you'll git a leetle of that pride rubbed off after you hit Abilene. But he said only, "No? Well, here's to you then, ma'am. The ladies—God bless 'em!"

The young man straightened up and for one brief instant the drummer thought that he saw enough fire flicker in his face to bring a start of fear. These Southern fools would just as soon kill a man as spit where a woman was concerned. But the moment passed, and Smith breathed again. Nope—not with that baby pout! He handed the bottle to the man next to him, a burly cowboy. "Have a snort and pass it on, brother."

The cowboy's eyes lit up and his throat worked compulsively as he swallowed. He gasped as he lowered the bottle and whispered, "Wow!" then passed the bottle to the man beside him.

"Thankee kindly." He was a mountain man, wearing worn, fringed buckskins, and he drank the whiskey smoothly as if it were lemonade. "Mighty fine panther spit." He grinned agreeably. "Yep, some whiskey would draw blisters on a rawhide boot—but now this, wal, it's so good you can taste the feet of the gal what hoed the corn it was made of!" He passed the bottle on, considerably depleted, and the two older passengers took their turns. They looked like clerks, with the sallow skin of men who seldom saw the sun.

Finally the bottle passed from a rawboned farmer wearing new overalls to Jeff Lindsey, who handed it on with a shake of his head. Reckon his mama won't let him drink with the men, Smith thought. The last passenger, a thin man dressed in a gambler's showy clothing, smiled through thin lips and took a pull, then handed the bottle back to Smith.

"Thanks." The gambler's voice was reedy and coarsened by a thousand nights of breathing harsh tobacco smoke and sipping raw whiskey. "How much farther to Rimrock?"

"Dunno," Smith said. He put the bottle away. "My first trip on this line. I usually take the Shawnee run."

"Not too fur," the mountain man said.

"How far exactly?" Jeff asked in the manner of one who liked his information in specific terms.

The eyes of the mountain man swung in his direction, taking in the black broadcloth coat, the string tie, and the patent leather shoes. He was silent so long that the young man's face began to burn, and finally he answered lazily: "Oh, it ain't but about two curves and a cuss fight, I reckon." He appeared not to see the anger in Lindsey's face as he added, "Jest a mite further than you can chunk a tater."

The stage gave a lurch, dipping so sharply to starboard that all the passengers were thrown in that direction. Jeff Lindsey attempted to catch himself, but the weight of the men to his right drove him against the slight form of his mother, crushing her against the varnished oak.

"Mother, are you all right?"

She fixed him with a steady stare. "Jeff, I haven't been all right since we left Dallas. And I don't expect to get better until you get this fool notion out of your head."

She had spoken in a low voice intended for his ears only, but Smith the drummer missed none of it—including the wince that the woman's sharp words drew from the young man. He shrugged and took out a cigar. Soon the fine dust that boiled in through the window mixed with the strong stench of the weed, but nobody protested.

For the next hour the coach jolted along, a crawling speck that moved slowly across the flat Kansas prairie. The fiery July sun seemed to penetrate the interior of the coach, so hot that all the passengers lay back in their seats gasping for breath. Twice they passed large herds headed north. The rolling dust gathered into clouds that rose high in the summer sky, then descended, coating the world with a coat of gritty gray film.

Finally the guard called out, "Stop ahead. One hour to redd up."

The weary horses managed a final burst of speed, which the driver halted with a squeal of brakes that pulled the stage to a halt beside a dreary building made of sawmill slabs and covered with sod. A rusty pipe rose through the dry grass, sending a faint trickle of greasy smoke listlessly across the sky, as if uncertain whether to rise or fall.

As the passengers stumbled out of the stage on legs grown numb, a fat, red-faced individual with a dirty red bandana covering his head came out. He counted the passengers, said in a sullen tone, "Grub's inside. Privy's over there."

"Let's walk a little," young Lindsey said. Taking his mother's arm, he led her past a barn and across a stretch of bare earth cluttered with rusty tin cans, chicken feathers, and several piles of decaying garbage.

"I suppose this is the garden spot of Kansas," Mrs. Lindsey said with a mirthless laugh.

"Oh, Mother, we've been through this a hundred times! You agreed to come!"

Her face softened, and the traces of a former beauty were caught in her smile. She touched his arm, saying in a gentle tone, "I'm sorry, Jeff. You're right. I did agree to come."

"It'll be better when we get to Rimrock."

"No, it'll be the same." She took a fine lace handkerchief from her pocket, wiped the dust from his cheek, then replaced the handkerchief with a frown. "When your father and I were first married, we lived in a series of towns like this one. They were all the same, Jeff. The most desolate places on the face of the earth!"

"That was over twenty-five years ago."

"Frontier towns never change. But I didn't leave your father and take you to civilization because life was boring. No, it was the utter contempt for human life, Jeff, that I couldn't bear!"

"Maybe if Dad hadn't been a peace officer—," he suggested, but she shook her head suddenly at the thought.

"That was part of it. I couldn't live every day of my life waiting for a deputy to come with the message that Jesse was dead on some barroom floor!"

They walked on slowly, and Jeff tried to think of a way to make his mother understand what he felt. He knew from bitter experience that the years his mother had spent as the wife of a small-town Texas lawman had marked her so deeply that nothing could ever change her. Finally he said heavily, "I wish you'd stayed in Dallas."

She stopped and held his arm with a surprising strength. "No! You—you're all I have, Jeff!" She bit her lip, shook her head, and made herself smile at him. "I won't complain again. I know this means everything to you. But I still say you would have been better off with Creasy's law office in Dallas."

"I guess we better get back." He turned her back toward the station and tried again to explain why he had left the security of a law office in a big city.

"You saw those big herds headed toward Rimrock, Mother? They're going to change this country! All during the war Texas sold no cattle to speak of. Now that the war is over, the East is hungry for beef. That's why all these trails headed to Kansas are running over with trail herds. And the action will be at little places nobody ever heard of—little towns like Dodge City, Hays, Abilene. All those trail towns have one thing going—they're on the railroad leading to Chicago and the East."

"I know all that, Jeff, but. . . ."

"Mother, if I'd stayed in Dallas at Creasy's, I'd have been one clerk out of twenty or a hundred. But if I go to Rimrock, I'll be one of a few lawyers, maybe even the only one. And how many times have we dreamed about my getting into office, Mother? I can do it at Rimrock! You know I can."

She brightened at that. "If you could do that, Jeff, it would be worth it all."

"We'll do it, Mother, you'll see! It'll be just like you always said it would be." He had the power to raise her spirits, and when they got back to the station she took her place and managed to eat some of the greasy beef and drink some of the strong black coffee.

Jeff smiled as he ate, pleased that he had finally found a key for keeping his mother happy. She had resisted his notion to go to Rimrock, especially since his father was there serving as marshal. He had never been able to gauge her feeling for the father he had seen only once on a brief trip to Oklahoma when he had been only fifteen. At times he suspected that although she had divorced Jesse Lindsey she still had strong feelings for him. Not that she ever said so, but she had never remarried and never shown more than a casual interest in another man.

Just as Jeff finished his meal, a door to the back of the room opened to what was obviously the station keeper's quarters. Jeff could see by the light of a single window a sagging bed and a washstand. The door was suddenly filled by a man who stood there looking out at them.

"Oh, yeah, I 'most forgot, Rainey," the station keeper grunted as he began collecting the dishes. "This here feller's horse up and died on him yestiddy. He's paid up to Rimrock."

The driver sopped the white gravy from his plate with a piece of cornbread, popped it into his mouth, and then swallowed it. He belched explosively, shoved his chair back, and pressed his hat down firmly on his head. "All who's goin' better git movin'."

He led the way to the stage where the guard held six fresh horses. They stamped and tossed their heads as the passengers mounted and were routinely cursed by the driver who snatched the reins.

The passengers all waited until Jeff handed his mother up and got

. to sit beside her. Then they hauled themselves aboard and waited for the new passenger to get in.

Jeff caught a view of the man as he picked up a saddle from the porch, moved across the yard, and stood just beneath the window waiting to toss it up to the guard.

He moved so slowly, almost painfully so, that Jeff assumed he was an elderly man, but as a slanting beam of sunlight illuminated the features, he saw his mistake.

The face beneath the low-crowned hat was wedge-shaped, tapering from a broad forehead to a chin which sloped forward aggressively and was punctuated by a shallow cleft. Heavy black brows shaded deep-set eyes, very dark and almost hidden by the shelter of the high cheekbones, and the same shade of raven black glistened in the hair that ran raggedly from beneath the hat. A dull pallor tinged the man's skin except for two red spots on his cheeks.

"Toss it up." As the guard spoke, the square hands holding the saddle tightened, and a ripple of muscle flexed, sending the heavy weight upward. There was an ease in the motion that hinted at power in the rather trim body, but suddenly the man swayed back and only by grabbing at the shoulder-high wheel did he save himself from falling to the ground.

"Dead drunk!" Ada said in disgust. "Jeff, we can't have him in here with us!"

Jeff nodded, but the mountain man said wryly, "Guess iffen you kept drinkin' men off stages, they'd all go bust."

"I'm afraid that's right, lady," the gambler said. "He can sit by us, though. Won't be any trouble to you."

"He'll have to behave," Jeff said sternly. But as he watched the painful progress the passenger made getting aboard, he saw that there would be no trouble. Grasping the edges of the door with both hands, he paused as if gathering his strength. He pulled himself through the door and spotted the space between the drummer and the gambler.

He fell into it with a gust of spent breath. His hands, they all saw, were trembling, and the whites of his eyes gleamed until he closed them and leaned back against the cushion without a word.

"Hyupp!" The driver sang out, and with a lurch the stage rolled out onto the road.

"Just a couple of hours to Rimrock," the farmer said. He was watching the face of the new passenger, as were the rest of them. "Ort to be in before dark."

The gambler moved slightly away, leaning back so that he could study the man's face carefully. His brow furrowed into deep lines. Finally he asked quietly, "Don't I know you, mister?"

The rolling of the stage moved the man's loose body from side to side, and it was obviously an effort for him to open his eyes and focus on the face of the gambler. "My name's Rossiter," the gambler added. "I think we must have met somewhere."

Slowly the man's lips moved, as if he were coming out of a deep sleep. When he did answer, the voice was slurred, the words running together. "Dunnoyou." Then the eyes closed and only the pressure of the bodies of the men on either side of him kept him from slumping to the floor.

"Dead drunk!" Ada snapped. "Shouldn't be allowed to ride with decent people!"

"Hope he don't puke," the drummer said. "If he starts gaggin', we better holler to the driver to stop."

Nothing like that happened, however, and soon all except the gambler Rossiter ignored the man. It was nearly an hour later and the sun was beginning to touch the flat horizon with streaks of crimson when Rossiter broke the silence.

"This man isn't drunk—he's sick!"

They all looked and it was obvious that the dark-haired man was ill. His face was flushed, and when the gambler touched his brow, he said, "He's burning up!"

"Fever." The mountain man leaned around to look at the lolling body of the man. He leaned across and pulled an eyelid up; there was no response as the white of the eye shone dully. "Got somethin' for sure."

"What!" Jeff was fully alarmed now. He leaned out the window and shouted, "Driver! Stop the coach!"

"Whut fer?"

"We have a sick man in here!"

"Wal, hold yer taters—they's an old shack down the road 'bout a quarter, and we need to water the hosses."

In less than five minutes the stage rolled to a stop and the driver peered in. Rolling a massive cud from one cheek to the other, he asked, "Whut's his trouble?"

"I think he's got scarlet fever," one of the pallid men answered. "There's been lots of it around."

"Does it look like this?" Mrs. Lindsey asked fearfully. She had seen that disease wipe out a large segment of a small Texas town once, and she knew that there was no defense, nothing a doctor could do for such a thing.

"Could be jest the flu," the pallid man said. "All them things look alike at the early stage. Could be cholera or diphtheria."

"Get him out of here!" Mrs. Lindsey said in a tight voice. She was not a flighty woman, but the fear of contagious disease was too much for her. "I will not ride with that man!"

"Ah, we're only 'bout an hour from Rimrock," the driver complained.

"I insist that you get him out of this stage!"

The driver stared at her, then spat out his wad of tobacco. He saw that the woman was verging on hysteria, so he said, "Wal, I guess we kin leave him here."

"Leave him here!" Rossiter said at once, anger in his voice. "Alone in this place?"

"Won't be fer no more than a couple hours," the driver snapped. He had had some experience with sickness himself, and it made sense to keep the man out of town if he really did have typhoid.

"Git him down!" The man's body was limp as they handed him down, his head bumping the floor of the stage. "Watch out! Don't brain the porc feller!"

Rossiter said, "Throw down his saddle." When it hit the ground, he pulled it into the shack, took the bedroll off, and made the unconscious man as comfortable as possible.

"This is wrong!" he exclaimed bitterly. "I wouldn't leave a dog out here alone like this!"

The driver cursed, spat, and said, "I ain't gonna argue with you. Everybody back inside!"

Jeff turned, avoiding the glance in Rossiter's eyes, and walked hurriedly back to the stage. Getting in, he said in a low voice, "I don't like this."

"What else can we do?" Ada asked. "You heard the driver—they'll send a doctor out right away."

Inside, Rossiter was staring down at the man, watching the chest rising and falling in a very shallow way. The others filed out quickly, and the driver said angrily, "You comin' or not?"

The slender back of the gambler was turned to the door, and he said in a low voice, "I'm staying. Put my bag off."

The driver stared at him, then called out, "Throw the man's bag down, Earl." Climbing back to his seat, he took the whip, cracked it over the head of the off horse, and the coach shot out into the falling dusk.

Inside, nobody said anything for ten minutes, then Smith said defensively, "Well, I can't hang around and play nursemaid!"

"Me neither," one of the sallow-faced men said, and the other nodded in agreement.

The burly cowboy said with a truculent edge to his voice, "Aw, that tinhorn ain't got nothing else to do!"

"Shet your filthy mouth!" The mountain man moved so quick the
movement of his hand was like a snake striking. Grabbing the husky
puncher by the collar, he said, "You ain't got no call to be proud—so
jest you open your face once more an' I'll be happy to redecorate it fer
yuh!"

The cowboy was obviously a pretty tough hand, but something in
the face of the older man, or perhaps the Arkansas Toothpick stuck in
the fringed belt, made him speak softly. "Well, what about you! I didn't
notice you stickin' around!"

The lean face of the mountaineer changed, and he dropped his
hand, muttering, "Yeah, that's plumb right. I reckon none of us air anything to write home about." He leaned back, and there was not
another word said as the stage rolled toward Rimrock.

Al Rossiter moved the saddle and his worn suitcase into the shack.
He found an oil lamp half-full and a rusty cookstove with three legs.
The nights were cold, and he knew that the fever would probably turn
to chills, so he made a sweep around the shack finding plenty of dead
wood. Going through the saddlebags of the sick man, he ran across a
blackened coffee pot, some coffee in a leather bag, and a chunk of
bacon. He dredged up a bent frying pan from a corner of the shack,
and went outside again with a tin pan that hung over a peg in the wall.
A small creek not a hundred feet away offered plenty of fresh water.
As the darkness closed in, he went back inside and sat down beside
the sick man.

Lighting a slender cheroot, he stared down at the pale face now
drenched with sweat, wondering what made him stay.

"Not my style," he said half to himself in the falling darkness.
"Never was one to give up much for anybody." He saw that the man
was beginning to shiver, so he got up, started a fire in the stove, and
put water on to heat.

The man's eyes opened, and Rossiter asked, "You awake?"

There was no answer, and the eyes were unfixed. Rossiter took some water in a cup, lifted the man up, and put it to his lips. He drank thirstily and then began to shake so violently that Al thought he was dying. He wrapped him tightly in the blanket and sat back, smoking, thinking, and wondering about his actions again.

The chills got worse, then began to modify as the fever took over two hours later. This time the eyes opened, and there was recognition in them.

"Feel pretty bad?" Rossiter asked.

The man said weakly, "They put me off?"

"Well—"

The dark eyes regarded him intently, and there was a trace of a smile on the broad lips. He said in a painful whisper, "You make a living taking care of sick cowboys?"

Rossiter grinned and said, "Maybe it's the beginning of a new career for me. You want a drink of water?"

"Yeah." He drank slowly and lay back exhausted. But his eyes were still intently fixed on Rossiter. He lay watching him for a long time, then said, "You sure are a funny sort of gambler."

The remark seemed to irritate Rossiter. He shrugged angrily, and there was no contentment in his thin face. He threw the cigar out the door and said, "Well, I ain't been a roaring success at that, to tell the truth." He had sharp features, like a hawk, with light blue eyes that moved restlessly, and his mouth was thin, almost a knife edge. He said, "I still think we must have met somewhere. My name's Al Rossiter."

He waited for the sick man to give his own name, but weariness struck him like a blow, pulling the lids down heavily. He managed to open them again, saying in a whisper, "Much obliged." Then he dropped into a heavy sleep that soon turned into a fever so fierce that it frightened Al. Once he had to hold the man down by force as delirium took him. He was yelling something about the round top and screaming for somebody to bring some guns up.

Finally he wore himself out, and Al took a pull from a silver flask he carried in his suitcase. He stared down at the face bathed in sweat and murmured softly, "With the kind of luck I been having, that driver and those sorry passengers will forget to send a doctor."

There was a dark streak of fatalism in the man, and he sat there staring through the single window, wondering what the lacy network of stars that decorated the sky had to do with Al Rossiter and his problems.

Books in the Reno Western Saga

From Gilbert Morris, the author of the Reno Western Saga and the House of Winslow series, comes a new Civil War series. . . .

The Appomattox Saga

Gilbert Morris is the author of many best-selling books, including the popular House of Winslow series and the Reno Western Saga.

He spent ten years as a pastor before becoming professor of English at Ouachita Baptist University in Arkansas and earning a Ph.D. at the University of Arkansas. Morris has had more than twenty-five scholarly articles and two hundred poems published. Currently, he is writing full-time.

His family includes three grown children, and he and his wife live in Baton Rouge, Louisiana.